DR

JACKKNIFE

JACKKNIFE

WILLIAM W. JOHNSTONE
WITH J. A. JOHNSTONE

PINNACLE BOOKS
Kensington Publishing Corp.
www.kensingtonbooks.com

PINNACLE BOOKS are published by

Kensington Publishing Corp.
850 Third Avenue
New York, NY 10022

Copyright © 2008 William W. Johnstone

PUBLISHER'S NOTE
Following the death of William W. Johnstone, the Johnstone family is working with a carefully selected writer to organize and complete Mr. Johnstone's outlines and many unfinished manuscripts to create additional novels in all of his series like The Last Gunfighter, Mountain Man, and Eagles, among others. This novel was inspired by Mr. Johnstone's superb storytelling.

All Kensington titles, imprints, and distributed lines are available at special quantity discounts for bulk purchases for sales promotions, premiums, fundraising, educational, or institutional use. Special book excerpts or customized printings can also be created to fit specific needs. For details, write or phone the office of the Kensington special sales manager: Kensington Publishing Corp., 850 Third Avenue, New York, NY 10022, attn: Special Sales Department; phone 1-800-221-2647.

This book is a work of fiction. Names, characters, businesses, organizations, places, events, and incidents either are the product of the author's imagination or are used fictitiously. Any resemblance to actual persons, living or dead, events, or locales is entirely coincidental.

PINNACLE BOOKS and the Pinnacle logo are Reg. U.S. Pat. & TM Off.

ISBN-13: 978-0-7860-1894-9
ISBN-10: 0-7860-1894-1

First printing: July 2008

10 9 8 7 6 5 4 3 2 1

Printed in the United States of America

*"Bravery is the capacity to perform properly
even when scared half to death."*
—General Omar Bradley

*"The enemy say that Americans are good at the long shot,
but cannot stand the cold iron. I call upon you instantly
to give a lie to the slander. Charge!"*
—General Winfield Scott

Tensions Increase
in Middle East

WASHINGTON, D.C., FEB. 14, 01:39 PM US/EASTERN, ASSOCIATED PRESS. In Washington today the mood is tense, as hostile rhetoric continues to fly back and forth between Tel Aviv and Tehran over the Iranian government's continued refusal to suspend its nuclear program. Israeli officials maintain that Israel will take whatever action is necessary to defend itself in the face of intelligence indicating that Iran intends to launch a nuclear strike at Jerusalem, while the Iranian Foreign Minister accuses the Israelis of paranoia, warmongering, and threatening the stability of the entire Middle East. Iran insists that its nuclear program is for peaceful purposes and not intended for military use. French, German, and Russian officials have called for a diplomatic solution to the crisis, urging the United Nations to step in and restrain Israel from taking any aggressive actions that might lead to war.

At the White House, the President remains in frequent contact with the Israeli Prime Minister and is said to be urging restraint as well. A White House spokesperson has quoted the President as saying, "War is not the answer. It has never been the answer, and it never will be."

PROLOGUE

A village on the Afghanistan/Pakistan border

Hamed al-Bashar felt his chest swell with pride as the bent, robed, and hooded figure of Sheikh Abu ibn Khahir shuffled along the line of freedom fighters, pausing to speak quiet words of encouragement to each of them. The sheikh had come to this remote hill village all the way from the south of France, where he lived. That alone was enough to tell Hamed how important the mission was that he and his companions were about to undertake.

The sheikh was the leader of Hizb ut-Tahrir, a shadowy but growing sect within the Islamic fundamentalist movement. The group had ties with other Islamic organizations throughout the world, but most people considered it a minor player in the ongoing war to cleanse the infidels from the face of the earth and restore Islam to its rightful place of dominance over all creation.

No one would see it that way after Hamed and his comrades concluded their mission, whatever it might be. Then everyone would know the power of Hizb ut-Tahrir and its devotion to the glories of Allah.

Sheikh ibn Khahir paused in front of Hamed and murmured, "You are willing to die for your faith?"

"Sheikh, I am eager to die for my faith," Hamed answered.

"And what gifts will you bring to the infidels?"

"A sword, and fire, and death."

A faint smile touched the sheikh's seamed, leathery face as he nodded in approval at the answer.

Hamed was speaking somewhat metaphorically, of course, and he knew it. A sword would do little good against the hated Americans. There were too many of them. The promise of a sword was only symbolic.

But fire and death . . . ah, those were real, as the Americans would someday know all too well. Someday soon, Hamed hoped.

"Where are you from?"

The sheikh's question caught Hamed by surprise. "Paris," he said. His parents had immigrated to France from Algeria before Hamed was born, and although he had been raised there, he had never felt French. His true nation was Islam, no other.

"I thought I recognized the accent," the sheikh said. "I live in France."

Hamed didn't know what to say. The sheikh's expression was hard to read. Hamed felt the old feelings of inferiority welling up inside him. It had always bothered him that he was not from Saudi Arabia, or Syria, or even Egypt. He was an Arab, not a filthy Frenchman! Even though the Muslim population of France was exploding, as it was throughout all of Europe, Hamed wished that he could have actually grown up somewhere in the Middle East.

But soon that would no longer matter. The twenty men who had been training with him here in this village for the past two months were from several different countries: England, France, Morocco, Egypt, Saudi Arabia . . . there was even an American among them, one who had been born and raised surrounded by filthy infidels.

None of that was important. When their mission was complete, they would all be the same—martyrs to the sacred cause of Islam. And they would be together in heaven, surrounded by beautiful virgins, enjoying all the rewards they would earn by dying. Nothing else mattered.

"What is your name?" the sheikh asked.

"Hamed al-Bashar."

The sheikh half-turned and pointed a bony finger at one of the villagers, a stocky, middle-aged man who was a minor official, one of the party that had greeted Sheikh ibn Khahir and escorted him here to this mud-walled compound on the edge of the settlement where the training had taken place.

"Do you see that man?"

"I see him," Hamed said.

"He is a traitor. The American CIA pays him to betray us."

The villager's eyes widened in surprise and horror. He began to shake his head, whether in denial of the accusation or shock at being found out, Hamed could not have said.

And it didn't matter, because the sheikh had said it and it must be so. One of the sheikh's bony hands came out from under the robes holding a jambiya knife.

"Deal with the traitor, Hamed al-Bashar." As the sheikh spoke, he held out the knife.

Hamed didn't hesitate. He took the knife and walked toward the accused villager, who began to back away in terror. The man's nerve broke and he turned to run.

He had no chance against the younger, faster, stronger

Hamed, who caught him from behind after only a few steps and looped an arm around his neck. Hamed jerked back on the man's head, exposing his throat. The knife flashed in the sunlight as it bit into the tight-drawn flesh. Hamed drew the blade across the man's throat in one deep, strong slash. A crimson fountain of blood spurted into the air and splashed across the sand. The man's body spasmed in Hamed's tight grip.

The sheikh barked a further command, and the knife grated on bone as the blade struck again, going deeper this time. The man's arms and legs flailed, but no one stepped forward to assist Hamed in the task he had been given by the sheikh. Hamed knew how to do this—in theory—but he had never had to put that knowledge into practice before.

Severing the spine posed some difficulties, but the rest of it was easy. Within a few moments the headless body toppled onto the sand and continued to pump blood from the grisly hole where the traitor's head had been attached. Hamed held that head up by the hair as the sheikh nodded approvingly. The men of the village cried out and fired their rifles into the air. Hamed's heart pounded in fierce joy at knowing that he had carried out Allah's will and eliminated a tool of the infidels.

How much more joyful would it be when he performed his holy mission and entered paradise knowing that he had helped to kill not just a single traitor, but rather thousands, perhaps tens of thousands, of those minions of Satan, those hated Americans, delivering unto them their richly deserved punishment for supporting the Israelis, those filthy Jewish interlopers.

O happy day that would be, Hamed thought as he looked at the contorted face of the blood-dripping head he dangled from his hand.

Middle Eastern Crisis Worsens

WASHINGTON, D.C., NOV. 15, 02:51 PM US/EASTERN, ASSOCIATED PRESS. After months of intense, behind-the-scenes negotiations, the agreement-in-principle between Israel and Iran regarding the development of nuclear weapons by Iran has collapsed. This agreement, which was brokered by representatives of the United States, would have opened Iranian nuclear facilities to United Nations inspectors in an effort to bolster Iranian claims that they are not manufacturing weapons of mass destruction. The recent rise to power by more fundamentalist politicians in Iran evidently fueled the collapse of the talks, although a spokesman for the Iranian government insists that there was never any such agreement to start with.

In Washington, the President issued a statement saying that this is only a temporary setback in the ongoing diplomatic process, and that she remains confident a peaceful solution to this crisis that threatens the stability of the Middle East will be found.

BOOK ONE

CHAPTER 1

The President said, "Those goddamn camel-jockeys never had any intention of holding up their part of the bargain."

"Don't let the press hear you using an ethnic slur like that," her husband said with a grin. "After all, you represent the party of tolerance and diversity."

She fixed him with the familiar steely-eyed glare he had seen so many times during their thirty-plus years of marriage. At first, he'd been scared shitless whenever she looked at him like that, because it was in those moments that he had been able to look into her and see her for what she really was.

Over the years, though, he had come to realize that maintaining the façade of a happy marriage was too important to her plans for her to ever direct the full force of her rage at him. All he had to do to remain safe was to exercise just the least bit of restraint and discretion. She had skated by on the edge of enough scandals, both personal and political, that she couldn't afford to let any sort of "accident" befall him, as had happened to others who had gotten in her way.

Besides, he truly did love her, despite knowing that to her, he was mostly just a useful prop. So when they were alone like this, in the upstairs quarters of the White House, he made it a habit to speak as plainly with her as he could. He wanted to help.

"You're right," he went on. "They were lyin' to you from the get-go, just stringin' you along with empty promises so you'd keep the Israelis off their back for a while longer."

She nodded. "Yes, but I believed them at first. I mean, why wouldn't I? They had no reason to fear U.N. inspections. Pulling the wool over the eyes of the United Nations is no great trick. Even a cheap thug like Saddam Hussein was able to do it for years. They never did figure out what he was up to."

"Don't let anybody hear you say that either," her husband advised, and he wasn't smiling now. "Everybody knows that Bush lied and Saddam never had any weapons of mass destruction. You don't want to go lettin' people think that the conventional wisdom might not be true."

She went on as if she hadn't heard him. "All they had to do was hide the real stuff and put on a dog-and-pony show for the inspectors. Then we would have had a good excuse for going along with whatever the U.N. said, and without our backing the Israelis would have had to accept it, too."

"Maybe you don't know the Israelis quite as well as you think you do."

"What do you mean by that?" she snapped.

"I mean that when those folks feel like they've been backed into a corner, they're liable to do almost anything."

The President shook her head. "They won't attack

Iran. My God, they're already surrounded by enemies who want them dead as it is."

"Then they don't have a hell of a lot to lose, now do they?" her husband said softly.

That shook her for a second; he could tell by the way she looked. She truly believed that every setback was only temporary, that in the end everything would work out the way she wanted it to because she was smarter than everybody else. Smarter, and more decent and moral, and anyone who disagreed with her was evil or stupid or both, and therefore destined to lose. Maybe she was right—he hoped she was—but he feared that the rest of the world might not cooperate.

She resumed the pacing that had sent her back and forth across the luxuriously appointed bedroom a dozen times so far during their conversation. "Why now?" she asked. "Everything was looking good. All the Iranians had to do was play along for a while. The whole situation would have cooled down, so that next year would be nice and peaceful leading up to the election. Why throw a wrench in the works *right now*?"

"Maybe they were just stalling for time. Maybe they don't need to anymore."

She stopped and swung around toward him. "You mean you think they're ready to . . . to *do* something?"

"I don't know," her husband replied honestly. "But I got a feelin' there's a shitstorm comin' . . . and we won't be able to deny our way outta this one."

CHAPTER 2

Hamed al-Bashar finished entering the data into the file and saved it, then clicked on the next item in the list and opened a new window to enter more information. The office around him was quiet on a Sunday afternoon. He was the only one who had come in today. Everyone else was home watching football on television.

Not Hamed, though. For one thing, he hated American football, just as he hated everything else about America. But football held a special place in his hatred, and had ever since he had seen news footage on French television of Arab mobs celebrating the deaths of thousands of infidels on 9/11.

One image he had witnessed on that glorious day remained seared in his brain. An Arab man was laughing and dancing for joy in the street in Baghdad or Damascus or some other city; Hamed didn't remember exactly where, and it didn't matter. Perched on the man's shoulders was his son, a boy of seven or eight years old.

And that boy wore a Dallas Cowboys sweatshirt.

The satanic influence of the Americans had wormed its insidious way so far into the Arab world that a child could wear a symbol of the infidels' national sport and not think anything of it. It was at that very moment that Hamed had known that peace was not possible, that Islam could never coexist with such evil. The only way to truly save the world was to cleanse it of all Western influences.

Europe was no threat to that glorious goal. The French? That thought made Hamed laugh. He had been around the French enough to know that they would never successfully resist anything for very long, not without someone else coming to their rescue. The Germans were not much better, and the Spaniards and Italians weren't worth even thinking about.

The British, though, might pose a bit of a problem, but they were already showing numerous signs of giving up. And nowhere in subequatorial Africa or South America was there enough cohesion to represent a threat to the march of Islam. As for China and Russia . . . well, oil and oil money could always buy them off. Anyway, they would be happy to be rid of America, too.

So America—and its godless infidel football—had to go.

There was another reason Hamed was working on a Sunday afternoon. He was a go-getter. That was what his supervisor called him. His instructions were simple— blend in and wait for the summons that would call him to perform the work of Allah.

When that summons would come, and the exact details of the mission he would be given, were unknown to Hamed, but he, like the other members of his group, was patient. Whether it took months or even years, he would be here, in Kansas City, Missouri, working in the transportation division of one of America's largest corporations, helping to coordinate the movement of goods throughout the nation by truck.

His passport, his work visa, and all his other papers were the finest money could buy. The paper trail, a mixture of fact and fiction, stretched back years and showed him immigrating from France to Quebec, where, according to documents in his possession, he had lived and worked for five years before applying for permission to enter the United States. His record was clean and beyond reproach.

Of course, he hadn't entered the United States by legal means, as all his phony paperwork indicated. He had come across the border from Canada in a remote location, along with several others from his cell. The rest of the group had been smuggled across the southern border from Mexico.

Homeland Security . . . what a joke! And the Americans' so-called crackdown on illegal immigration was equally amusing. None of the American politicians, especially those currently in power, really wanted to stop the free flow of illegals from Mexico. Doing so might cost them Hispanic votes. As for the Canadian border, that was just too long and porous to even pretend that any sort of enforcement was possible.

What sort of country was it, Hamed had often wondered, that not only allowed its deadliest enemies to enter it, but practically invited them in?

And the answer was . . . a country of fools.

No wonder the United States would soon be nothing but a bad memory.

"Why, Hamed, honey, what the hell're you doin' here on Sunday?"

The voice took him by surprise and brought him out of a very pleasant vision of America in flaming ruins.

He turned and saw a woman standing by the office door. She wore shorts and a shirt with no sleeves and a pair of those rubber sandals Americans called flip-flops. Her blond hair was pulled back in a ponytail. Hamed secretly burned with shame at the sight of so much female flesh and an uncovered female head, but he forced himself to smile back at her.

"I just thought I'd get a head start on those bills of lading for tomorrow morning's shipments," he said.

"Honey, you're just a workin' fool," the woman said. Her name was Mandy Armitage. She was one of his supervisors, and Hamed burned with shame because of that as well. In an Islamic America, females would have no such positions.

"What are you doing here?" he asked, knowing that he had to make small talk with her so she wouldn't be suspicious of him. Americans chattered incessantly.

"Would you believe it? We're goin' to Arrowhead to watch the Chiefs play the Colts this afternoon, and I went off and left the tickets in my desk." She went across the big room to her cubicle, which was smaller than some but larger than most, to retrieve the tickets. When she had them, she turned and gave him another smile. "Don't work too hard now, hear?"

"Don't worry about that," he told her.

She paused in the doorway. "Say, maybe you'd like to go to a game sometime. We can always get tickets through the company, even when the stadium's sold out."

She was looking at him with lust in her eyes again, he thought. He knew he was not unattractive to American women, with his olive skin and his thick dark hair and his neatly trimmed mustache and beard. He was in superb physical shape. With the least bit of encouragement on his part, Mandy Armitage would lie with him, and she wasn't the only one.

That was out of the question, of course, and even considering such a thing was sinful. But Hamed managed not to show the revulsion he felt as he said, "Sorry, I don't know anything about American football. I wouldn't have the slightest idea what was going on."

"That's right, where you come from people play soccer, don't they? That's what you call football."

That's what 90 percent of the world calls football, you stupid American cow, he thought, *but with your typical arrogance you believe that you're right and everyone else is wrong.*

"I could explain the rules to you," Mandy went on. "I've got four brothers who played varsity, and I was head cheerleader. I'd have you knowin' the difference between a blitz and a post pattern in no time."

"I'll think about it," Hamed promised, with no intention of wasting even a second's thought on such worthless drivel.

"All right, honey. See you tomorrow."

Hamed smiled and waved as Mandy went out, then turned back to his computer. "And I'll see you in hell, you foolish infidel bitch," he said to himself as he went back to work.

CHAPTER 3

McCabe saw the woman as he rolled the big rig into the truck stop parking lot. She was a lot lizard—a hooker, of course. The tight, cutoff blue jean shorts, the equally tight tank top, and the high heels told him that much.

But it was the middle of the night and she was running and she looked scared. McCabe brought the truck to a stop with a hiss of air brakes, opened the door, and called to the woman, "Lady! Over here!"

She hesitated, as if she thought she might be trading one threat for another, but then she veered toward him. He had stepped down from the cab, and she must have thought he looked trustworthy.

What he probably looked like was tired as hell. He'd been on the road since early that morning, pushing the consecutive-hour limit and then busting right through it, risking getting in trouble if he was pulled over and the troopers checked his log. But he was stopped now, ready to crash for the night.

As soon as he dealt with whatever had gotten the hooker so frightened. Couldn't be anything good.

She trotted up to him, pushed her lank blond hair out

of her face, and said, "Mister, just get back in the truck and let's go."

McCabe shook his head. "Nah, I'm stopped for the night."

She clutched his arm. Her long fingernails dug into his skin through the sleeve of the khaki shirt he wore.

"Some people are after me. I'll make it worth your while. You won't even have to pay me. I'll be paying you, I guess you could say."

McCabe looked at her and thought about his wife and said, "Honey, what I got at home, you can't even come close to matching."

She looked surprised and angry as she said, "Well, then, why'd you call me over here, asshole?"

McCabe's voice was mild as he replied, "You looked like you were in trouble."

"The only way you can help is to get me out of—"

"Hey, there she is! Hey, Lindy!"

Three men emerged from behind one of the big tractor-trailer rigs scattered through the parking lot. They started toward McCabe and the woman, moving fast. In the yellow glare of the sodium lights that washed over the parking lot, McCabe saw that they were all tall and muscular. They towered over his medium height, and their shoulders were broader, too. They had youth on him as well. None of them looked to be over thirty.

But their guts were soft. McCabe noted that right away. Big muscles and soft guts . . . not the best combination in the world.

"Oh, hell," the hooker said. "Better go while you still can, mister."

She turned to run again before the three men could reach her.

McCabe stopped her with a hand on her arm. "Stay here," he told her.

She tried to pull away, but couldn't get loose. "You bastard!" she hissed. "You're gonna give me to them."

McCabe didn't say anything.

The three men slowed from their trot to a stop as they came up to the truck. "Thanks, buddy," one of them said to McCabe. "This little lady tried to run out on a business deal after she took our money."

Lindy stopped struggling in McCabe's grip and glared at the three men. "I didn't know what you had in mind," she snapped. "I may be a whore, but there're still some things I won't do."

The man who seemed to be the spokesman for the trio returned the glare. He wore a John Deere cap and had a goatee. "We paid you good cash money," he said as he reached for her. "Now you come on with us like a good girl."

McCabe moved so that he was between the men and the woman. He didn't get in a hurry about it, but he was there before any of them seemed to know what was happening.

"Hold on a minute," he said. "You mean she took your money and ran off?"

"Damn right," one of the other men said. He took his cap off and wiped a hand over his mostly bald head. "That's thievin', in my book."

"Yeah, it is," McCabe agreed. He turned to Lindy. "Give them back their money."

"We don't want the money," Goatee said.

"We want her," the third man said. Tufts of red hair stuck out from under his cap.

"Well, she doesn't want to go with you, so I think she should just give you your money back and we'll all just say that the deal is off." McCabe looked at Lindy. "How about it?"

She was sullen and obviously reluctant to part with the money. "What if I don't give it back?" she wanted to know.

McCabe shrugged. "Then I'll go on inside and get that cup of coffee I've been wanting for the last hundred miles, and you can work things out with these gentlemen on your own."

Before Lindy could say anything else, Goatee said, "You just don't get it, mister. We don't want the money back. We want the girl."

"Yeah," Red said, grinning.

Lindy looked at the three of them, then started to open the little purse she carried. "All right, all right, I'll give them the damn money."

"Now hold on," Baldy began.

"That's the deal," McCabe interrupted. "You boys get your cash back, and you leave the lady alone."

Red said, "Who died and left you in charge, hoss?"

"I'm tired o' this shit." Goatee started to reach past McCabe. "Come on, bitch—"

McCabe put a hand on the man's broad chest. "She said she'd give the money back. That's it. Deal's off."

"What the hell's wrong with you, old man?" Goatee demanded. "You in the mood to get your ass kicked or somethin'?"

McCabe knew what they saw when they looked at him—a guy on the wrong side of forty, with some gray in his dark hair and a decent enough build in his work clothes but nothing special. Just another truck driver, and worn out from a long day on the road.

True enough, he supposed, but it wasn't all the story. They didn't know the places he'd been, the things he'd done.

Goatee thrust his jaw out and said, "I asked you a question, you sumbitch. You lookin' to get your ass kicked or somethin'?"

"Or something," McCabe said.

Then he punched Goatee in that belligerent jaw, as hard as he could.

Goatee went backward. Not far, just a couple of steps, because he was a big man with a lot of weight to move. But that gave McCabe enough room to operate. He half-turned to the left and snapped a kick with his right foot into Baldy's belly. The guy's gut was as soft as McCabe had figured. Baldy doubled over so fast that his cap went flying. He stumbled backward and collapsed on the pavement, curling up in a ball.

Red came at McCabe with fists flying. He was fast and strong and McCabe was no miracle worker. One of the punches got through and clipped him on the side of the head. The impact stunned him.

But instinct and training had taken over by now. McCabe could take some damage and keep functioning. He had taken a lot worse than a punch to the head before. He stepped inside Red's mad rush and brought the base of his left hand up under the man's chin. McCabe overcame his instincts and pulled the blow at the last second so that it wouldn't break the guy's neck and either kill him or leave him a hopeless cripple for the rest of his life. Instead, it just sent Red flying off his feet to crash down onto the concrete on his back.

Goatee had recovered his balance. With a roar he lunged at McCabe and got his arms around the smaller man. Those arms were like tree trunks, and they closed with bone-crushing force.

McCabe broke Goatee's nose with a head butt. Goatee screamed, then screamed again as McCabe's knee smashed into his groin. He let go of McCabe, stumbled around in a wobbly, bent-over circle for a second, and then folded up like a puppet with its strings cut.

McCabe was breathing a little hard. He turned to see Lindy cowering against the rig. "You . . . all right?" he asked her.

"How . . . how did you . . . there were *three* of them!" Her eyes were wide with amazement.

The commotion had drawn some attention. Several men approached from the direction of the truck stop. They were all drivers, and McCabe recognized a couple of them.

One of the men let out a low whistle as he looked around at the three bodies sprawled on the parking lot in various stages of semiconsciousness. He grinned at McCabe and said, "Should've known you'd be mixed up in this trouble, Jackknife."

"It was their idea," McCabe said. "Tried to get 'em to back down, but they were stubborn about it."

"Damn fools, if you ask me," the other man said.

McCabe turned to Lindy. "Why don't you call it a night and go home?"

She still looked a little dazed by what she had seen. After a moment, she nodded and said, "Yeah. Yeah, I might just do that."

"Before you go, though," McCabe said, "get out the money they paid you."

That brought her back to earth. "You mean I really have to give it back to them?"

"Seems like that would be the fair thing to do, considering."

"Do you know what those bastards wanted to do to me?"

McCabe shook his head. "Nope. And I don't want to know. Just get out the money they paid you."

Grumbling, she dug several wadded-up bills from her purse and tried to give them to McCabe. He pointed to the driver who had greeted him earlier and said, "Give it to Roy here. He's honest, and he'll see to it that the money gets back to its rightful owners."

Grudgingly, Lindy handed the bills to the driver called Roy. "Now what?" she asked McCabe.

"Now you go home and don't be around when these fellas recover from our little dance. And I go get some coffee and something to eat and some sleep for what's left of the night."

Lindy watched him go and said, "I don't get it. He was worried about me being here when those guys wake up, but *he's* staying."

"That's because he knows he can take care of himself," Roy told her. "Those dumb bastards picked the wrong guy to tangle with."

Lindy frowned. "He's just a truck driver, isn't he?"

"Just a truck driver?" Roy laughed. "Honey, that's Jackknife McCabe. Ex-Special Forces. He was in Desert Storm, then went back to Iraq years later, after stopovers in Afghanistan, Pakistan, and probably half a dozen of those other 'istan places that used to be part of Russia. Lord knows where-all he's been and what he's done, because he won't talk much about it. But I'll tell you this much . . . those fellas who were hasslin' you, they're lucky to be alive right now. I reckon a lot of bad guys who've run up against ol' Jackknife . . . ain't anymore."

Israeli Jets Hit Iranian
Nuke Facilities

WASHINGTON, D.C., Nov. 16, 03:42 PM, US/EASTERN, ASSOCIATED PRESS. Sources at the White House and the Pentagon, as well as in Tel Aviv, confirm that Israel has launched an air strike against the Iranian nuclear facility in Bushehr. Israeli fighter jets armed with conventional missiles and bombs attacked the facility before dawn this morning. Sources within the Israeli air force say that the target was completely destroyed. However, a spokesman for the Iranian government issued a statement claiming that damage was minor and that the only casualties were innocent civilian workers.

The facility has long been rumored to be an important part of Iran's nuclear weapons program. Speaking on condition of anonymity, an Israeli intelligence officer said,

"We have set them back at least five years with this action."

Iranian officials called the attack an act of wanton, lawless aggression against a peaceful nation and called on the world community to express its outrage over this unilateral assault by Israel. The Secretary General of the United Nations has convened the Security Council and has promised a full investigation of the incident.

The White House is withholding comment for the time being. Press Secretary Davisson said, "I assure you, the President is on top of the situation and will be issuing a statement as soon as she is certain that she has all the facts concerning this incident. I can tell you, though, that she considers this situation to be very grave, and that the response of the United States will be measured and appropriate."

CHAPTER 4

The President's index finger stabbed angrily at the remote control as she switched through the channels on the TV monitor that had been set up in the Oval Office. The story was the same on every network.

". . . aggression by the Israelis . . ."

". . . unconscionable arrogance . . ."

". . . unprovoked act of war . . ."

Well, almost every network.

"You're an absolutely terrible singer. Just appallingly bad."

The President jabbed the button that turned the monitor off. One by one, she looked at the advisors gathered around her.

During the campaign that had gotten her elected, she had promised a rainbow administration, and she had followed through on that promise. The Vice President was young, handsome, and black. The Secretary of State was Hispanic. The National Security Advisor was a striking Chinese American woman who was rumored to be bisexual. The Secretary of Defense was female, too, a former general in the Air Force. The Chairman of the

Joint Chiefs of Staff was the only white male in the
room other than the President's husband, who sat quietly in a corner, if the Oval Office could really be said
to have corners.

Despite the carefully calculated diversity of the
group, at this moment, after being called to this emergency meeting in the White House, they all had a couple
of very important things in common: They were scared,
and they didn't know what to do.

"Well?" the President snapped. "What's our response
to this going to be?"

"How bad is it really?" the Vice President asked. "In
military terms, that is."

The President looked at the Secretary of Defense,
who said, "The Israelis blew the crap out of the place.
Leveled it. It was a good clean strike, too, with little or
no collateral damage, despite what the Iranians are
saying. Our satellite imagery confirmed all of that."

"What about civilian casualties?" the President asked.

The SecDef shrugged. "I'm sure any workers who
were inside the plant at that hour were probably civilians. But they were civilians who knew damned good
and well that they were working on nuclear weapons
that were intended to one day blow Israel off the face of
the earth. I wouldn't call that innocent."

"What about the civilian workers at *our* nuclear facilities?" the President shot back. "Wouldn't you consider
them innocent?"

"Of course I would."

The President folded her arms across her chest. "Well,
the Iranians feel the same way about their people." She
prided herself on being able to empathize with other
points of view—especially those of America's enemies.
"I don't see any way we can support Israel on this."

"What about sixty years of friendship between the United States and Israel?" asked the National Security Advisor. "Doesn't that count for anything?"

The President frowned. She wasn't sure she liked or trusted the NSA. The woman had a brilliant mind and all the proper academic credentials, as well as mixed ethnicity, debatable sexuality, and camera-friendly looks. She was freakin' perfect, as the President's husband had put it . . . except for the fact that the President had come to realize that she didn't fully share all of the administration's views. Neither did SecDef, but being a good soldier, she would go along with whatever her commander in chief said.

"Israel is still our friend," the President said as she looked at the NSA. "But that doesn't mean we have to be one hundred percent in favor of anything Israel happens to do."

The Asian American woman shrugged. "Respond however you want, of course, but if you condemn Israel's action it'll be a slap in the face. The Israelis won't forget it. *And* it'll make you look like you're waffling and soft on the threat of Islamofascism."

"We don't use *that* word in this White House," the President snapped.

"Why not? It's a perfectly good, descriptive word. Or did you mean the word *waffling*?"

The President heard something, and glanced around to see that her husband had his hand over his face. He was trying to look solemn, but she could tell that the big bastard was actually stifling a chuckle. He loved seeing someone get the better of her, even for a moment, probably because he had never been able to.

"All I've tried to do is repair some of the damage that the previous administration did to this country's standing in the community of nations," she said to the National Security Advisor.

"Oh, sure, that's what the rest of the world *says* they want from the United States," she responded, much as she would have slashed right through some feeble argument from a student in one of her classes. "They want us to make nice and consult them on any action before we ever make a move and do whatever they tell us. But when we behave like that, they don't see a strong but cooperative nation. They see a patsy, a pushover. They see an impotent giant without the balls to do what needs to be done." The NSA shrugged. "I'm sorry if that's not politically correct enough for you, Madame President, but you hired me to tell you the truth as I see it—and that's the way I see it."

For a long moment, the President thought about firing the arrogant bitch on the spot. Nobody talked to her like that and got away with it. Nobody. Even her husband would be licking his wounds—literally as well as figuratively, in his case—if he ever dared to speak to her in that tone of voice.

But the slant-eyed slut had a point, the pragmatic part of the President's brain insisted. Ever since the bloody debacle in Iraq caused by the total troop pullout as soon as she took office, America's enemies around the world had been licking their chops, just waiting for the right opportunity to humble the giant even more. So far it hadn't happened, but according to the intelligence briefings from the CIA and Homeland Security, it was only a matter of time. Of *when,* not *if.*

But maybe she could postpone the day when some other rogue nation or organization would spit in Uncle Sam's face. Maybe a show of strength now really *was* what was needed. For one thing, it would take the rest of the world by surprise. It was good to keep your enemies off balance, a little unsure of what to expect.

The atmosphere in the Oval Office following the NSA's comments was thick with tension. The President broke it by turning to the Secretary of State and asking, "What's the diplomatic response by the Iranians going to be? Can they do anything except whine to the U.N. and get the French and the Germans and the Russians to feel sorry for them?"

The heavyset man shrugged his shoulders. "What else *can* they do?"

The President looked at the SecDef and the JCS Chairman. "Militarily?"

"They don't have the capacity to do much of anything," the SecDef replied. "The Israelis wiped out any shot they had at delivering a nuclear strike, and while their conventional forces are fairly strong, they're not up to invading Israel."

"About all they *can* do," the Chairman added, "is turn off the oil spigot."

"Shut down the Strait of Hormuz, you mean?" the President asked.

The man nodded. "That they can do with their navy and air force . . . if nobody's there to stop them."

"What are our assets in the area?"

"A few," the Chairman said. He was an old Navy man, an admiral, and his eyes glittered with the desire to get into the action. "And we can get our carriers in the Mediterranean over there in forty-eight hours."

The President looked at the Vice President, but the gesture was more out of courtesy than anything else. They both knew who was going to make the decision here. But he was strong-willed enough to register an opinion anyway. "I don't see that you have any real choice, ma'am."

The President wanted to look at her husband and see if she could tell what he thought, but she suppressed the impulse. He wasn't the commander in chief here; she was. Her head jerked in an abrupt nod as she looked at the Chairman and said, "Get those carriers to the Gulf, Admiral."

She could tell that he fought to keep from grinning as he snapped to attention and said, "Will do, ma'am."

"All right, everybody out," she went on as she stalked over behind the desk. *Her* desk. The President's desk. The ultimate seat of power in what was still the most powerful nation in the world. "I've got a statement to write. Somebody tell my Chief of Staff to advise the networks I'll address the nation at eight tonight."

She sat down and pulled a legal pad and a pen over to her as they all filed out of the Oval Office, even her husband. He lingered until last, and then looked at her with his bushy eyebrows lifted questioningly, as if he were unsure whether she really wanted him to go, too, or if she might want his help on the speech she was going to have to deliver to the American people.

She flipped an impatient hand at him, shooing him out with the others, and paid no attention to the hurt-puppy-dog look on his face. She had important work to do here . . . at the President's desk.

God, despite all the annoyances, the power felt good. As if she were born to it.

CHAPTER 5

"Accordingly, American aircraft carriers and other elements will be traveling to the Persian Gulf as quickly as possible in order to peacefully secure the region."

Nate Sawyer called from the living room, "Mom, where's the Persian Gulf?"

"Oh, I don't know, it's over in the Middle East somewhere," Allison Sawyer told her son. She was folding laundry on the kitchen table in their little apartment and not paying much attention to the TV. She knew the President was on, talking about that crisis overseas. There was always a crisis somewhere overseas, it seemed like.

"Where's the Middle East?"

"You know, Iraq and Iran and Israel, all those places. Don't they teach you this stuff in school?"

Nate grinned. "I know all those countries you just said start with I. Wanna hear me say the alphabet?"

"You've been saying the alphabet since before you even started to school."

"I could read before I started to school."

Allison wasn't so distracted by the laundry that she

failed to hear the pride in her son's voice. She smiled at him and said, "You sure could, champ."

And she could take some pride in that, too, since she was the one who'd read to him every day since he was a baby. She was convinced that was why he had learned to read by the time he was four and now read at a higher level than any of the other kids in his third-grade class. She knew she wasn't supposed to make too much of a fuss about that; the teacher had told her so. Doing that might foster a sense of elitism in Nate and ultimately damage the self-esteem of the other kids in the class, and you couldn't have that. The whole public education system was geared toward leveling the playing field and making all the kids as much alike as possible.

But facts were facts, and Allison's kid was *smart*. She wanted to make sure he knew it, too.

Maybe that way he wouldn't make the same sort of dumb mistakes that his mom had made, like marrying a self-centered asshole—

"Are we gonna have a war?"

"What?" Allison set aside the laundry she was folding and walked into the living room. Maybe she ought to pay more attention to what the President was talking about, she thought.

"The President said there was gonna be a war between Israel and Iran. Are we gonna be in it?"

Allison sat down on the edge of the sofa beside Nate. "Surely that's not what she said."

"Uh-huh! Just listen."

The camera, steady as a rock, showed the President sitting behind her desk in the Oval Office. She had some papers in front of her, but she wasn't reading from them. Instead she gazed into the camera with an earnest, worried expression on her face.

". . . deeply regret that Israel was forced to take this action by Iran's continued refusal to allow United Nations inspectors in its nuclear facilities. I spoke to the Prime Minister of Israel a short time ago, and he personally assured me that it was imperative action be taken now, without delay. According to information received by the Israeli intelligence services, Iran was less than a week away from launching a missile carrying a nuclear warhead at Tel Aviv."

"See?" Nate said. "A nuclear warhead."

"That doesn't mean there's going to be a war," Allison told him.

But if it was true, it meant that Israel and Iran had come damned close to a war. And it might happen yet if Iran tried any sort of payback for the Israeli air attack. Allison didn't keep up with politics all that much—Nate and her job kept her too busy for that—but there was such a bombardment of news and information all the time now that you couldn't help but be aware of what was going on in this crazy world. Today especially, TV and radio had been full of stuff about what was going on in the Middle East. As usual for that region, things seemed to be teetering on the brink of Armageddon.

"Maybe you should go on to bed," Allison suggested. "You're already up past your bedtime."

"No! I wanna watch the rest of this."

"You don't really care about somebody making a speech, even the President."

"Well . . . there might be somethin' good on afterwards."

Not likely, Allison thought. All the talking heads would have to yammer for another hour about everything the President had said. Politicians and military experts from both parties would be interviewed. The ones from the

President's party would agree with everything she said; the ones from the opposition party would disagree. And none of them would see that if the situation had been exactly the same—hell, if the words of the speech had been exactly the same—and only the party affiliation had been reversed, then their reactions would have been exactly the opposite. That was what Allison hated about politics and why she didn't bother to vote anymore.

"I don't think there's going to be anything else good on tonight," she told Nate. "You go on to your room. I'll be in to read a story to you in a few minutes."

"I can read to myself, you know."

"I know you can." She put an arm around his shoulders and hugged him to her. "But I still like to do it. Let me do it for a while longer, okay?"

"Okay." He trudged off toward his room. He didn't have far to go because the apartment was so small.

Allison leaned back against the sofa cushions and watched the last few minutes of the President's speech. It was full of flowery rhetoric about respecting the rights of sovereign nations and abiding by the rule of law and not allowing ourselves to descend once more into barbarism. All that stuff meant that the President didn't want to go to war. Everybody knew that. The woman's antiwar credentials went way back. And everybody had seen what had happened in Iraq as soon as she took office, too. She had cut and run, choosing sure defeat over possible progress someday. Allison couldn't really fault her for that; that war *had* been poorly run, from what little Allison could see from her civilian standpoint.

That was just it, she thought as the President signed off with the usual "Good night, and bless the United States of America." She, Allison Sawyer, was a civilian. All this stuff going on didn't have anything to do with her. She worried about her son, and her job, and coming up with enough money to pay all the bills at the end of the month . . . with maybe a little left over for an occasional treat. Christmas was coming up after all. It was only a few days until Thanksgiving, and then it would be less than a month until Christmas, and Allison hadn't even started her shopping yet.

But luckily, there was a new MegaMart, one of those giant UltraMegaMarts, only a few miles away, on the Interstate between Fort Worth and Denton, and it was about to have its grand opening on Friday, the day after Thanksgiving. There would be a lot of sales and specials—there always was on what was traditionally the biggest shopping day of the year—but the prices would be even better at the UltraMegaMart on that day. Allison tuned out the talking heads on TV and started thinking about what she might be able to get Nate for Christmas. There would be a huge mob there, of course, but she might have to brave it anyway.

She would do whatever was necessary to make this a good Christmas for her son.

CHAPTER 6

Although the Prophet had taught his followers to practice moderation, Hamed al-Bashar's reaction to what he was hearing and seeing on the television had no moderation to it.

Indeed, he wished he were there in the Oval Office with a sword in his hand—the holy sword of Islam—so he could kill that Zionist bitch.

Hamed had little use for Iranians, of course—they were Shiites, and he was Sunni—but right now his hatred for the Shiites was subordinated to his even greater hatred of the filthy Jews. At the training compound in the hills of Pakistan, his superiors in Hizb ut-Tahrir had taught him that tribal differences had to be put aside for now, because all of Islam faced an even greater threat. It was the goal of the West to wipe out the entire Muslim world, the leaders said, to obliterate all the Prophet's holy teachings, and that was why the cause of jihad was so important. That was why the infidels had to be wiped out first.

The Jews' attack on Iran was just one more example of lawless aggression against the Muslim world. And instead of condemning it, the American President was supporting Israel. In fact, she was sending warships to the Persian Gulf to further suppress the Iranians and interfere with their right to enforce their will in their own waters.

It made Hamed seethe with outrage. He wanted to pick up one of the new Adidas shoes he had bought earlier in the day and throw it through the television screen. Instead, he sat in his apartment in Kansas City and fumed.

After a while, his anger faded and was replaced by depression. He had been in America, living and working with these godless devils, keeping to himself and not doing anything that might make anyone suspicious. Those had been his orders, and he had followed them faithfully. He assumed that the other members of his cell, scattered through the Midwest and the South, were conducting themselves in the same manner. They were probably feeling the same frustration he was.

He was ready for action, ready for the call that would summon him to his mission, whatever it might be. Ready to strike back against the Great Satan.

Ready to die for his holy cause. Eager to die. *Eager* for the day when he would inflict the same sort of pain and suffering on the Americans as they had inflicted on his people. On his brothers—using the word loosely— in Iran, and in all the other places where Westerners had attacked Muslims. Eager as well for the beautiful virgins who would be waiting for him in paradise, but really, that was just a minor consideration. What was important was striking back against the Jews and the Americans. The same thing really. They were all Zionists. Filthy Zionists.

The shrill ringing of the cell phone in his pocket made Hamed jump.

He had bought it in a drugstore in Crosby, North

Dakota, not far from the Canadian border, on his first day in the United States. Along with it, he had bought a time card that was good for a year, and had activated both the phone and the card from a computer in the public library that was connected to the Internet.

Then he had written the phone's number on a piece of paper, put it in a get-well card he had also bought at the drugstore, sealed the envelope that came with the card, addressed it to Bob Wilson at a post office box in St. Petersburg, Florida, bought a stamp from a coin-operated machine in the local post office, and dropped the card in the mail.

There was no Bob Wilson, of course. Well, there probably was, almost certainly was in a country like this, but the owner of that post office box in St. Petersburg most assuredly was not really named Bob Wilson. But once the get-well card arrived, he would have the number of the cell phone that Hamed had carried with him at all times ever since.

But it had never rung, not once, until now.

Hamed fumbled the phone out of his shirt pocket and checked the little display window. UNKNOWN CALLER, it read, just as it should have. He opened the phone, thumbed the button to answer the call, and said, "Hello."

"Hey there, boy. It's your Uncle Billy down in Fort Worth." The male voice was . . . what was it they said on television? As American as apple pie? "How y'all doin'?"

"I'm sorry, you must have the wrong number," Hamed said. The words were burned into his brain. "I had an Uncle Billy, but he passed away a few years ago."

"Aw, I'm sorry to hear to hear that. Sorry to bother you, too. Y'all have a good evenin' now, hear?"

The connection cut off. The call had lasted only a few seconds. But it had accomplished its purpose. Fort Worth,

Hamed thought. That was in Texas. He had studied maps of the United States for endless hours back at the training camp. He knew where every major city in the country was located, and which highways to take in order to get there.

He would start tonight. His tiredness from the day's work was gone. It had vanished in an instant. The call to action had come at last, and further instructions would be waiting for him in Fort Worth. If he drove straight through, stopping only for gas, he could be there in less than a day. Some of the other members of his cell were probably even closer to the rendezvous point. Hamed was already looking forward to seeing them again.

His coworkers would wonder why he didn't show up at the office in the morning. He had been an exemplary employee, right from the start. But he didn't care anymore, now that he had gotten the summons he'd been waiting for ever since he came to this despicable nation.

Those godless infidels at the Midwest Regional Transportation and Freight Division of MegaMart, Inc., would just have to get along without Hamed al-Bashar from now on.

CHAPTER 7

Brad Parker crouched behind a large rock and peered down at the village, which was little more than a cluster of mud huts sprawled at the base of the hillside . . . except for the large, stone-walled compound at the edge of the settlement. Parker's eyes, normally a light bluish-gray, darkened to the color of steel in moments of stress, tension, or anger.

They were the same shade as a battleship now as they narrowed in concentration.

"That's the place?" he asked the man hunkered beside him.

"Yeah, dude, that's it."

The tone of voice sounded odd coming from a man who looked even more like a native of these hills than Parker did—and Parker was burned so dark by the fierce sun that he could pass for a Pakistani hill man when he had to. His companion really had been born and raised in these hills, but Oded Hatali—"Call me Odie, like that dumb dog in the comic strip, man"—had spent years in California working in the computer industry before being recruited by the Company. He had taken to American life like a duck to water, too, finding himself right at home in the Granola State.

Odie was a natural linguist, speaking not only Urdu and Punjabi but also a dozen different tribal dialects and variations on Pakistan's two main languages. When he put on the loose trousers and the long shirt common to Pakistani men, the outfit known as the *shalwar-qamiz,* and pulled a fur cap onto his head, he blended right in with the rest of the country's teeming population.

Brad Parker wore the same sort of garb, only he had a turban wrapped around his dark blond hair, conceal-ing it. His face, all hard planes and angles, was dark enough for him to pass as a native if not too much atten-tion was focused on him. He usually let Odie carry the ball whenever they had to talk to anybody, although technically Parker was the senior member of the duo. He was thirty-five, had joined the Marines at eighteen, fought in Desert Storm, moved over to SpecOps when he was twenty-five, joined the Company at thirty.

So he had spent nearly half his life in the ragtag back-waters of the world, doing the dirty jobs that kept not only the United States but also the rest of the Western world safe—or at least, safer than it would have been otherwise. If the details of some of his missions had ever been made public, the crybaby left-wing politicians and the equally whiny news media would have pitched a shit fit . . . even though some of those self-righteous sons of bitches would have died in terrorist attacks, too. They had no clue how close to disaster they had come at times, no idea how things would have gone straight to hell without Brad Parker and a lot of other men and women like him, nameless, faceless heroes who fought the good fight in the far corners of the world, knowing all the while how reviled they would be by certain elements of society if the truth about their activities ever came out.

Parker didn't give a rat's ass about any of that. He just wanted to protect his country from the bad guys, whatever it took.

And if what he and Odie had discovered was true, there were some mighty bad guys down there in that compound.

"The villagers you spoke to can be trusted?" Parker asked now.

"Yeah, I think so. It's not like they don't have an ax to grind, though. From what they told me, the headman at Jihad U. down there had one of his merry little suicide bombers kill one of the village elders. Sawed the poor bastard's head right off with a knife. The sheikh said the guy was working for the CIA."

"Was he?" Parker asked.

"No, dude, that's what makes it so bad. It was just a mix-up." Odie grinned. "It was another of the elders who was passing intel to us. But he's dead, too, now. Accident. Rock slide got him."

"You sure it was an accident?"

"Yeah, there were witnesses, and I trust 'em."

"What's the connection between the man who was decapitated and the ones who told you about all this?"

"They're his sons," Odie explained. "So they've got a blood debt marked up against the Jihadists. They're not crazy about Westerners, but they hate the sheikh and his people even more."

Hatred was the fuel that ran this entire part of the world, Parker reflected. The feel-good liberals back in the States insisted that everybody was alike under the skin, that there were no real, fundamental differences between people from different cultures. Deep down everybody was human and wanted the same things, said the doctrine according to the Sixties, still the religion of the left.

But that was bullshit, Parker knew. Sure, the people of this region loved their families. But they loved hating their enemies even more. The smallest grudge could bring on a bloody, lifelong war between two factions. How the hell could you even hope to deal rationally with somebody who hated their neighbors and wanted to kill them because of something somebody's ancestors had done to somebody else's ancestors a thousand or fifteen hundred or even two thousand years ago?

The answer was, you couldn't deal rationally with them. But you couldn't let yourself be seduced by their culture of hatred either. You just did your job. Pragmatically, even ruthlessly when you had to, but you didn't let yourself hate these people.

Because that would make you just as bad as they were.

The bleeding hearts had *that* much right anyway, even though they would never understand the realities behind it.

"How many men in the compound?" Parker asked.

"The sheikh went back to France and took his entourage with him. But they've got a new crop of homicidal-maniacs-in-training down there, plus the instructors . . . say thirty to thirty-five, give or take a few."

"And how many fighters can your contacts muster?"

"Twenty-five tops."

"So we're going to be outnumbered."

"Yeah, but we'll have the element of surprise on our side," Odie said. "Those guys think they're safe since the Americans gave Afghanistan back to the Taliban."

"The Americans didn't give Afghanistan back," Parker growled. "One woman did."

"The people put her in office."

"Yeah, and they're already damned sorry they did it. I've got a hunch they'll be even sorrier before it's all over." Parker shook his head. They weren't here to talk politics. "I could call in some air support, but then the Pakistani government would get its panties in a wad. Anyway, if I did that, then it would look like something *we've* done. I want *those* people to do it."

He pointed at the village.

"Al Qaeda, Hamas, Hizb ut-Tahrir . . . those are all local cancers, when you get down right to it," Parker went on. "If we cut 'em out, they'll just grow back, more malignant than ever. But if the locals rise up and get rid of them, maybe then we might see some real progress."

Odie nodded. "A holistic approach to the war on terror. I like it."

Parker's hand tightened on the rifle he carried and his expression grew solemn. "Pass the word to your contacts. We'll hit the compound an hour before dawn."

The night was cold and quiet. It sometimes snowed in these hills during December, but that was rare because overall the climate was too dry for much precipitation to fall. The temperature could get bone-chillingly cold, though, especially when the wind swept down from the Hindu Kush and whistled through the Khyber Pass.

When Brad Parker was a kid, he had read adventure stories about this region by authors like Talbot Mundy and Robert E. Howard. He would have given a lot to have some guys like Athelstan King—"King of the Khyber Rifles!"—or Francis Xavier Gordon with him tonight. Gordon, also known as El Borak, Howard's Texas gunfighter turned American agent in the Hindu Kush, would have known how to handle terrorists. Hell, he probably would have been able to ferret out Osama bin Laden.

But that was fiction, and long-ago fiction at that. This was real. This was now.

This was the time when the killing was about to start again.

Parker and Odie and twenty-two other men were pressed against the wall of the compound. Millions of stars glittered in the frigid heavens above the village. The light from those stars failed to glitter on the barrels of the M-4 rifles the men held, because the metal surfaces of the weapons had been rubbed down with soot. They could be cleaned up later, when this early morning's work was finished.

Odie had led Parker to the house where the tribal fighters were gathered. They were fierce, dark-faced men. Most sported jutting black beards. Black cloaks concealed their lighter-colored clothing. Their eyes had burned with hatred in the lantern light inside the house. The only electricity in the village was in the compound, powered by a generator. But that allowed the whole place to be lit up with floodlights whenever danger threatened, Haj al-Barmuz explained to Parker. Haj was the eldest son of the man who had been beheaded at the orders of the foreign sheikh.

"The first thing we'll need to do is knock out that generator," Parker had said in the local tribal dialect to Haj and the other men. He wasn't as fluent in that tongue as Odie was, but they didn't expect him to be. They knew he was an American and were willing to forgive that, since he was also the enemy of their enemy. Nor had the older men among them forgotten how the Americans had helped the mujahideen in neighboring Afghanistan fight back against the invading Soviets, more than a quarter of a century earlier.

Of course, the mujahideen had repaid the Americans for that aid by fostering some of the most virulently anti-American terrorists to be found anywhere, and Parker hadn't forgotten *that*. These men who were his allies tonight might want to behead him as a godless infidel to-morrow . . . but he would worry about that once the Hizb ut-Tahrir training compound had been destroyed.

Odie had referred to the place as Jihad U., and that was a good description of it. Fanatics from all across the Middle East and even as far away as Europe came here to learn all the skills necessary to carry out terrorist strikes anywhere in the world. Hizb ut-Tahrir meant "the party of liberation," and while the group's original purpose had been to assist the Palestinians in driving out the Israelis, in recent years their goal had grown to include forcing all the foreign devils off Islamic soil.

These efforts were aimed mostly at the American military, which still had a considerable presence in Saudi Arabia and elsewhere in the Middle East, but some of the European countries, notably England and France, had come in for their share of grief. Members of Hizb ut-Tahrir had their bloody hands in all sorts of pies; even when other groups claimed responsibility for terror attacks, like the recent deadly bombings in Liver-pool and Marseille, the operations had been financed by Hizb ut-Tahrir and the suicide bombers had been trained in their grisly work right here at this very compound.

When Parker had mentioned taking out the generator, Haj had grinned and motioned for a couple of his men to open a wooden chest in a corner of the room. From it they took a pair of RPG launchers. Parker recognized the weapons immediately. They were older models, but the rocket-propelled grenades they fired still packed a punch. Parker gave Haj an approving nod, and didn't bother asking where the men had gotten the launchers. He didn't care, as long as the damned things worked.

"We know the building in which the generator is located," Haj had explained. "Two of my men will blow it up, and then the rest of us will attack."

Those two men would be taking a big chance, Parker had thought, but he didn't bother saying it. The guys would know what they were letting themselves in for.

The group had a three-quarter-ton truck. The plan called for that truck to crash through the gates of the compound, carrying a driver and the two men who would handle the grenade launchers. As soon as the gates were breached and the generator had been knocked out, the other men would enter the compound and begin killing everyone they could find before placing explosive charges to level the place.

The current class of trainees gave the enemy a numerical advantage, but the would-be jihadists hadn't been there for very long. They were raw, mostly untrained, and untested when it came to their fighting skills. The odds against Parker's group of ten were not insurmountable.

Death and destruction were the main goals, but acquiring intel was *always* vital. Parker planned to scour the place from one end to the other as soon as all the occupants were dead and see what he could find before they blew it up. You never knew what a raid like this might uncover. The plans for 9/11 had been floating around for quite a while before the day itself arrived. All those deaths could have been prevented with a stroke of luck here and there.

Odie touched Parker's arm and leaned close to his ear in the darkness. "The truck's coming," Odie said.

Parker heard the low grumble of the engine, too, and thought that if he could hear it, so could the guards inside the compound. But they wouldn't think anything of it, he told himself. This was an agricultural area. The guards would think that one of the local farmers was coming in early to get a jump on everybody else at the market.

Parker squeezed Odie's shoulder. "Pass the word," he whispered. "Tell everybody to be ready to move."

Parker's heart slugged hard in his chest. After all this time, all the covert actions, all the firefights, he still felt adrenaline coursing through him and was grateful for it. If he ever reached the point where his heart *didn't* beat fast before going into battle, it would be time to give up this job. Go back to Langley and stand in a classroom and teach other agents how to carry out ops like this.

Yeah, like that was going to happen.

Like he would ever live that long.

The truck rounded a corner, starting to pick up speed as it came into view, and headed straight toward the gates. The guards inside tumbled pretty quickly to what was going on. Parker heard them yelling to each other in Arabic. Floodlights mounted on the walls blazed into life, illuminating both the interior of the compound and the area outside the walls. Parker squinted against the glare. Guns began to pop and bullets pinged off the front of the truck, which had steel plates bolted to it to serve as primitive armor. Men inside the compound screeched in surprise and outrage.

You ain't seen nothin' yet, boys, Parker thought as he tightened his grip on his rifle.

CHAPTER 8

The truck never slowed down, even though several bullets found the windshield and spiderwebbed the glass. That meant either the driver wasn't hit or if he was, he was still able to keep his foot on the gas pedal. The truck hit the gates with a shattering, rending crash of metal and wood.

The volume of fire from inside the compound increased. Even though Parker couldn't see what was going on from where he was, he had been over the plan enough times with Haj and the other tribal fighters to know what was happening. The two men with grenade launchers were drawing beads on the building that housed the generator, exposing themselves to the fire of the guards so they could get a clean shot . . .

Parker heard the *whoosh! whoosh!* of both weapons being fired, followed a heartbeat later by twin explosions that shook the ground under his feet. The floodlights went off as if someone had thrown the switch. Parker knew that wasn't the case, though, because he could no longer hear the steady *chug-chug-chug* of the generator. The RPG guys had blown it to hell.

"Go, go, go!" Parker called in English to Odie, who relayed the order in the local dialect, not that all the tribal fighters needed the translation. Parker figured most of them would understand the tone of his voice.

The men dashed toward the gates in the sudden darkness. Another *whoosh* sounded, and something blew up inside the compound. At least one of the men with the grenade launchers had lived long enough to get off a second shot. But no more explosions came as Parker, Odie, and the men from the village darted through the opening where the wrecked gates had stood and split up around the now-stopped truck. The rifle fire continued unabated, though.

The compound's defenders couldn't see what they were shooting at with the generator knocked out and the floodlights off. Parker and Odie wore night-vision goggles that they had pulled down over their eyes once the floodlights were out. That gave them an advantage. As they hurried past the stalled truck, Parker glanced into the cab and saw the motionless shape slumped over the steering wheel. The odds had caught up to the driver.

The same was true of the men with the grenade launchers. Both of them were sprawled on the ground, one on each side of the truck. They were riddled with bullets. But they had lived long enough to do their jobs. The building that had housed the generator was a blazing ruin. Parker didn't look directly at it because the flames would have been blinding through the goggles.

He spotted several men standing outside one of the other buildings, firing rifles and machine guns toward the place where the gates had been. The terrorists knew that was where the follow-up attack would come. They were just a little too slow in concentrating their fire there. Parker snapped his own rifle to his shoulder and began

squeezing off shots. The volley rolled out smoothly from
the weapon, and every time it bucked against his shoulder, another of the compound's defenders folded up or
went over backward as Parker's bullets tore through him.
He killed five of the goat-humping bastards in a handful
of seconds.

Then, as bullets whistled past his ears and kicked up
dust at his feet, he whirled away from the barrage and
leaped behind the corner of a building. He reached
under his cloak, found one of the grenades attached to
his flak jacket, and leaned out from cover to fling it
through an open doorway. He heard men shout in alarm,
but their cries were drowned out a couple of ticks later
by the eruption of the blast.

Parker had done his part, killing enough of the terrorists so that the odds should now be even between them and
the local fighters. But he had never been one to sit on the
sidelines, even for a moment. He spotted Odie crouched
behind one of the jeeps that was parked inside the compound, and called to his partner. When Odie looked
around, Parker gestured toward the largest building, which
was probably where the local leaders of Hizb ut-Tahrir
lived, along with being the administrative center for the
group.

Parker and Odie darted out of cover and sprinted
toward the building, swerving back and forth to throw
off the aim of anyone trying to draw a bead on them.
The battle was going on all over the compound now.
Muzzle flashes split the darkness, the flames from burning buildings rose higher in the predawn gloom, and the
chatter of automatic-weapons fire was interspersed with
the screams of dying men.

The sounds were ugly, even to a man of Parker's experience. He tuned them out as he bounded onto a porch

attached to the front of the largest building. The structure was made of wood instead of mud or stone, wide planks of raw, unplaned lumber that must have come from the trees on the mountains that loomed over the village. Parker kicked the door open and went through with his rifle held ready to fire.

He and Odie found themselves in a long, barrackslike room. Give these guys credit, Parker thought. They didn't live high on the hog, like old Saddam had over in Iraq. Their cause meant more to them than luxurious surroundings or personal possessions. Parker could have almost admired them for their courage and devotion to what they considered their duty . . .

If that "duty" hadn't included slaughtering thousands of innocent men, women, and children, and doing it in the name of their god at that. They were death-loving lunatics, and no amount of flowery rhetoric could cover that up.

Parker held up a hand to stop Odie in his tracks. "Listen," he hissed.

From somewhere in the building, he heard a familiar whining sound. That was a shredder being worked, Parker realized. Fearing that the compound was under attack by the American military or CIA, one of the group's headmen was trying to dispose of vital documents.

Parker knew that, and he didn't want any more papers to go in the shredder. He pinpointed the sound as best he could, and than ran to the end of the barracks room, where he found a narrow set of stairs.

He and Odie went up the stairs as fast as they could. Parker knew whoever was up there could hear the clumping of their boots on the steps, but that couldn't be helped. He paused before he reached the top of the staircase and searched under his cloak for another grenade. Selecting it by its shape and feel, he armed it and tossed it, then ducked his head and covered his ears. A couple of steps below him, Odie did the same.

The flash-bang grenade went off with devastating effect, blinding and deafening anyone who wasn't ready for it. The eye-searing, ear-numbing blast lasted only a second, and then Parker and Odie were moving again. They lunged up the rest of the stairs and came out in a room with several desks in it. Three terrorists were stumbling around, pawing at their eyes, obviously disoriented. Two carried rifles and one had a pistol. The man with the pistol bumped into one of his fellow terrorists, yelled in alarm, and turned and started shooting, jerking the pistol's trigger in panic-stricken fashion. The unlucky bastard who'd bumped into him flew backward, half his head blown away by the bullets.

Dumb jackass, killing his own man, Parker thought as he lifted his rifle. That just made it easier for him and Odie. He sent a two-round tap coring through the pistol-wielder's skull while Odie shot the third and final terrorist in the chest. They stepped over the bodies to get to the desks.

Parker became aware that the sounds of battle from outside in the compound had slowed down. The firing was more sporadic now. He hoped that meant his team had just about won. "See how the others are doing," he told Odie, "while I see what I can find in here."

Odie nodded and hurried back to the stairs. Parker started pawing through a heap of papers piled on the desk where the shredder was set up. It stood to reason that the terrorists would have started disposing of the most important papers first, but that wasn't a hard-and-fast rule. Who knows what might be scattered in this mess?

Parker read Arabic fairly well, and was able to start

making two piles as he sorted through the documents, one for papers that were obviously unimportant, just mundane details of running the compound, the other for documents that might contain valuable intel. He scanned the writing that resembled chicken scratches, picking out familiar names and places. Islamic terrorism was like a spiderweb, with strands going every which way and connecting one group to all the others. He was beginning to get the idea that Hizb ut-Tahrir was at the center of that web, even more so than Al Qaeda.

He stiffened in shock as he stared at one document. It appeared to be notes of some sort, made during a meeting of the organization's top planners. The plot they set forth was so hideous that it shook even Parker, who had thought that he knew the depths to which these bloodthirsty madmen could sink. But now he saw that he was wrong. Worse yet, this plan appeared to be on the verge of being implemented, to strike back against the United States for its support of the Israeli air attack on Iran's nuclear bomb factory.

Parker's eyesight blurred slightly. The night-vision goggles made it hard to read. He ran a finger along a line of Arabic scrawls, seeing the characters that translated, at least loosely, into the term "sleeper cell." Hizb ut-Tahrir had agents already inside the United States, waiting for orders. It had long been known in the intelligence community that Al Qaeda had agents in the U.S. Many of them had been identified, and the FBI and Homeland Security kept tabs on them as best they could without tipping off the agents that their identities were known.

But as far as Parker knew—and admittedly, he could be behind the curve on this—the Powers That Be were unaware that Hizb ut-Tahrir agents were already in the

country. This was important stuff, especially considering
what that crazy sheikh was planning for them to do.
Parker stuffed the handful of papers inside his jacket. He
had to get out with these and pass them on to his superiors, no matter what else happened. Somebody had to
warn the folks back home.

The sudden burst of automatic-weapons fire somewhere close by made him jerk his head up. He saw Odie
backing up the staircase and shooting at a figure below.
The young California transplant reached the top of the
stairs and stumbled, sitting down hard. Odie twisted
around and yelled in English, "Get out of here, dude!
Now!"

Parker saw the bloodstains on Odie's clothes. They
were black through the goggles. He took a step toward
his partner as Odie tossed a grenade down the stairs.
The blast stopped the shooting.

Odie turned to him again and motioned weakly
toward the windows. "Courtyard's clear, and the C-4's
planted. Get out while you can, Brad."

"We're both getting out," Parker insisted. "I'll call for
choppers—"

"I'm hit too bad for that, and I think some of them are
still alive down below. They'll be comin' up the stairs in
a second. I'll hold 'em off—"

A cough wracked Odie, and blood gushed from his
mouth.

"Go on, man," he half-whispered. "I don't know if
you found any good intel, but if you did, you gotta get
it out of here."

Parker had found some good intel, all right. Vital
intel. And Odie was right—it had to be extracted.

But that meant leaving a man behind, and doing that
went against every instinct in Parker's body.

"Damn it, Odie—" Parker began as he took another step toward his partner.

The firing from below began again. Odie swung the muzzle of his rifle from side to side and sprayed lead down the stairs as he shouted, "Burn in hell, you pricks!"

Then he went over backward as more slugs ripped into his body.

Parker knew he had no choice. He opened the window and started climbing out. He glanced back to see that Odie had been able to push himself upright again, even as badly wounded as he was, and was still firing at the enemy.

That image was burned into Parker's brain as he dropped the dozen feet or so to the ground.

He was running as soon as his boots hit the sand. He'd been forced to leave behind a lot of documents that might have proven to be important in the ongoing battle against terrorism. But he had the most important paper of all, the notes detailing the latest and most heinous plot hatched by the bastards since 9/11.

Bodies of the tribal fighters were sprawled everywhere, along with the dead homicidal-maniacs-in-training, as Odie had called them. It looked to Parker like the two sides had pretty much wiped each other out. Unfortunately, a few of the terrorists had survived. They were the ones who had killed Odie—and now they spilled out of the building Parker had just left, giving chase as he sprinted toward the gates.

There were only four of them, he told himself. He could stop and fight. But with the information he was carrying, getting away was more important, even if it went against the grain. He darted around the truck that had been used to crash through the gates.

As he did, he was hit. The blow felt like a giant hand

slapping him in the side. He spun out of control, hit the ground, rolled over a couple of times. As he came back up on his knees, he told himself to ignore the fiery pain in his side and squeezed the rifle's trigger. Set on full auto, it spewed death at the onrushing terrorists. Two of them were knocked backward. Another stumbled forward a few steps before falling on his face. But the fourth man kept coming.

Parker's rifle ran dry.

There was no time to slap another mag into the weapon. The only break Parker caught was that the other guy's gun was out of bullets, too. The jihadist flung it aside and jerked a knife from behind the sash around his waist. Parker grabbed the guy's wrist in both hands as the blade slashed at him. The terrorist's momentum carried him into Parker, and the collision sent both of them to the ground.

From there on out, it was a desperate, hand-to-hand struggle. *Mano a mano,* Parker told himself crazily as more thoughts of El Borak came back to him. He hung on for dear life with one hand and used the other to slam a hammer fist into the guy's head. A heave of Parker's body sent the terrorist toppling to the side. Parker lunged after him, still hanging on the wrist of the guy's knife hand, twisting his arm, forcing it down . . .

The man let out a sharp, short cry, then a long sigh as his knife went into his own chest. Parker bore down and buried the blade as deep as he could. The terrorist's head fell back. Parker had seen enough men die to know that the guy was done for.

He left the knife where it was and struggled to his feet. His hand went to his side to check the wound, but surprisingly, he didn't find any blood. When he reached into his jacket, he pulled out fragments of his radio.

Well, he couldn't call any choppers in to extract him

now, he thought. The radio had saved his life by stopping the bullet. The impact had been enough to knock him down and hurt like hell, but the slug hadn't penetrated.

It might have doomed him anyway, though, since he was a hell of a long way from anywhere, with no transportation but his own two feet. He would have to make his way back to what passed for civilization in this backwater country on his own.

But at least no one would be chasing him. As he looked around, he seemed to be the only person left alive in the compound. In the nearby village, the inhabitants would be cowering in their beds, waiting to see if the shooting was going to start again.

Maybe he could find another truck that was in running order, Parker thought as he reloaded his rifle. Lord knows the one they had used to bust in here was shot all to hell.

He broke into a stumbling run that steadied somewhat as he loped off into the darkness. He hoped it wouldn't take him too long to contact his superiors. The intel he carried had to be passed on to the proper people ASAP.

Parker hoped it wasn't already too late.

The American never looked back, so he failed to see one of the wounded men inside the compound lift his head. Ibn bin Suleiman hurt terribly, but he didn't think he was so badly wounded that he would see paradise this day. Still, he would have welcomed death—if it had not been for the fact that the American might have discovered what was being planned for that nation of infidels. Suleiman had meant to shred those notes, but he hadn't gotten to them yet when the dogs burst in . . .

He pushed himself to his feet. He had heard one of

the Americans say something about C-4. That was an explosive, Suleiman knew. He was quite familiar with it, in fact, having taught scores of young men how to blow themselves up with it, along with as many of the godless as possible. Suleiman knew now that he had to get out of here. He had to warn his friends that their plan might have been discovered. And if possible, he had to stop that American and make sure that he didn't tell anyone about what had been planned here.

Suleiman stumbled through the wrecked gates and started toward the village.

He had gone less than fifty meters when the explosions began behind him. The concussion knocked him to the ground, and as he pressed his face to the sand, he thought that it sounded as if the entire world were coming to an end . . .

CHAPTER 9

"Hey, it's not like it's the end of the world, old buddy-roo," Ellis Burke said into his cell phone as he inched along in the heavy traffic on the interstate. "Trust me, this is just a minor setback. We'll still get everything we want from those bastards at the insurance company. You remember everything I told you, right? You don't ever step outside the house without that collar around your neck? *You stupid asshole!* . . . No, no, not you, Mitch. I'm talkin' to this guy in front of me who won't get off his brakes . . . Yeah, you just do like I say, and payday's a-comin' . . . Hey, who's the lawyer here, you or me? I've handled hundreds of these cases. Thousands! Those insurance sons o' bitches'll cave. You'll see . . . Okay. No, that's all right, no need to apologize. Of course you worry about it. You're out of work. Your family's future depends on this settlement."

So did the next payment on Burke's Caddy, but he didn't say anything about that to the client. It was always best to keep it all about *them,* and never remind them that *he* stood to collect a big chunk of change from this case, too. He needed the money as much as Mitch Sherman did; otherwise, he was gonna have to choose between the car payment and the child support payment. Couldn't make 'em both this month.

But he was confident that the insurance company's lawyers would give in once they'd strutted around and acted like hard-asses for a while. They had to make it look like they were worth that big retainer the insurance company paid them. Ellis Burke didn't know why, instead of paying off legions of high-priced attorneys, insurance companies didn't just deal fairly with the folks who filed claims against them. Hell, they had all the money in the world to start with. It was only fair that they spread some of it around.

"All right, Mitch, all right, I'm glad you called. I'll be in touch . . . Nah, at this point, we can't really expect any movement until next week. It's Thanksgiving in a couple of days. People are already thinking about turkey and football and Christmas shopping, instead of lawsuits. Gimme a call on, like, Wednesday if you haven't heard anything from me, okay? Okay-doke. Bye-bye."

Burke closed the phone, slid it into his shirt pocket, and thought, *Asshole.*

He told himself he shouldn't be that way. It wasn't Mitch's fault that he'd been born and raised in a state full of gun-nut, execution-loving assholes . . . and assholes who didn't know how to drive at that.

"Can't you just go on and get out of the friggin' way!" Burke shouted at the drivers clogging the highway in front of him. Traffic hadn't come to a dead stop, but it was really creeping along. Burke wished he was back in New York, where people had the good sense to use public transportation. You'd think with all the ugly, empty space in Texas, the highways wouldn't be so damned crowded.

That was because too many "damn Yankees" had moved down here, to hear the local yokels tell it. He got fed up with them getting mad whenever somebody with some common sense—namely him or somebody else from an actual *civilized* state—tried to explain that you couldn't keep doing things the same way just because that was the way Cousin Zeke and Uncle Jed had done them for the last hundred and fifty years. Frickin' Wild West lunatics with their gun racks and their racist Confederate Rebel Nazi bumper stickers and their love affair with the death penalty. What was he doing down here in this Lone Star Insane Asylum anyway?

Fighting for justice, that's what.

He couldn't let himself forget that. His was the voice of blue-state reason and sanity, crying out in the red-state wilderness.

When his wife had said that she wanted to move back home, back to Texas, at first he'd said forget it, that he wouldn't be caught dead in such a backward place. But since she was pregnant, she wanted to be closer to her mama—and that was the way she had phrased it, too, closer to her mama—and Burke supposed he could understand that. So he'd agreed, figuring that as smart as he was, he could run rings around those cracker lawyers down South.

What he hadn't reckoned with was the good ol' boy network that ran from the very bottom to the very top of the Texas legal system. The bastards shut him out because he wasn't one of them. He couldn't get the important cases, the cases where he might be able to make an actual difference and do some good for the common man.

No, he was reduced to taking on personal-injury lawsuits on a contingency basis, and not even the big-money tier of those. He supplemented what he made there with

DUI and drug-possession and hot-check defenses, which pretty much assured that he was stuck dealing with world-class bubbas and bubbettes. He told himself that he was doing some good by getting fair settlements for people who deserved them . . .

But it was a far cry from saving the world as he'd set out to do, wasn't it?

Since the traffic wasn't moving, he glanced at himself in the rearview mirror. When had his face gotten so broad and red and beefy? When had those lines appeared around his eyes? What the hell was that gray doing in hair that was supposed to be thick and black? He'd been in Texas less than ten years, and already that handsome young liberal firebrand who had come out of law school in New York was gone.

He never should have listened to Rebecca. He should have insisted that they stay right where they were. If they had, he would have gone into politics by now. He'd be a congressman, or maybe even a senator. He'd be in Washington, where he could really accomplish something, instead of creeping along a crowded interstate north of Fort Worth, just another ambulance-chasing shyster.

And the thing that really sucked about it was that Rebecca was gone. She'd gotten tired of him and left, taking their daughter with her. Burke had had no shot at getting custody, not with the affairs he'd had and the drunken-driving charge—even though he'd been able to get it dismissed—and all the other crap Rebecca had threatened to dredge up if she had to. He went along with what she wanted, so that Vicky wouldn't have to be dragged into a nasty court fight.

And if he wanted to be honest about it, he wouldn't have had a whole lot of ammunition to use against Rebecca anyway. She was a smart woman . . . just not smart enough to realize that she shouldn't have married some handsome young crusading attorney when she went off to New York to study art.

Burke took both hands off the steering wheel since the car wasn't moving anyway, spread his fingers, and said, "Where the hell did all these people come from anyway?"

When he and his wife and daughter had moved north of Fort Worth, this area wasn't even the suburbs. It was country. So much country that the quiet at night creeped Burke out. But DFW Airport was close, and the cities of Fort Worth and Dallas weren't much farther away. They called it a megalopolis now, stretching for almost a hundred miles from east to west, and still growing.

In recent years that growth had exploded northward, taking in Denton, a picturesque little university town. Alliance Airport, a sprawling complex that was an air-freight hub for the entire region, had gobbled up thousands of acres of what had once been farm and ranch land. A NASCAR track was built not far away. Housing and shopping, hotels and restaurants had soon followed.

Just in the time that Ellis Burke had lived here, the country had disappeared, replaced by mile after mile of the worst urban sprawl. The air pollution and traffic were so bad that people were already starting to call the area Little L.A.—but it didn't have any of L.A.'s benefits because it was populated by a horde of mouth-breathing rednecks.

Burke did his best not to let them corrupt him with their racist attitudes and rampant consumerism. He still read the *New York Times* instead of any of the local rags, and he donated money to the local PBS station every time they had a pledge drive. He listened to NPR. He wished he could drive a more fuel-efficient car, maybe a hybrid, but he'd found that he needed the Caddy for his image. People down here didn't take a lawyer seriously unless he drove a Cadillac or a Lincoln. But he tried to fight back with bumper stickers that savaged the previous administration and boosted the current one. He'd found that a surprising number of the locals agreed with him, proving that not *everybody* in Texas was a reactionary, knuckle-dragging conservative.

Despite everything, though, sometimes you had to just go with the flow. Like today, when he found himself driving around looking for the one thing his daughter wanted most for Christmas, some sort of singing, dancing puppet thing that was overpriced and probably made in Taiwan by slave labor in some sweatshop run by a corrupt dictatorship propped up by American military and financial aid. But Vicky wanted it, so he was going to do his best to find it.

No luck so far. They hadn't made enough of the little bastards in that sweatshop. Either that, or the company was holding them back to create more demand so they could jack the price up higher.

That was the sort of thing companies did all the time, having learned their lesson from Big Oil. It would serve the corporations right, Burke thought, if everybody stopped buying for a while. Just stopped buying everything, to teach the fat cats a lesson. See how long the consumer-driven economy could stand *that*. The thought made him grin.

But of course it would never happen, because little girls like his daughter wanted toys. Everybody wanted toys. So the corruption rolled on, and Ellis Burke was part of it whether he wanted to be or not.

If worse came to worst, he told himself as he wiped

sweat from his forehead, he knew where he could get the thing Vicky wanted.

They'd have it at the new UltraMegaMart that was about to open just up the road a couple of days from now on Friday. Going to that high temple of American excess would be an ordeal, but he supposed he could do it for his daughter. It would have to be Friday, too, the day after Thanksgiving, because after that they might be sold out of the thing he wanted.

That eased his mind a little. Sure, he hated the thought of braving a crowd of unwashed rednecks, especially after they'd spent the entire day before stuffing their faces with Thanksgiving dinner and drinking beer and rooting for the damned Dallas Cowboys, but he could do it. For Vicky. For his little girl.

How bad could it be?

CHAPTER 10

Traffic was really backed up in the northbound lanes of the interstate. The southbound lanes were moving a little faster. Hamed was grateful for that. He was anxious to reach his destination. Fort Worth was not far ahead of him now. In fact, as his car topped a long rise, he was able to see the tall buildings jutting up from the prairie ahead of him, still some five or ten miles to the south.

He took the prepaid cell phone from his pocket. Before he'd ever entered the country, he had been given a phone number to commit to memory. The plan called for him to use it when he reached the destination to which he was summoned when the call to action came. He thought he was close enough now. He hadn't programmed the number into the phone; that would have been too risky. But he had no trouble thumbing the ten digits and then hitting the connect button while he was driving.

He heard the phone on the other end ringing. Wherever it was, whoever owned it would see the number of Hamed's phone and would know who was calling. So he wasn't surprised when there were no preliminaries, just a neutral-sounding voice that spoke an address when the call was answered. Hamed repeated it back, and the connection was broken. Quickly, so that there was no chance of him forgetting it, he entered the address into the GPS unit mounted on the car's dashboard. A moment later a map popped up on the unit's screen.

Hamed followed the turn-by-turn directions given to him by the computer-generated voice. They led him around Fort Worth on a loop to the east, into the densely packed suburbs between the cities of Dallas and Fort Worth. Everywhere he looked were housing developments, apartment complexes, and shopping centers dominated by the so-called "big box" stores. He saw perhaps a dozen different MegaMarts and grimaced each time he passed one of them. These American cities were nothing like Paris. They had no charm, no grace, and the starkly ugly MegaMarts were the perfect symbols of everything that was wrong with the American infidels and their godless culture.

The voice from the GPS unit instructed him to leave the highway. He did so, and followed a route of twists and turns into the mazelike apartment complexes. He recognized the name of the street he was on. He had to be close to the address he was given.

He found it a few minutes later. The apartment complex was not new, not fancy, but it appeared to be fairly well cared for. The parking places were not reserved, so he slid his car into one of them and stopped. He had been on the road for a long time, so his back was stiff when he climbed out of the vehicle. As he stretched, trying to unkink the sore muscles, he was aware of the gun tucked behind his belt at the small of his back, its butt covered by the tails of the loose shirt he wore. He hadn't carried it there for the whole trip, of course; that would have been too uncomfortable. But as he approached his destination he had taken the weapon from between the car's bucket seats and concealed it under his shirt. He didn't know what he was walking into, but he wasn't going to do it unarmed.

The apartment number was 427, but the building had only two stories. It was arranged in a square around a central courtyard that contained a swimming pool. Signs were posted on each leg of the square, giving the numbers of the apartments it contained, so Hamed had no trouble finding 427. It was on the second floor, overlooking the pool, which had been drained and stood empty at this time of year. It looked forlorn somehow. Dead leaves from the trees in the courtyard had blown into it.

Hamed knocked on the door and was surprised when a woman opened it—a very attractive woman at that, although her long, raven-black hair should have been covered instead of displayed so openly and shamelessly. Hamed concealed his reaction and said in English, "Hi. I'm looking for Steve."

"Sure, he's here," the woman said as she stepped back from the door. "Come in."

Hamed did so—then froze as the woman shut the door behind him and pressed what felt like the barrel of a gun against the back of his neck.

CHAPTER 11

McCabe was glad to be home. The rest of the run had gone just fine, no problems, after that little fracas a couple of nights earlier at the truck stop. He'd made it on down to Jacksonville, delivered his cargo, and deadheaded back to Fort Worth, something of a rarity in this day and age when every precious drop of fuel had to be used efficiently. Somebody in Transportation up in Kansas City had fouled up, because McCabe wasn't supposed to pick up another load at the distribution center at Alliance Airport until Monday.

But that was MegaMart's problem, not McCabe's. He was just looking forward to spending the Thanksgiving holiday at home for a change, instead of carrying merchandise across the country. Maybe they would even do some shopping. Seemed fair, when you considered that he spent most of his days delivering things for *other* people to buy.

He'd had his own truck and been an independent for a while after retiring from the military, and he'd liked it. After being part of a group for so long, it felt good to be on his own, responsible for nobody but himself.

Problem was, he *wasn't* responsible just for himself. He had a wife and a daughter to take care of, too. And he felt like Terry and Ronnie deserved the best possible life he could give them, since they had spent so many years pretty much taking care of themselves on various military bases around the country, while he was off on the missions that had taken him around the world, to some of the most hellish spots on the face of the earth.

But they'd had it rough sometimes, too. Low pay, endless red tape, frequent moves . . . Terry and Ronnie had had to deal with most of it alone. They had always come through, though. His guys, he called them because of their masculine nicknames. They didn't want to be Theresa and Veronica. They preferred Terry and Ronnie.

Not that there was anything remotely masculine about them except their nicknames. At thirty-eight, Terry still had the same earthy, cowgirl-type beauty as the coltish twenty-year-old that McCabe had fallen in love with when he first saw her. She wore her blond hair a little shorter these days, but there was no gray in it and her body was almost as lithe and supple as it had ever been.

Ronnie had inherited her father's darker looks—and darker moods, if the truth be known—and at sixteen she was turning into a lovely young woman. McCabe had already had to put the fear of God and the Special Forces into a couple of boys that Ronnie had dated. They'd seemed like good kids, so he hadn't tried to scare them off entirely, but he'd made sure they knew he had been trained to kill with his bare hands, in any number of lethal ways. After Ronnie had gone off with her dates, McCabe and Terry had shared some good laughs at the way the boys' eyes had widened while he was talking to them.

It was because of the two of them, the two most precious people in the world to him, that he had gone to work for MegaMart. As an independent trucker, he'd had to be on the road too much just to make a living. Terry and Ronnie had spent enough time alone while he was in the military. True, as a driver for MegaMart, he was still gone quite a bit, but at least his schedule wasn't as erratic and he was usually able to get home several days each week. Sometimes he even managed to be home for four or five days in a row, like now.

He was in the living room of their house in River Oaks, one of Fort Worth's older suburbs, with his feet up, the newspaper in his lap, and his eyelids getting heavy. It was Wednesday, the day before Thanksgiving. Ronnie was out of school today—when McCabe was a kid they had gotten Thanksgiving Day and the Friday after it off from school, but never Wednesday—but she and Terry had been busy all day on some sort of project that was due right after the holiday in Ronnie's biology class. McCabe was willing to help out, but Terry was better at that sort of stuff. She'd been a teacher herself at one time, although at the elementary level, not high school biology.

McCabe gave up on trying to hold his drowsiness at bay and closed his eyes. They had been shut for only a few moments, though, when Ronnie came into the room and said, "Daddy, we're going shopping on Friday. You wanna come with?"

McCabe tried not to grimace. Since when did kids who lived in Texas talk like streetwise New Yorkers? Of course, Ronnie had lived in lots of different places, on lots of different bases. It wasn't like she'd been raised here in Texas. But McCabe, himself a Texan, born, bred, and forever, had heard kids who had lived here all their lives talking the same way.

It was because of all the TV and movies they watched

and all the time they spent on the Internet, he supposed. American culture was blending together, with the distinctive pockets of how people in different parts of the country spoke and acted slowly fading away. That was good in its own way, he supposed, but regrettable, too. Like the seasons, the differences in people made for welcome changes.

He opened his eyes and repeated, "Shopping? On Friday? Black Friday? The busiest shopping day of the year?"

Ronnie nodded. "Yeah. We thought we'd go to the grand opening of that new UltraMegaMart."

McCabe bit back a groan. He saw enough Mega-Marts in his line of work. "You and your mother can go and have a great time," he said. "I think I'll pass."

"You sure? It's supposed to be the biggest MegaMart in the world. It's as big as a mall all by itself."

"If you're trying to convince me, you're going about it the wrong way," McCabe said, but he grinned to take any sting out of the words. "Besides, I've seen the place. I know how big it is. I even delivered a truckload of stock there a couple of weeks ago."

"Oh, yeah," Ronnie said with a grin of her own. "You work for MegaMart. I forgot."

"Sure you did."

Ronnie grew more serious. "I need some stuff for my project. You think they'll have it?"

McCabe didn't bother asking what sort of "stuff" she needed. If the world's first UltraMegaMart lived up to all of its hype, it would have what Ronnie needed, whatever that might be.

"Don't worry about that," McCabe told her. "I'm sure you'll find just what you're looking for."

CHAPTER 12

Parker saw the lights of Islamabad ahead of him as the ancient Volkswagen bug bounced along the potholed road that passed for a highway here in Pakistan. He tried to miss the worst of the craters for fear that they'd knock the car's suspension out. If he'd been in America, he would have said that a vehicle this old was held together with spit, baling wire, and bubble gum, but he didn't know what the Pakistani equivalent of that phrase was.

All he knew was that he had to get to the American embassy, and get that document in the hands of people who could do something about it, before it was too late.

It might be too late already. Here in Pakistan the hour was just after midnight. That made it Thursday. Thanksgiving. Although to the Pakistanis it was just another day. Pilgrims and parades, turkey and pumpkin pie didn't mean a damn thing to them.

What it meant to Parker was that he had somewhere between thirty-six and forty-eight hours to prevent mass murder. In this age of instant communication, that was an eternity. Plenty of time to do what needed to be done.

But if things went wrong, if he failed to deliver the intel, those hours could speed by like minutes.

He had caught a break when the guy who owned this Volkswagen stopped to ask Parker if he needed a ride. Parker had been double-timing it along the road east of the village where the Hizb ut-Tahrir training compound had been located. The compound was gone now. Parker had heard the explosions, had felt the ground tremble under his feet, had seen the flames leap high into the air as the explosives went off.

It was several hours later, around midday, when the car came along. The driver had seen what appeared to be a fellow Pakistani jogging along the road in the middle of nowhere and had stopped to generously offer him a lift.

Parker had been shocked as hell when he heard the car and turned around to see a Volkswagen bug approaching. How it had wound up here in Pakistan at least thirty years after it had been manufactured, he had no idea. But it ran, even though the engine didn't sound too good, and it would be faster than walking.

Keeping his rifle hidden under his cloak, Parker circled around the front of the car as the driver cranked the window down. The guy had barely opened his mouth to offer a ride when Parker hit him. It was a short, sharp punch that knocked the Pakistani senseless without doing any permanent damage. Parker hauled him out of the car and left him lying on the side of the road.

It would have made more sense to kill the driver. That way, if there was any pursuit, he wouldn't be able to tell them that Parker had taken the car and describe the vehicle. Parker considered it very seriously for about ten seconds.

Then he sighed, climbed into the bug, and put it back

in gear. He was no Boy Scout, but the cold-blooded murder of an innocent civilian had to be a last resort, if the country he was defending was to mean anything.

The liberals never got that right either. They thought everybody who worked in SpecOps, especially the covert branch, was a bloodthirsty rogue.

Over the next twelve hours, Parker had wondered several times if he'd been wrong about his assessment of the vehicle's speed. Maybe it wasn't faster than walking. The engine had a definite knock to it that got worse every time he pressed down too hard on the gas. He had a feeling that everything under the hood in the rear would fly to pieces if he pushed the car too fast.

So he had to settle for creeping along, wrestling with the poor steering around the worst of the potholes, and hoping that the Volkswagen would hold up until he reached Islamabad. Once he made it to the embassy and turned over the information he had found in the compound, the problem would be out of his hands. Somebody else would have to deal with it.

And now, another half hour tops and he'd be there. He allowed himself to feel a slight sense of relief as the lights of Pakistan's capital drew closer.

That was a mistake, he realized as a pair of headlights popped up behind him and began to close in rapidly on him. He shouldn't have jinxed himself like that.

There had been other traffic on the highway, other cars and trucks he'd met and some that had come up behind him and passed the battered old bug. Parker's instincts told him that this was different. He sensed menacing purpose behind those lights that were growing larger in the flyspecked rearview mirror.

He kept his left hand on the wheel and reached down with his right to the automatic rifle that lay on the seat beside him. His foot pressed harder on the accelerator. Once again the pinging from the rear-mounted engine behind him grew louder, but there was nothing he could do about it.

Nothing but pray that the Volkswagen held together long enough for him to reach the capital and lose himself in the maze of Islamabad's streets.

Parker's eyes darted back and forth between the road ahead and the rearview mirror. The headlights were only a few hundred yards behind him now, and still closing steadily.

Suddenly, the rear window shattered. Glass flew across the backseat and stung the back of Parker's neck. He crouched lower behind the wheel and cursed. His pursuers were impatient. They had opened fire before they were right on top of him. And they were pretty good shots, too, judging by what had happened to that back window.

But now the gloves were off. He didn't have to wait to make sure he wasn't just being paranoid. Now there was no doubt they were after him.

One-handed, he swung the rifle up and around and fired a burst through the rear window while continuing to drive toward Islamabad as fast as he could. He paused and then squeezed off another dozen rounds or so, craning his neck to look behind him as he fired.

This time he was rewarded by the sight of one of the headlights going out suddenly. Luck had been with him, because under the circumstances it sure as hell hadn't been skill that had caused one of his bullets to hit its mark. The remaining headlight veered sharply to the left, toward the edge of the road, and Parker allowed himself to hope that he had also hit either a tire or the driver.

The tire would have been better, but no such luck. The

pursuing vehicle pulled back onto a straight course after him. That meant he had either winged or killed the driver, but the rest of the bunch had hauled the guy out from behind the wheel and somebody else had taken over.

Parker emptied the rest of the clip at the vehicle, but didn't think he did any good. He kept his left hand on the wheel while he used his right to dump the clip and ram home a fresh one.

Bullets thudded into the bug's chassis, and the racket from that competed with the knocking in the engine. The now-one-eyed vehicle behind him was only fifty yards back, close enough for him to see the flickering muzzle flashes. It was a toss-up what would happen first—the Volkswagen's engine would give out on its own, the pursuers would knock it out of commission with their bullets, or they would shoot out one or more of Parker's tires.

He guessed he should have slit the throat of the guy who owned this ancient Beetle. No question he had to be the one who had put these bastards on Parker's trail.

He wondered fleetingly if any of the terrorists back there at Jihad U. had survived the battle and the explosions. That was always possible. He hadn't had time to put a round through the head of each and every one of them.

The answer to that question didn't matter. Parker heard a loud bang and felt the bug lurch hard to the right. There went a tire. With a huge clatter, the engine gave up the ghost a heartbeat later, while Parker was trying to hold the Volkswagen on the highway's almost nonexistent shoulder. The old car weaved back and forth crazily as it lost speed. More glass sprayed around Parker as a slug shattered the driver's side window.

The pursuing vehicle swerved to the left and zoomed closer, coming alongside the struggling Volkswagen.

Parker knew that in a second the killers inside it would riddle the bug—and him—at close range. He glanced over as he switched hands on the wheel, saw that it was a pickup with several heavily armed men in the back. He even caught a glimpse of some of them grinning evilly at him.

Then his left hand came out from under his jacket where he had found his last grenade. He yelled, "Catch this, fuckers," as he tossed it through the broken window at the jihadist assassins. None of them caught the grenade. He saw it fall among them as he jammed his foot on the brake and dove for the floorboard. Bullets smashed the windshield and punched through the doors and stormed around him like a swarm of angry bees.

He didn't see the explosion, but he heard it, an ear-splitting roar followed immediately by an even heavier blast that told him the pickup's gas tank had gone up, too. Even as that registered on Parker's stunned brain, he felt the Volkswagen tipping.

The highway was built on a slight embankment, and there was enough of a slope so that the car started to roll as it veered off the shoulder's edge. The bug went up and over, up and over, metal denting and crumpling under the impact, sand flying, axles snapping, hubcaps spinning off the tires and sailing through the air.

The old German car finally came to a shuddering halt on its top, a good thirty or forty yards from the road where the wreckage of the pickup blazed brightly. None of the Volkswagen's windows were still intact, and in the flickering light that came from the burning pickup, it seemed that not a single square inch of metal on the smaller vehicle was undented. But it wasn't on fire, and after several moments a groan sounded from inside the Volkswagen as

Brad began struggling to pull itself out through the jagged opening where the windshield had been.

Parker wasn't sure how bad he was hurt. He knew he'd been hit by some of those flying bullets, and he'd been thrown around all over the inside of the car as it was tumbling off the road. Bones had to be broken, and he tasted blood in his mouth along with the sand and grit that seemed to fill it.

But he was still alive, and as he hauled himself free of the wrecked bug, he told himself he was going to stay alive until he turned over that intel. He felt under his coat and found the documents he had taken from the compound. Still there, and they weren't soaked with blood . . . yet.

With the lights of Islamabad to guide him, Parker struggled to his feet and stumbled off into the darkness. He had help. He felt them hurrying him along and giving him strength . . .

All those Americans who would die if he failed. They didn't know it, but they were right there with him in the Pakistani night, urging him on.

CHAPTER 13

Hamed didn't try to reach for his weapon. He knew if he did the woman would kill him. Instead, he stood as still as humanly possible and listened as she spoke to him in Arabic, asking him his name. He told her, giving her his real name instead of the fake one that was on all of his fake identity papers. He didn't relax until the gun went away from the back of his neck—and he wasn't fully at ease even then. He was angry that he had allowed anyone to get the better of him like that, especially a woman.

"All right, you can turn around," she said in English. She had no trace of an accent.

Hamed turned toward her. She held the gun down at her side. She wore a sweatshirt with the big letters UTA on it and a pair of blue jeans. The shirt was baggy and at least somewhat decent, but the jeans were immodestly tight. She lifted the hem of the sweatshirt, exposing a few inches of smooth, golden-brown belly, and tucked the little pistol into the waistband of the jeans.

"I'm Shalla," she said as she pulled the shirt down again. "Shalla Sahi."

"Iranian," Hamed said, not bothering to keep the disdain out of his voice. She was Shiite.

"My parents are Iranian. I was born here." A note of bitterness came into her voice. "My father was a doctor in Tehran until he was forced to flee the Shah. Here he drove a taxicab for twenty years before a crackhead murdered him one night to steal less than thirty dollars."

Hamed sneered. "We all have our stories."

"Don't take that tone with me . . . Frenchman." Her dark eyes blazed with anger.

"Children." A new voice came from a doorway leading into one of the apartment's other rooms. "We are all on the same side here, remember? The infidels are our enemies, not each other."

Hamed turned and saw a familiar face. The last time he had seen this man had been at the training compound in Pakistan. He was one of Sheikh Abu ibn Khahir's lieutenants. Mushaff al-Mukhari was his name. Older than Hamed, he had a lean face, balding head, and neat goatee that gave him a look the Americans would have called satanic. To Hamed, though, the sight of Mukhari was a very welcome one indeed. It meant that the head of Hizb ut-Tahrir was taking a personal interest in this mission by sending one of his top men to oversee it.

Mukhari came into the room and embraced Hamed, pounding him on the back. Other men emerged from the room where Mukhari had been waiting, and they were familiar, too. Hamed greeted his fellow graduates of the training compound with smiles and hugs and backslaps. He counted quickly. Ten men were crowded into the small apartment. That was only half of the force that should be gathering here. The others hadn't arrived yet.

"We would have food and drink," Mukhari said to Shalla in Farsi. For a second she looked like she wanted to tell him to get it himself, Hamed thought. Clearly, the evil Western ways had embedded themselves in her, causing her to no longer know her proper place. That was apparent from her dress as well as her attitude. But then she shrugged and went into the tiny kitchen to do Mukhari's bidding.

"You have come to tell us of our mission, Sheikh?" Hamed asked Mukhari, since the man was entitled to that term of respect as well.

Mukhari held up a finger and waved it back and forth as he smiled. "Later, my impetuous young friend," he said. "When all the others have arrived."

Hamed nodded with downcast eyes. He *was* impetuous. It was one of his failings. He was just so eager to strike a blow against the infidels and die for Allah that he could barely contain himself, especially after living and working among the decadent Americans for months that had seemed like an eternity.

So now he had to be patient. He told himself that he would be, with the help of the Prophet. He waited with the others for the rest of the cell to arrive.

To help pass the time, he asked Shalla Sahi, "What is your part in this?"

"I told you, my father was murdered by a drug addict. If this country had accepted him as it should have, he would have been working in a hospital somewhere, saving lives with his medical knowledge, instead of driving a cab in the worst parts of Dallas."

"I am sorry for your loss," Hamed told her, trying not to sound grudging about it. "This tragedy led you to become a believer in our cause?"

"I've always been a follower of Islam," she said. "I know, I may look like one of them, but I still believe. I still think America is the Great Satan."

It figured that she would quote the Ayatollah. Hamed said, "You could return to Iran. Such things can be arranged, even now."

"Why would I want to do that? My family is all dead. I've never set foot in that land. It's not my home. This is. But that doesn't mean I hate the infidels any less."

"You just don't want to give up the advantages they give to women. You don't want to don the burka and live as a proper Muslim female should."

Her face darkened again with anger at the disapproving words, but before she could say anything, Mushaff al-Mukhari lifted a hand and smiled. He didn't have to remind them that they all had a common enemy.

The doorbell rang. Mukhari came to his feet and motioned for all the men to go into the other room while Shalla answered the door and made sure that the newcomer was one of their group. If not, she would send whoever it was away.

The man at the door was Rahjif, one of Hamed's best friends from the compound. Again there were hugs and backslaps of greeting. Then Najul arrived, and Ogan, and Khalid . . .

By eight o'clock that evening, all twenty members of the group were there, packed into Shalla's apartment like sardines, as the Americans would say. Like Shalla and the sheikh and Hamed, they all wore American clothes, and although their ancestry was apparent by looking at them, there were millions of fellow Muslims in this country. They would do nothing to stand out, and although some of the infidels would look at them with hatred and suspicion, no one would think that they represented a real threat until it was too late—much too late—to stop them.

Because most Americans would look at them and see

convenience-store clerks and software engineers and believe that these were some of the *good* Arabs, the ones who had adopted Western ways and beliefs, the ones who were glad to be here earning money and buying DVD players and iPods and sending their children to American schools. The only Arabs who really represented a threat were the ones who wore robes and spoke among themselves in foreign tongues and bowed to Mecca five times a day.

At least, that was what the infidels believed in their arrogance. They thought so highly of themselves and their culture that they assumed just a taste of it would be enough to seduce anyone into accepting their ways. It never occurred to them that someone wearing Levi's and Nikes could be a warrior of the Prophet.

They would find out, Hamed thought as the group gathered around the sheikh to learn the details of the plan. To their everlasting regret, they would find out . . .

CHAPTER 14

Private Rigoberto Gomez loved being a Marine. He had even loved the physical, mental, and emotional challenges of boot camp at Parris Island, because every day he survived those challenges was one more day he wasn't spending in the barrio. Instead of being back there with the 'bangers and the lowlifes, worrying about drive-bys, watching his friends die from drugs or violence—*like Little Chuy, man, his best amigo since they were kids, bleedin' out from that bullet wound in his neck while 'Berto sobbed and held his hand over the hole with all that red pumpin' out, sayin' don't die, Chuy, don't die, man*—instead of that, Private Gomez was doing something with his life. Accomplishing something. Putting all that gang shit far behind him.

Of course, now the Marines had him standing guard at the U.S. embassy in Islamabad, Pakistan, where you never knew when one of those crazy suicide bombers might try to crash through the gates with a truck full of explosives and blow himself to hell in the ultimate drive-by, along with as many Americans as he could take along for the ride. Those Al Qaeda dudes were as mean and nasty as any of the gangs back in East L.A., man. But 'Berto Gomez was a Marine now, which meant he had the whole damn Corps at his back.

That didn't keep him from getting sleepy, pulling the graveyard watch like this. Nothing was going on. The streets around the embassy were empty at this time of night. Islamabad might be the capital of this country, but it was still a small town in many ways.

Well, the streets weren't exactly empty, Private Gomez realized as he stifled a yawn. Somebody was walking toward the main gate in the wall around the embassy compound, where Gomez was posted. Just one guy, but that didn't mean anything. He was wearing one of those long cloaks like the Pakistani men wore, which meant he could have a lot of explosives strapped to his body. He could be a walking bomb.

And he was coming straight toward Gomez.

Bartosowicz, a private from Cleveland, was on duty at the gate with Gomez. He didn't look like he had noticed the guy yet, so Gomez called across to him, "Yo, Barty, one of the locals comin'."

Bartosowicz jumped a little and said, "Shit, you think he's a suicide bomber?"

"I dunno." Gomez thumbed off the safety on his weapon and lifted the rifle. He knew how to say "Halt!" in both Urdu and Punjabi. He tried Urdu first, calling out to the approaching figure. The man kept coming. He was shambling along at an unsteady gait, Gomez could tell now, like he was sick or hurt or something.

Or maybe he was just a little scared because he was about to blow himself up. That would be enough to put a hitch in anybody's step.

Gomez yelled at the man in Punjabi next, telling him to stop right where he was and not come any closer.

When that didn't work, Gomez started to get impatient and shouted in English, "Stand down, my man! Right there! Come any closer and we'll shoot!"

Bartosowicz glanced over nervously at Gomez and asked, "Are we really gonna shoot him?"

"Damn right we are," Gomez responded without hesitation. "Maybe he's just drunk, but I'd rather take a chance on cappin' him than let him blow us to hell."

Still, Gomez thought as his finger lightly touched the trigger of his rifle, it wasn't easy to shoot a man down in cold blood. He'd never killed anybody in his life. Not back in the streets of East L.A., and not here in Pakistan. But all it would take, he realized as he drew a bead on the cloaked, shambling figure, was just a little more pressure on the trigger . . .

The guy croaked something. Gomez couldn't understand the words, but he thought the man sure *sounded* like he was hurt or sick.

He yelled again in Urdu, then Punjabi, and finally in English. "Stop right there and get down on the ground!" To his fellow sentry he added, "Barty, call the lieutenant!"

"Already did," Bartosowicz replied. "He's on his way."

Gomez wished the officer would hurry up and get there, so the decision whether or not to kill this guy would be taken out of his hands. But he would make it if he had to, Gomez told himself. If the stranger took two more steps—

Again the cloaked man lifted his head and said something, and this time Gomez was able to make out the words. A shock went through him as he realized that the guy had gasped out, "Semper . . . fi . . ."

Bartosowicz had heard it, too. He said, "Shit, Gomez, he's one of us!"

"Not necessarily," Gomez warned. "These guys can

learn to speak English, just like we learn to speak their lingo." He kept his rifle trained on the figure as he shouted, "Hey, man, if you understand what I'm say in', stop right where you are! Don't come any closer or I'll shoot you, I swear to God I will!"

The man stopped and slowly raised his hands. He was close enough now so that Gomez could see his face in the glow from the floodlights that illuminated the grounds of the embassy compound. It was the same sort of dark-skinned face Gomez saw hundreds of times a day on the Pakistanis, except this guy didn't have a beard like most of the men around here.

The man began fumbling with the turban wrapped around his head. Bartosowicz yelled, "He's got a gun in there!" His rifle came up.

Some instinct made Gomez say, "Wait! Hold your fire!" He didn't think the guy was going for a weapon. He watched as slowly, unsteadily, the man began unwrapping the turban. As the cloth fell away, it revealed hair that was a dark shade of blond, but definitely blond nonetheless.

A grin creased the guy's gaunt, haggard face. "I'm . . . an American," he said. "Got to see . . . the ambassador."

Then his eyes rolled up in his head and he pitched forward, either passed out cold—or dead.

As Gomez pushed the buttons on the keypad that would open the heavily reinforced iron bars of the gate, he hoped the guy had just passed out.

Gomez wanted to hear the story of how a blond American dressed like a Pakistani came wandering up to the U.S. embassy in Islamabad in the middle of the night. Gomez was willing to bet it was a good one.

CHAPTER 15

So I'm not dead after all.

That was Brad Parker's first thought when consciousness seeped back into his brain. He had fully expected to wake up either at the Pearly Gates or the gates of Hell, depending on how harshly his sins were judged. But the first face he saw didn't belong to either St. Peter or Lucifer.

It belonged to J. Gordon Keyne, United States Ambassador to Pakistan.

Keyne was a balding, stuffy-looking black man who had once been a university professor—and looked it. He glared down at Parker, who seemed to be in a bed of some sort, and said, "Young man, you'd better have a good excuse for showing up unannounced on my doorstep at three o'clock in the morning."

Parker recalled that he and the ambassador had never met, although Parker certainly knew what Keyne looked like. Parker's lips and tongue didn't want to work at first because they were so dry, but after a moment he managed to husk, "I need to talk to . . . Ford."

Keyne frowned. "You mean Larry Ford?"

"Y-yeah."

The expression of disapproval on Keyne's face deepened. Lawrence Ford was a deputy attaché at the embassy. At least, that was the way he was carried on the books.

But he really worked for the Company, and Keyne knew it. He probably didn't like it much. Diplomats seldom liked to acknowledge that there were some problems in the world that couldn't be solved by negotiations. But a CIA presence in American embassies worldwide was a fact of life.

Keyne looked at somebody Parker couldn't see and snapped, "Get Ford in here. Now."

When Keyne turned his attention back to the man in the bed, Parker asked, "How bad . . . am I hurt?"

"My medical people tell me that you have three broken ribs, a concussion for sure and possibly a hairline fracture of the skull, a bullet hole in your left arm, a couple of deep grazes on your right arm and right side, and enough scratches and scrapes and bruises for a regiment. In other words, son, you're lucky to be alive, and depending on how bad that head injury really is, we're not sure what kind of shape you're in." Keyne paused, and his voice was a little more sympathetic as he went on, "What's your name? Or are you allowed to tell me that?"

"B-Brad Parker . . . sir."

"I suppose it would have been too much to expect for someone in Washington to let me know you were over here in Pakistan."

"Things sometimes . . . develop pretty fast . . . sir." There was no point in telling Keyne that he had been in Pakistan for months, working with Odie to develop intel and do whatever needed to be done. Parker knew that, by and large, it was better to keep the paper-pushers in the dark as much as possible.

Another man bustled into the room. He was tall, broad-shouldered, starting to develop a little paunch. A pair of glasses perched on his nose. "Brad, old buddy," he said, "you look like you just went six rounds with a buzz saw."

Parker grinned, even though it hurt. "Yeah, well . . . at least I . . . didn't start out lookin' this way . . . Fargo."

Lawrence "Fargo" Ford had picked up his nickname because of his hometown in North Dakota. He chuckled, even though his eyes were deadly serious behind the glasses. When he glanced at Keyne, the ambassador gave a frustrated grimace and said, "I know, I know, I need to leave you two alone."

"I'll debrief Mr. Parker and then be in to talk to you, Mr. Ambassador," Ford promised.

Keyne just grunted, nodded, and left the room.

When Parker and Ford were alone, Ford drew a chair closer to the bed and sat down. Parker asked, "Is this room . . . clean?"

Ford reached into the pocket of the robe he wore over his pajamas and brought out a small black box with a tiny lever on it. He pushed the lever and said, "It is now. We sweep the whole place for bugs pretty regularly, and even if we missed something, this little gizmo will take care of it."

"Even the ones that . . . our side planted?"

Ford grinned. "Even them. Now tell me . . ." He leaned closer to the bed. "You ran into trouble in that village? The one where Hizb ut-Tahrir has its training compound?"

"Had," Parker said. "No more Jihad U."

"Damn! That's good work, Brad. I'd heard rumors that something big had happened over there, but I hadn't been able to confirm them yet. What about Odie?"

"Didn't . . . didn't make it."

Ford took a deep breath and then shook his head. "I'm sorry. He would've been a hell of an agent someday."

"He . . . already was." Parker lifted a hand and reached out toward Ford. "Got to tell you . . . documents hidden in my jacket . . ."

Ford nodded and said, "I've already got 'em, but they're, uh, sort of soaked in some of that blood you lost. We haven't been able to translate them yet. Under the best of circumstances, it's hard to dig the details out of all that chicken-scratching they call writing—"

Parker clutched at the arm of his friend and comrade in the shadow war against terror. "I can tell you," he said as urgency lifted him in the bed. "They're going to . . . blow up something . . . in the States . . . on the day after Thanksgiving."

"What is it? A political target? Part of the infrastructure?"

"Worse," Parker said. His head pounded fiercely with a sudden pain that sent black flashes across his vision. He was about to say, *They're going to blow up the biggest damn MegaMart in the world,* when something burst inside his skull, flooding it with agony. The whole world was red, then black—

Then gone.

"According to a story by the Associated Press datelined Washington, D.C., November 27, there was a brief confrontation today between American and Iranian airplanes over the Persian Gulf. According to a Pentagon spokesman, the Iranian planes attempted to turn back an oil tanker heading into the Strait of Hormuz with radio warnings that if the tanker proceeded, it would be fired upon. American fighter jets from one of the carriers in the Gulf arrived only moments after the warning was given, and the Iranian jets departed from the area. The tanker was able to proceed on its course without incident.

"Spokesmen for the Iranian government in Tehran immediately issued a statement claiming that their planes were fired upon without warning or provocation, but the Pentagon denies that any shots were fired by either side. The Pentagon also released a recording of the Iranian pilots threatening the oil tanker.

"White House Press Secretary Davisson

stated that while the President remains committed to finding peaceful solutions to the problems in the Middle East, the United States will not permit any disruption of shipping in the Persian Gulf, a statement which the Iranian government decried as meddling in the affairs of sovereign nations. Iran has long insisted that the Strait of Hormuz belongs to it, and that it can be shut down at any time.

"In other news, the war scare in the Middle East appears to be having little effect on the American economy. With the Christmas shopping season poised to officially begin tomorrow, the day after Thanksgiving, retailers are looking forward to booming sales, as all indicators point to a retail bonanza, as people will be shopping more and spending more this year. . . ."

CHAPTER 16

"Madame President, you'll be leaving shortly to go to the soup kitchen," her Chief of Staff reminded her as she stood at the window behind the desk in the Oval Office. The glass was bullet-proof, of course. In fact, it was so heavily reinforced that it might as well have been a sheet of armor.

But it couldn't keep out the bad news. Nothing could.

"I don't suppose I could beg off this year," the President said. "Given the circumstances in the Middle East."

"Well, you *could,* I guess," the Chief of Staff said. "But you've made it a tradition to help feed the homeless on Thanksgiving. It would look bad to the press if you skipped it, unless we were actually at war or something."

"Or something," the President muttered. She had been roused from sleep before dawn with the news that Navy fighter jets and Iranian planes had almost started shooting at each other before the Iranians decided to turn tail and run instead.

Would they do the same thing next time? Who knows? That was the problem with fanatics—you never could predict with any reasonable sort of accuracy what they would do.

Washington was gray and overcast on this Thanksgiving morning, matching the President's mood. The leaden sky looked like it might produce some snow later in the day. By then she would be back from the homeless shelter where she would dish up turkey and stuffing, cranberry sauce and giblet gravy, to the unfortunates who had nowhere else to go on this holiday. Or any other day, for that matter. Nothing said compassion like a photo op of the President helping out the homeless.

And right now, returning to her roots as a champion of the unfortunate and disenfranchised wasn't a bad idea, because fresh polling data showed that the electorate had very little faith in her ability to handle the crisis in the Middle East. That came as no surprise considering her antiwar, antimilitary background. People expected her to roll over and give the country's enemies whatever they wanted because . . . well, because that was exactly what she had done in Iraq, wasn't it?

But she had done that because the polls said that was what the country wanted her to do. It wasn't fair for people to turn on her just because things had turned out so badly there. It wasn't her fault. Nothing had ever been her fault. It was all because of her enemies and the conspiracy among them . . .

She took a deep breath and forced those thoughts out of her head. She didn't have time to get bogged down in them now. She had homeless people to feed. All the evening newscasts, broadcast and cable, would lead with the footage of her standing in the homeless shelter in an apron, dishing out Thanksgiving dinner. People would see that and know how good and moral she was.

They wouldn't be thinking that she was liable to let things in the Persian Gulf spiral out of control.

At least it was still almost a year until the election. By then people would have forgotten all about this little glitch in the Middle East, and they would return her to office for a second term.

As long as nothing else bad happened between now and then.

CHAPTER 17

Allison Sawyer was up early on Thanksgiving Day. Even though it was just her and Nate, she wanted to fix a traditional Thanksgiving dinner, complete with turkey and all the trimmings. Her parents lived in Waco, and she and Nate could have driven down to spend the day with them, but Allison knew all too well how easily spending time with her parents could lead to an argument.

Her folks had never approved of her marriage and had never been shy about letting her know that, and still weren't. Of course, as it turned out, they had been right about her choice of a husband being a bad one, but that didn't mean she wanted to hear about it over and over . . .

So she got everything cooking and then woke Nate so they could watch the Macy's Thanksgiving Day Parade together. He always got a kick out of the giant balloons, and to tell the truth, so did Allison. And at the end of the parade there was Santa, and his appearance always made Allison think of that old movie *Miracle on 34th Street*.

It was a pleasant way to spend the morning, and after

dinner, she could read or nap while Nate watched the Cowboys play on TV. Allison had been a Cowboys fan when she was a teenager, but she'd sort of lost interest in the sport after Troy Aikman retired, which she supposed meant that she had never been all that interested in the games themselves, just a certain Number 8 . . .

Nate surprised her that afternoon by asking, "Hey, Mom, can I go with you to MegaMart tomorrow?"

"Well, I don't know," Allison said. "I'd planned to get Mrs. Sanchez to watch you while I was gone." Their neighbor in the apartment house babysat for Nate pretty often. They got along well.

"Yeah, but I want to go. It's the grand opening."

Allison hesitated. The real reason she couldn't take Nate with her was because she intended to do all his Christmas shopping at the new UltraMegaMart. There was a huge ad for the place in this morning's paper, and in the few looks she had sneaked at it, she had already seen several things she thought he might like as presents. She couldn't very well get them, though, if he was right there at her side. That would spoil everything.

"No, it'll just be a big mob of people," she said, putting a note of firmness in her voice. She didn't do that very often, but she wanted him to know that she had made up her mind and wouldn't be swayed by whining or complaining. "You wouldn't enjoy it. I'll take you there later, on a day when it won't be quite so busy."

"But, Mom—" he began.

"I've already asked Mrs. Sanchez to have you come over, and she said she'd be glad to. You wouldn't want to disappoint her, would you?"

"What about me being disappointed?"

She reached out to tousle his hair. "Don't be like that. You've got your whole life to go to MegaMart, because

I promise you, they're not going away. Now, is it still halftime in the game?"

"Yeah."

"What's the score?"

"Cowboys are ahead, fourteen to three."

"Good," Allison said. "Maybe they'll win."

CHAPTER 18

People told Ellis Burke that he was lucky to have gotten the house in the divorce. Burke didn't see it that way. He knew he had gotten it only because Rebecca hadn't wanted to put up a fight for it. She *wanted* to move out and get a fresh start, she'd said. Sure, it meant taking Vicky out of the only home she'd ever known, but Rebecca hadn't cared about that. As usual, Burke had thought bitterly at the time, his wife wanted what was best for *her,* and if anybody else didn't like it, that was just too bad.

So he was left to live in the ten-year-old brick house that looked like all the other ten-year-old brick houses in the vast subdivision, with all its memories of good times—and bad.

The housing market was in a slump, even with all the fantastic growth in the area. No way he could get what the house was actually worth. So he couldn't afford to move, not with the child support he was paying.

He woke up on Thanksgiving morning in the bed he had once shared with his wife. He walked down a hall-way that had once been littered with toys, and ate break-fast at an island countertop in the kitchen where his daughter had once eaten cereal every morning. Then, faced with a long day of having nothing to do except go over paperwork from various cases he was working on, he went into the den and made himself a drink.

If he had been home in New York, he could have gotten together with friends. Watched the parade from somebody's penthouse. Gone out on the town. Taken in a show. But in this cultural wasteland there was nothing to hold his interest. He brought in the newspaper and flipped through it. Ninety percent ads, which was why he subscribed to it in the first place. He certainly didn't rely on it for actual news coverage.

The thick ad for the new UltraMegaMart caught his attention. He went through it carefully, and sure enough, there on page five was the puppet-thingy that Vicky wanted, and for a really good price, too. Burke suppressed a groan as he saw the small print reading *Limited to Quantities on Hand—No Rain Checks.* He turned back to the first page of the section. *DOORS OPEN AT 6 A.M.*

Shit, he thought. Anybody who got up at a reasonable hour and arrived at the store at, say, ten o'clock in the morning would be out of luck. All the good stuff would be gone by then, and he would be faced with forcing his way through a mob of sweaty rednecks looking for something, anything—confident only in the fact that whatever he got, his daughter wouldn't like it nearly as well as the freaky-looking puppet.

Burke tossed back the rest of his drink and thought that he would just forget the whole thing. He made a good living. He could afford to go out somewhere and pay more for the thing later, without ever venturing into Redneck Central.

But if he did that, he told himself, he ran the risk of not being able to find it anywhere else either. He had seen stories on the news in past Christmas seasons about near-riots at toy stores when people tried to get their hands on that year's hot toys that were in short supply.

Like it or not—and he didn't—he decided that his best course of action would be to drag himself out of bed early and head up the interstate a few miles to that grand opening. It would be an ordeal, but he told himself he could stand it . . . for Vicky's sake.

With that decision reached, he made up his mind about something else. He got up and went to pour another drink.

CHAPTER 19

There was nothing special about this Thanksgiving, and that's what made it seem so nice, McCabe thought as he and Terry and Ronnie sat on the sofa and waited to see if the Cowboys placekicker was going to make the field goal that would win the game.

Just Thanksgiving dinner with his family, followed by a nice nap, and then a football game that turned out to be close and exciting. He wasn't on the road somewhere, hauling a truckload of goods along the interstate. Nor was he freezing his ass off in some mountains or sweltering in a jungle or scorching in a desert while people who hated the United States and everything it stood for did their damnedest to kill him. He had spent more than one Thanksgiving like *that,* too, and it was no fun.

"He's gotta make this kick," Ronnie said as the opposing team called a time-out to let the Dallas kicker stew some more. "He's just gotta." McCabe's daughter was a die-hard Cowboys fan. As for himself, he liked to see them win, but he wasn't going to lose any sleep either way over something like a football game.

The teams lined up. Neither side had any more time-outs. Three seconds remained on the clock. The ball was on the forty-yard line. That would make this a forty-seven-yard field goal. Difficult, but certainly possible. The Cowboys were two points behind. The new stadium, which had opened just a year earlier, was packed with screaming fans. They were all on their feet as the ball was snapped.

McCabe felt some of their urgency, and leaned forward on his sofa as the kicker stepped into the ball and swung his kicking leg. The camera followed the ball up and up as the announcer on TV yelled, "It looks like it's long enough . . . It's good, it's good! No time left on the clock! No penalty flags down! The Cowboys have won!"

Ronnie jumped up and did a little dance, pumping her fists in the air. Her parents grinned at her, but she was too excited to notice.

"Well, that was certainly a thrilling finish," Terry said. "I think I'll make myself a turkey sandwich. Anyone else want one?"

McCabe rubbed his stomach and groaned. "I'm still too stuffed from dinner to even think about eating again. How can you be hungry already?"

"I have a healthy appetite," Terry told him.

"I'll say."

She punched him on the elbow, then stood up and headed for the kitchen. The phone rang while she was on her way there, so she detoured a few steps to answer it. McCabe wondered who would be calling on Thanksgiving Day. Probably one of Terry's relatives, he thought. He didn't have any close relatives left. That was one reason he had made the military his career for a long time.

It took him by surprise when she held the phone out toward him and said, "Jack, it's Keith Gossage."

McCabe frowned. Gossage was one of his supervisors. As he stood up and went to take the phone from his wife, he wanted to ask what the hell they wanted with him on Thanksgiving, but she hadn't covered the receiver with her hand, so he didn't.

"Hey, Keith, what's up?" he said into the phone.

"Sorry to bother you on Thanksgiving, Jack," came the voice in his ear, "but at least I waited until the Cowboys game was over."

"Yeah, I appreciate that." McCabe didn't say anything else, just waited to see what Gossage wanted.

"I know you thought you were off until Monday—"

McCabe couldn't hold back a groan. "Aw, no. Don't tell me."

"Sorry, buddy. Hiram Stackhouse needs you."

Stackhouse was the founder of MegaMart, a multibillionaire, an elderly man who was either a colorful eccentric or a crazy old coot, depending on who you asked about him.

"Uncle Sam needed me, too, and that like to got my head shot off."

Gossage laughed. "Well, at least you won't have to worry about that tomorrow. And you won't have very far to go either. You just have to pick up a load of freight at the Alliance distribution center and take it to the new UltraMegaMart that's opening tomorrow. Won't take you more than an hour or so, I'd guess."

"That store's not even open yet," McCabe pointed out. "It should be fully stocked. They can't be running short of anything yet."

"That's where you're wrong. The guys in Marketing have been running the numbers. They've decided that the turnout for the grand opening is going to be even bigger than they thought at first. So they've ordered up some extra stock in certain areas."

McCabe didn't care what the stock was. It could be anything from diapers to automatic transmission fluid to hairspray; it didn't make any difference to him. All that mattered was that he had to get it from Point A— the distribution center at Alliance Airport—to Point B—the brand-spanking-new UltraMegaMart. And on a day that was supposed to have been time off for him.

"I reckon it's too much to ask if you've got anybody else who can handle this job."

"You're the best, Jack. You know that."

His superiors in SpecOps had said that very thing to him on more than one occasion, especially when they were sending him into some dangerous Third World shithole from which they didn't expect him to come back. But he had fooled them. He had come back every time, and usually relatively intact at that. Not always, and he had the scars to prove it, but usually.

Gossage made the job of driving a truck some five miles sound just as vital. And McCabe supposed it was, to Gossage and *his* bosses, all the way up to Hiram Stackhouse. McCabe had heard rumors that the old man himself was going to be on hand tomorrow for the grand opening, although that hadn't been officially announced yet. Stackhouse liked to just show up with little or no warning. That was part of that eccentric charm of his.

McCabe sighed. "All right, Keith. I'll take care of this for you. But you'll owe me."

"Extra time off later? You've got it, buddy."

"I was thinking more along the lines of a bonus."

"Well . . . I'll see what I can do." Gossage didn't sound too hopeful about that, however. Like George

Halas, the old-time NFL big shot who had once owned and coached the Chicago Bears, Stackhouse had a reputation for throwing nickels around like manhole covers.

"What time do I need to pick up the load?"

"Eight o'clock. It'll be loaded and ready to roll. See, I told you this won't take very long, and then you'll have the rest of the day off just like you planned."

"Okay. I'll be there."

"I knew I could count on you, Jack. Thanks."

McCabe said his good-byes and hung up. Terry was watching him. She said, "Don't tell me . . . you have to work tomorrow."

"Yeah."

"I was counting on you going with us to the grand opening."

McCabe chuckled. "Well, that's where I'm going. I have to pick up a truck full of extra stock at Alliance and drive it over to the store."

Terry smiled. "That means you can meet us there and go shopping with us after all."

McCabe was starting to feel trapped, in more ways than one. "I, uh, already told Ronnie that I thought I'd pass."

"But now you have to be there anyway, so you don't have any excuse for disappointing your loving wife and daughter, now do you?" she said, her smile growing even sweeter.

That didn't fool McCabe for a second. "You're right," he said, giving in. "Things are really working out for the best, aren't they?"

CHAPTER 20

The plan was, in a way, simplicity itself, Hamed thought. Of course there would be security at the target, that temple of American decadence known as the Ultra-MegaMart, but it would be directed more at stopping shoplifters inside the store and car burglaries in the parking lot. Americans were such idiots. Just because they had not been attacked on their own soil since 9/11, they thought it would never happen again. Even though Homeland Security and the FBI had been lucky enough to uncover several small-scale plots by near-amateurs in time to stop them, people paid no attention.

The group crowded into Shalla Sahi's apartment spent the entire day, Thanksgiving Day, going over the plan. It had several different components, and everything had to occur perfectly for maximum effect.

"Car bombs will be placed here, and here, and here, and here," Sheikh Mushaff al-Mukhari said as he pointed to the map that was spread out on Shalla's kitchen table. He placed pushpins at the site of each bombing. "A police station, to strike at American authority. A post office, to strike at American bureaucracy. A bank, to strike at the American economy. And this last one—"

"A day-care center?" Shalla asked with a frown.

The sheikh looked up at her. "You are not wavering in your zeal to serve Allah, are you?"

"No, of course not," she answered quickly. "Not at all."

Hamed wasn't sure he believed her. This was a perfect example of why women could not be trusted to play an important part in this holy war. They were too weak, too emotional. Instead of being clear-eyed servants of the Prophet, they allowed their feelings to influence their actions.

"And a day-care center," Mukhari went on, "to strike at the hearts of the Americans. To make them feel the same pain that untold thousands of our people have felt at the loss of our children, not only to American guns and bombs, but to the satanic culture that seduces them away from the true tenets of Islam."

"But these explosions," Hamed dared to say, "they are only a prelude, yes?"

The sheikh nodded. "Yes. A prelude. So the Americans will take us seriously when we take over the Ultra-MegaMart and issue our demands."

The timeline was straightforward. The bombs would go off at nine forty-five on Friday morning, when targets such as the bank, the post office, and the day-care center would be busy. Then, fifteen minutes later, at ten o'clock, the group of heavily armed sleeper-cell Hizb ut-Tahrir agents would take over the UltraMegaMart, killing anyone who stood in their way. There would be hundreds, perhaps thousands of shoppers inside the sprawling store, and only twenty warriors, but that would be enough.

The plan called for them to enter the store individually, along with the crush of Americans, starting when the doors opened at six a.m. The four hours before they struck would give them plenty of time to move throughout the store and plant the small but powerful bombs they carried at every entrance point. Once those bombs were armed, delicate sensors would trigger them if a large number of people approached from outside, like a force of American police or military. Of course, the Americans might think about *trying* to trigger them in some fashion, so they could launch an attack once the bombs had gone off, but they would reconsider when they saw the hostages secured right next to each of the explosive devices. The Americans would not deliberately blow up any of their own people—especially on camera.

And there would be plenty of cameras, Hamed thought, once the sheikh contacted the American news media and issued the group's demands.

Demand, actually, because there was only a single major one.

All United States presence—military, corporate, what have you—was to be withdrawn from Islamic soil. American business interests in Muslim countries would be turned over immediately, not to the governments of those countries, but rather to the Caliphate, the new Islamic order that would unite all Muslims everywhere and lead them to their rightful place of dominance in the world. If what it took to accomplish that goal was the death of every infidel on the entire planet, then so be it. Allah willed it. *Allahu akbar!*

But kicking the Americans out had to be the first step. Their godless power would be broken. They would have to give in.

Or else Hamed and his comrades would detonate the "dirty" briefcase nuke that Mukhari had brought with him, and where the UltraMegaMart now stood would be nothing but a radioactive crater, a blight on the already ugly Texas prairie that would last for hundreds of years.

So, yes, Hamed thought, the plan was simple, but there were plenty of things involved in it that could go wrong. They would need the blessings of the Prophet to strike this blow for jihad, this opening gambit in the rise of the Caliphate. But he was confident that they would have those blessings. Allah would not desert them now, not when they were so close to their goal.

Most of the men had not slept much in the past few days. The sheikh instructed them to rest that evening. They dozed in chairs and on Shalla's sofa and on the floor.

Hamed tried to sleep as well, but he was too restless. He got up, made his way to the kitchen, and opened the refrigerator, looking for something to eat.

"You're having trouble sleeping, too?" a voice asked quietly.

He straightened and looked around the refrigerator door to see Shalla standing there. She had gone into her bedroom earlier. Her thick dark hair was tousled, as if she had been tossing and turning. She wore a long T-shirt that ended just below the tops of her thighs, leaving her legs mostly bare. The sight of all that smooth brown flesh was extremely disturbing to Hamed. It was immodest and sinful, of course, but he was also bothered by his reaction to it, which was that of a normal man. He felt himself becoming aroused, and by sheer force of will dragged his gaze away from her.

"You should return to your room," he snapped.

"Why?"

"Men are trying to sleep here."

"This is my apartment," she said. "Who are you to tell

me what to do?" She stepped in front of the refrigerator, her hip bumping his as she did so. "Anyway, I'm hungry."

She bent over to search for something to eat, and as she did so the T-shirt pulled up in the back, revealing the bottom half of a nicely rounded rump clad only in thin panties. Hamed looked at it without meaning to, then closed his eyes and prayed for strength. Being surrounded by beautiful virgins in paradise was one thing; even a holy man could wish for that. But he had to remain strong and pure in this world and not succumb to the temptation of earthly pleasures.

Shalla straightened and glanced over her shoulder. "Do I bother you?"

She was tormenting him on purpose, Hamed thought. There was no other explanation for her behavior.

"You are nothing to me," he said, making his voice as cold as possible. "I am devoted to the holy cause of jihad."

"As am I. I told you what happened to my father."

"And you blame the Americans for that."

"Of course! His death was their fault. I want only to see them suffer as I and my mother have suffered. I want them to feel the same pain of loss, as Sheikh al-Mukhari said."

Keeping his eyes fastened on hers so that he wouldn't be tempted to look at her body, Hamed asked, "Your mother, she still lives?"

Shalla shook her head. "Without my father, she was nothing. She mourned him for six months before she went on to join him in paradise. But I promised her, on her deathbed, that I would avenge them both. That is why I will be with you tomorrow."

A shock went through Hamed at her words. "With us?" he repeated.

"Of course." She smiled at him. "Did you think that

I was merely providing a place for you to meet?" She shook her head. "I received the same sort of training as you, Hamed al-Bashar, and I have been in this country even longer. And I am just as willing to die in the service of Allah."

Hamed's mind was whirling now. He knew that females had served as freedom fighters in the past, and they could be as devout in their beliefs as any male.

But for some reason, he had assumed that the group taking over the UltraMegaMart would all be male, his cohorts from the training compound in Pakistan. The idea that a woman who had adopted some of the Americans' ways, who even dressed like an American slut, would be with them when they carried out their glorious mission simply had not occurred to him.

The more he thought about it, the less he liked it.

"I will speak to the sheikh," he said stiffly. "You should not accompany us. There will be much danger—"

"I don't care about that, as long as I get to kill some Americans before I die. I fully *expect* to die, you know, just as you and all the others do."

"But . . . but you should not."

"Because I am female?" Shalla made a curt gesture of dismissal. "All are the same in the eyes of Allah."

"This is not true. Women are delicate flowers to be protected."

She sneered. "Do I look all that delicate to you?"

In truth, she did not. Her arms and legs, despite being rounded and feminine, were also strong with sleek muscles. No doubt she could, as the Americans said, "kick ass." But that still didn't make it right.

She moved closer to him, brazenly defiant. "By this time tomorrow, we'll probably both be dead," she went on. "I'm not hungry anymore. Not for food."

Yes, she had definitely been around American women too much, Hamed told himself. Otherwise, she never would have been so forward.

But even as he was embarrassed by her scandalous behavior, he was also drawn to her, and although he hated to think that he could be so weak in his resolve, he was actually considering her blatant proposition when the sheikh came into the kitchen, taking them both by surprise. Hamed and Shalla jumped a little as they turned to face the older, distinguished-looking man.

"You children should be resting," Mukhari said with a faint smile. "Perhaps you are nervous. You should ask the Creator to grant you peace."

Hamed nodded. "Yes, of course. I will return to the living room."

Shalla shrugged, and Hamed didn't miss the way her unbound breasts moved under the soft fabric of the T-shirt. "I guess I'll go back to bed, too," she said. She added, "Good night."

Hamed gave her a curt nod and didn't say anything.

He lingered as Shalla left the room. Without a note of reproach in his voice, the sheikh said, "Even a man who is truly devoted must guard against distractions."

"This is true," Hamed agreed. He was grateful that Mukhari had come in when he did; otherwise, who knows what might have happened.

Now he could go to his death unsullied, if that was what Allah willed.

And nothing would happen to ruin the plan.

CHAPTER 21

"What's the verdict, Doc?" Lawrence "Fargo" Ford asked the chief medical officer at the American embassy in Islamabad. "How long is he going to be out?"

The doctor shook his head. "It's impossible to say. By doing surgery, we were able to stop the bleeding in his brain and repair the fracture in his skull. But Mr. Parker's brain is still swollen, and in all likelihood the swelling will have to go down before he regains consciousness. That could be a few hours, or days, or even weeks or months. We just can't predict something like that."

Ford and Ambassador Keyne traded looks, and then the ambassador said, "Thank you, Doctor. I'm sure you did the very best you could under the circumstances."

"I don't mind telling you, I would have rather been performing that surgery in an American hospital, rather than a Pakistani facility. It would have helped to have a real neurosurgeon, too." The doctor shrugged. "But even though everything wasn't state-of-the-art, we managed to get the job done."

"When can he be moved back here to the embassy?"

"Not for several days," the doctor said. "And he probably shouldn't be moved even then. Is that all?"

"Yes, thank you," Keyne said.

The medical officer gave the two men a brusque nod, then left the ambassador's office. Ford sank down wearily into a chair in front of Keyne's desk.

"I take it you have Mr. Parker under guard," Keyne said.

"As best I can with Pakistani security forces," Ford replied. A hint of bitterness and anger crept into his voice as he added, "I can't very well surround his room with United States Marines, much as I'd like to. Might offend our hosts, and not offending anybody seems to be the most important consideration in Washington these days. Wouldn't want to damage our standing in the world community again so soon after it's starting to be repaired."

"The President that you're disparaging appointed me to this position, you know," Keyne pointed out.

Ford spread his hands. "Disparaging? Who said I'm disparaging anybody?"

"I know how you people feel about her," Keyne snapped.

"'You people'? That's sort of a discriminatory thing to say, isn't it, Mr. Ambassador?"

"You know what I mean. You Company men who think you know more about what's in the country's best interests than the people who were elected to lead it."

"Let's just say that sometimes we have a better grasp of the real world," Ford drawled. His manner became more brisk as he sat forward and clasped his hands between his knees. "And here's something from that real world for you, Mr. Ambassador—Islamic terrorists are planning to attack a target *inside the United States* . . .

and we don't know what it is. Parker risked his life to bring us that intel, then lost consciousness before he could pass it along."

"I understand that."

"Have you told Washington about it?"

Keyne scowled. "What is there to tell? We don't have any concrete evidence of anything. Your people haven't managed to decipher those documents that Parker was carrying, have they?"

"Not yet," Ford admitted with a sigh. "The blood they were soaked in obliterated a lot of the writing. The blood Parker shed in getting here, I'd remind you."

The ambassador grimaced. "You don't have to remind me."

"We've been able to make out words here and there," Ford continued, "enough to tell that it's some sort of operational plan. But we haven't figured out what the target is. That means Parker is probably the only one who knows, at least on our side."

"All we can do is wait for him to regain consciousness."

"Yeah, that's all well and good . . . except for the fact that he said the attack was going to take place the day after Thanksgiving."

Keyne glanced at his watch. "It's nearly Friday morning in the States."

"Yeah. I know. That's why I sent a signal of my own to Washington."

A sharply indrawn breath hissed between Keyne's teeth. "You went over my head?"

"Sorry, Mr. Ambassador. Homeland Security, and my bosses at Langley, had to be alerted. They'll keep it on the down-low so that they won't cause a panic, but at least this way the authorities will have *some* warning."

"This administration doesn't play politics with terror," Keyne said.

Ford managed not to laugh in the man's face. *All* administrations played politics with *everything*. That was one of the first things you learned when you took up arms in the shadow wars. But the current occupant of the White House lived and breathed politics, especially the politics of power. She had never done anything in her adult life that hadn't been aimed at getting her elected to the highest office in the land, and now that she occupied that office, her sole concern was getting reelected. Ford had already begun hearing worried rumors that she might not want to go peacefully when her time was up.

If something like that ever happened, Lord knows what would happen to the country. But it wouldn't be anything good, that's for sure.

"I won't forget what you've done," the ambassador went on. "In the meantime, keep trying to translate those documents. And keep an eye on Mr. Parker."

"Yes, sir. I thought I'd go on over to the hospital now. My people don't really need me here. I'm not a document expert. My specialty is more in, ah, field operations."

"You mean you're a killer," Keyne barked.

"I prefer to think of myself as a warrior, sir. One of the last lines of defense between us and the barbarians."

Ford sometimes wondered if that battle could really be won, that ages-long struggle between civilization and barbarism. He had a bad feeling that he already knew to whom the ultimate triumph would belong.

But until that day came—or his time ran out—he wouldn't lay down his sword and shield. Not while America's enemies were still out there, coiled in their dens like snakes, plotting their evil.

CHAPTER 22

Walt Graham carried a little more weight through the midsection these days than he had when he was playing power forward for Texas A&M, but he liked to think that he wasn't *that* far out of playing shape. He knew he could still whip his son in a game of driveway one-on-one.

But he had to admit that he was more winded afterward, and sometimes his knees ached. He wasn't old, though. Far from it. He was in the prime of life, and an FBI agent, just as he had always dreamed of being, and he had a pretty wife and three fine kids. Life was good.

Which was more than enough reason right there to be worried. Nothing gold can stay, some poet had said. Robert Frost? Graham couldn't recall for sure, but he remembered the line from one of his college literature courses and he knew it was true. Life starts looking too rosy, you better run for the damn hills . . . 'cause all hell was probably about to break loose.

Knowing that, Graham didn't feel the least bit surprised when he walked into the Dallas office of the Federal Bureau of Investigation at five o'clock in the morning and saw the upset expression on the face of

Eileen Bastrop, the Assistant Special Agent in Charge who had called him at four fifteen and asked if he could come to the office.

"What is it, Eileen?" he asked in his deep rumble of a voice.

She handed him a curling sheet of fax paper. "This came in about an hour ago."

Somebody with a long memory for old comic strips had once referred to them as Mutt and Jeff, since Graham was six-five and Bastrop barely topped the five-foot minimum height requirement for female agents. Of course there were considerable differences between them other than their height, the most immediately noticeable being that he was a black man and she was a white woman with such pale blond hair that it almost appeared to be silver.

Both were well-trained, highly competent agents, though, and all business most of the time. When they overheard that Mutt-and-Jeff line, the glares they both sent at the perpetrator insured that it never happened again.

Graham's eyes efficiently scanned the fax, and even though the words it contained were shocking, none of that shock was visible on his face. His customary unflappable expression remained in place.

But he was feeling it inside. Man alive, was he feeling it.

He looked up from the curling paper and said, "This isn't a false alarm, is it, Eileen?"

She shrugged. "Who knows how these things will turn out? There have been plenty of warnings in the past that came to nothing. This could be another one. But we have to take it seriously either way."

"Oh, I take it seriously, all right," Graham said. "I've got a bad feeling in my gut about this one. Those cameljockeys have been waiting a long time to hit us again."

Bastrop pointed at the fax. "That says Hizb ut-Tahrir is behind whatever is being planned to go down. They're what you call a pan-Islamic group. In other words, they not all Arabians or Egyptians. They could come from just about anywhere that there are Muslims."

"So I shouldn't call them camel-jockeys?" Graham asked with a slight smile.

"It would be politically incorrect, not to mention inaccurate, for you to do so."

"All right, point taken. Will 'crazy bastards' do instead?"

Bastrop nodded. "Crazy bastards will do just fine."

She perched a hip on the edge of a desk. They were the only ones in the office at the moment. A couple of young agents had been holding down the fort on the graveyard shift. They had called the ASAC when the high-priority fax arrived from Langley, and once she had seen what was going on, she'd sent the kiddies down to the break room so she could talk this over in private with the Special Agent in Charge.

"What now, Walt?"

"We follow protocol," Graham said. "Notify the antiterrorism people at all the local law enforcement agencies, as well as the State Troopers and the Texas Rangers. Tell them to keep things as quiet as possible. We don't want a panic on our hands."

"The news media will get the story anyway," Bastrop said with a resigned look. "They always do."

Graham sighed. "I know. And those valiant defenders of the public's right to know won't even entertain the notion of keeping their traps shut for a change, or that everybody might be better off in the long run if they practiced a little discretion."

"If it bleeds, it leads," Bastrop said. "Freedom of the press and all that."

"Oh, I believe in freedom of the press. I surely do. But it wouldn't hurt those folks to show a little common sense every once in a while."

"Might hurt the ratings or the circulation numbers, and that would anger the gods of the bottom line."

Graham snorted. "We could commiserate all day about the sorry state of the mainstream media, Eileen, and it wouldn't change a blasted thing. Get the Boy Scouts back in here and get 'em to work on the phones."

Bastrop straightened from her casual pose and said, "Will do, Boss. It's more work for us now that all the different agencies try to share their intel, isn't it?"

"Yeah, but it gets better results." Graham stifled a yawn. "I think I've got a turkey hangover. I didn't want to wake up when the phone rang. Didn't much want to crawl out of a warm bed with my wife next to me either."

"We all have to make sacrifices."

Graham happened to know that Eileen Bastrop lived alone, didn't have any family in the area, didn't have a steady boyfriend. He wasn't sure she even dated anybody. Most of the time he figured that the FBI was pretty much her entire life. Every so often he wondered what she did for fun, but that was none of his business, so he just didn't think about it much. She was a damned fine agent, and that was all that really mattered.

Graham went into his private office while Bastrop and the two young agents got busy alerting the local law enforcement agencies about the terrorist threat. He took the fax with him and studied it, trying to parse more meaning out of the simple words.

The intel Langley had received from one of the CIA's agents overseas was sketchy. There was a confirmed threat from Hizb ut-Tahrir, not just against American interests, but against American soil. The bastards wanted to hit us again, somewhere right in our own backyard. But where exactly that might be, nobody knew.

So the word had gone out to the entire country. Be on the alert. Be ready for trouble. The enemy is out there, and he's poised to strike.

Lord help us, Graham thought, *if we're not ready for him.*

CHAPTER 23

The stockers had been working around the clock for days, getting merchandise on the shelves in all the departments. Cash registers and bar-code scanners had been tested and retested, calibrated and recalibrated. Electricians finished up last-minute wiring jobs. Plumbers tightened the connections on toilets in the restrooms. Here and there a little more fresh paint was dabbed on. The floors were mopped and buffed. Frozen foods and perishables were carted in and put in the proper places. Outside on the parking lot, the last stripes and arrows were painted on the asphalt. More than a hundred people had labored through the night to put all the finishing touches on the spanking-new store.

As long as two football fields, behind a massive parking lot, it ran roughly north and south on the west side of the interstate. The property was located at the top of a long, fairly gentle rise. Looking to the south, one could see the skyline of Fort Worth in the distance. To the north lay the vast sprawl of Alliance Airport, and beyond it, also visible from the high ground, rose the grandstands of Texas Motor Speedway, the NASCAR track. Stretching for miles along either side of the highway were residential and retail developments, but this was perhaps the prime piece of real estate in the area, easily accessible by millions of people, and the advertising blitz had made certain that every one of those people knew the store was having its grand opening today. There would be no "shakedown" opening to get the bugs out. When the doors slid back for the general public at six a.m., it would be for the first time ever.

Minnesota had the Mall of America. Texas was going it one better. The Lone Star State had the first Ultra-MegaMart. Hiram Stackhouse wasn't finished either. On several thousand acres around the store, he planned to build restaurants and hotels, apartment complexes, even a golf course and resort. Anything that anybody would ever need or want would be found right here by the time Stackhouse was through. And this would be only the first in a series of such complexes that he would build all across the country, ensuring him a lasting legacy as America's greatest entrepreneur. Maybe the greatest of all time.

The lights illuminating the parking lot could be seen for miles in the predawn darkness. Normally the interstate wasn't too busy at this hour, but today a river of red taillights stretched as far as the eye could see in both directions as traffic backed up on the highway. Shoppers waiting to get into the parking lot lined the frontage roads, and those lines spilled over onto the exit ramps and shoulders of the highway itself. Security guards waved flashlights and directed traffic, but getting that many cars off the road and into the parking lot was a slow process. Once shoppers finally found a place to park, they left their cars and joined the lines in front of the store's five main entrances. They would have lined up on the loading dock and gone in through the service entrance if they could, but guards were posted at the rear corners of the store to keep unauthorized people from venturing back there.

The doors were still closed and locked, but after six o'clock came they never would be again, except on Christmas Day. Other than that, the store would be open twenty-four hours a day, every day of the year, including Thanksgiving, Easter, and Fourth of July.

It was like a holiday in the parking lot this morning . . . the bright lights, the crowds, the sense of anticipation in the air . . . Everything made it seem a little like Christmas morning, in fact, as everyone waited anxiously to unwrap the shiny present that was the new UltraMegaMart store.

Later in the day, Hiram Stackhouse himself would be here. Bands would play, merchandise would be given away, there would be free food and drink—within reason, of course—and the celebration would just grow larger as the day went on.

But for now, people just wanted to get in there and see what bargains they could grab. News choppers from the local TV stations circled overhead, sending back live shots of the crowd for their morning shows. No doubt more than one news director wished that the crowd would get so impatient to start shopping that they would rush the doors and a riot would break out. What great footage that would be! Visions of local-news Emmys and triumphant ratings books danced in their heads.

The constantly growing crowd was well behaved, though, and nothing of the sort happened. Sure, folks were anxious to get inside and start shopping, but a spirit of camaraderie extended through the mass of people. They were all in this together, and years from now, they could tell their children and grandchildren that they had been there when the UltraMegaMart opened its doors for the first time.

Talk about your historic occasions.

CHAPTER 24

"Do you really think Dad's gonna show up?" Ronnie McCabe asked her mother as they stood in line in front of the store's middle entrance, about a hundred yards from the doors.

"He said he would," Terry replied. "He usually keeps his word, if he can."

"Yeah, but I know how much he hates crowds and shopping."

Terry smiled. "He doesn't *hate* it. He just has that typical male gene that prevents him from understanding how important shopping is."

They shared a laugh as Terry checked her watch. Less than ten minutes to go before the doors opened.

Jack wasn't supposed to get here until eight o'clock, which meant that Terry and Ronnie would have to kill a couple of hours until he arrived. That shouldn't prove to be too difficult, Terry thought. It would probably take them a while to even get inside the store, and once they were there the aisles would be crowded. No use getting in a hurry. She and Ronnie could afford to take their time.

When you came right down to it, they had all day.

* * *

Allison Sawyer heard a cheer go up, following immediately by a swelling chorus of excited shouts, and she knew the doors must have swung open. She looked at her watch and saw that the digital readout said 5:59. Either the watch was a little slow, or the UltraMegaMart employees had jumped the gun by a minute or so. She didn't care which was the case. The only thing that mattered was that soon she would be inside and could start shopping for Nate's Christmas presents.

She kept a tight grip on her purse, and had her arm wound through the strap to make it even more difficult for anybody to snatch it away from her. She had been putting money aside for months now—not easy to do when her salary as an assistant manager at a movie theater didn't do much more than cover their bills every month—and she had 148 dollars saved up to spend on her son. Right now that seemed like all the money in the world to her.

Nate hadn't even opened his eyes when she carried him next door and left him sleeping on the neighbors' sofa. With luck she might be back at the apartment before he woke up.

But that was pretty unlikely, she thought as she looked around her at the crowd. Barricades had been set up at the store entrances to funnel people into manageable lines, so that there wouldn't be a dangerous stampede when the doors opened. Those lines were moving slowly. The one Allison was in hadn't budged yet. Like a long line of cars at a traffic light, it took a while for everybody to start moving once the light turned green—or in this case, once the doors to the UltraMegaMart opened.

"Come on, come on," Allison muttered under her

breath. People were already in there, grabbing up the good stuff, she thought.

All she could do was hope that there would be enough left over for her once she finally made her way into the store. She didn't want anything to ruin Nate's Christmas.

There ought to be a law, Ellis Burke thought. A law against greedy, stupid people. Of course, if there was, the legal system in Texas would be even more bogged down than it already was, because then cops would spend all their time arresting people for being rednecks.

He wished he had gotten here earlier. But judging from the crowds in the parking lot and in front of the doors, he would have had to arrive before five o'clock to be anywhere close to getting in. He was just going to have to stand here with all these yokels and wait his turn. That annoyed the hell out of him. He deserved better than that. He wasn't one of the mob.

But like it or not, today he was.

At least it wasn't raining, he told himself, or too cold. The temperature was probably in the upper forties, just chilly enough so that a jacket felt good. And the doors were open and the lines were moving, also a plus. Burke shuffled along with the thousands of other would-be shoppers.

To occupy his mind, he tried estimating how many people were in line in front of him and how fast that line was moving, so he could make some sort of educated guess about how soon he would reach the doors and be able to go on inside. After a few minutes he gave it up as a hopeless task. There were just too many people. He couldn't keep up with all of them.

Where were they all going to go once they were inside

the store? he asked himself. Sure, the place was big, but was it big enough to hold everybody who was out here? Of course, some shoppers would be leaving as others went in, but it might take a while for that ebb-and-flow effect to kick in. Most of them probably planned to spend at least an hour on their shopping, maybe more. In an hour or two's time, would so many people try to crowd in there without enough people leaving so that all the space would be taken up? Burke got this crazy image in his head of the walls of the UltraMegaMart beginning to swell, to bulge out more and more, until finally they couldn't stand the strain any longer and they exploded outward, spewing rednecks in every direction in a tidal wave of blue jeans and gimme caps . . .

A sudden shout jolted that bizarre image out of Burke's head. He started to look around as a frightened voice cried, "Oh, my God! What's that man doing? What's he got? Stop him, for God's sake, somebody stop him!"

CHAPTER 25

All the foreign embassies in Islamabad were located in the northeastern corner of the city, in the so-called diplomatic zone. Stretching to the west from there was the administrative zone, the center of Pakistan's government. Since the hospital where surgery had been performed on Brad Parker was run by the government—like practically everything else in Islamabad—it lay in this sector of the city, about two miles from the American embassy.

Even at what would be thought of in the United States as rush hour, there weren't all that many cars and trucks on the roads in Islamabad, because the rank-and-file Pakistanis, the low- and medium-level government workers who made up most of the city's population, couldn't afford a vehicle. But that didn't mean the streets weren't crowded. Ford had to dodge numerous pedestrians, bicyclists, and even the occasional donkey-drawn cart as he maneuvered his car toward the hospital.

Despite his name, his family wasn't related in any way to the automobile manufacturers, at least as far as he knew. Growing up, he'd taken some ribbing from friends because even though his name was Ford, he had driven Chevrolets, Dodges, and whatever else he could afford at the time. Most of them were junkers because, after tearing up his knee in his freshman year of college, he had lost his scholarship. It had taken a lot of scrambling and long hours and struggling to make it through college and then law school.

His high marks, his athletic ability, and an indefinable something had drawn the attention of government recruiters. He could have gone to work for either the FBI or the CIA, but since he had grown up in North Dakota, he'd decided that he wanted to see the world, so he had opted for the Company.

He had seen the world, all right . . . all the ugly, dangerous places in it.

At the moment, making his way through the streets of Islamabad, he was in a little Japanese car that belonged to the embassy. He didn't like it very much; his height and broad shoulders made the car seem cramped.

But it was what he had, and he'd learned to make do. As a veteran of numerous backwater postings since he'd gone to work for the Company, he had become good at doing more with less—less funding, less political support, fewer assets on the ground. Ever since the nineties, when the American intelligence community had been gutted along with the military, it had been a constant struggle for the shadow warriors to rebuild their capabilities. You would have thought that 9/11 would have served as a true wake-up call for the politicians. They needed to give the intelligence services adequate backing and *by God start paying attention when those services tried to warn them about something*.

But of course the effects of that terrible day in September had worn off pretty quickly once the news media grew tired of promoting them and the opposition party realized that a weakened, feeble America was better for them in the long run. The current occupant of the White House was proof of that. She never would have been elected without the constant drumbeat of negativity from her party and their loyal lapdogs, the mainstream media.

Ford grimaced as he braked and let one of those donkey carts cross in front of him. Modern, glass-sided buildings rose on both sides of the street. The dichotomy of such a sight was common in the Third World, and Ford had long since stopped letting such things throw him off stride. The modern and the primitive went hand in hand here. That was just the way it was.

As Ford drove on toward the hospital, he visited some scorn on the so-called conservatives, too. It was easy to blame the liberals for everything, and in truth, most of what was wrong with the country was their fault. But the other side wasn't totally blameless either. When they'd had their chance to govern, they hadn't quite mastered the competence required for such a job, nor had they been able to resist the temptation to pander to the opposition, to waffle on their convictions, to try to please everybody instead of doing what was best for the country. Partisanship and the never-ending electoral process had come close to wrecking what had been a pretty good system for a couple of hundred years.

Close . . . but no cigar. The United States still functioned, and for all its problems, it was still the greatest country in the world. Deep down, all the carpers and naysayers, both at home and abroad, knew that. That was one reason their never-ending bitching and moaning had a hollow ring to it.

And it was also one reason that, despite all the annoyances and the real dangers, Lawrence "Fargo" Ford was going to continue devoting his life to protecting his country.

He pulled into the hospital's small parking lot, hoping against hope that Brad Parker had regained consciousness, even though it was unlikely. Until Parker could tell them exactly where the terrorist threat was aimed, the only precautions the folks back home could take were general ones, the same sort of things that everybody tried to do these days.

Like all the buildings in Islamabad's administrative zone, the hospital was fairly new, a three-story building with lots of glass and chrome, surrounded by small but neatly kept lawns. Ford locked the car and followed a concrete walk to the main entrance. Automatic doors slid aside. He walked into the lobby, past a guard station where a turbaned member of the Pakistani Army was posted with a machine gun looped over his shoulder by its strap. The soldier called to Ford in Urdu, asking him to please stop for a moment.

Ford did so, showing the guard his identification papers. The man nodded and waved him on. Ford supposed that news of the American patient on the third floor had gotten around the hospital. Hell, given the efficiency of the grapevine that operated in the capital city, speculation was probably rife by now that Parker was an American intelligence agent, a member of the CIA or Special Forces.

That was why Ford planned to stay at Parker's side from now until the guy woke up. He had already taken a big enough chance going back to the embassy to brief the ambassador on what was going on. Keyne was an officious, sanctimonious son of a bitch—a typical appointee of the current administration, in other words—and had insisted that Ford fill him in personally.

There was only one elevator in the lobby. Ford pressed the button to summon it and waited. After several minutes he pushed the button again, and began to frown as the elevator still didn't come. He glanced up at the numbers above the door. The one for the third floor was lit up. It stayed lit up.

Suddenly, Ford turned and lunged across the lobby toward the door that led to the stairs.

Behind him, the guard at the entrance shouted a command to stop. Ford didn't even slow down. A volley from the machine gun ripped through the air, the bullets slamming into the wall next to the staircase door as Ford threw it open. He dived through and started bounding up the steps, taking them three at a time.

Whatever was going on up on the third floor, the Pakistani soldier was part of it. That came as no surprise to Ford. Most of the army was loyal to the government, but like every other segment of society in the country, it was also riddled with sympathizers and outright supporters of the radical Islamic fringe groups. In this part of the world, almost anybody could be a terrorist—or want to be one.

Ford knew that he hadn't been hit. He wouldn't be moving as well as he was if he had been. He also knew that his heart was already pounding wildly in his chest. He wasn't as young as he'd once been, despite his efforts to keep in top shape. He thought he could manage three flights of stairs without having a coronary, though.

He had to, if Brad Parker was going to have a chance.

Ford wondered if the burst from the machine gun had been heard on the third floor. It was certainly possible. Even if it hadn't been, the turncoat soldier would be alerting his friends up there even now. Ford would probably find a reception committee waiting for him.

That was why he slowed down as he rounded the bend in the middle of the third and final flight of stairs. He reached under the tails of his coat to the small of his back and took out the little flat nine-millimeter automatic he carried there. He always had the 9mm either on him or within easy reach, all the time.

When he got to the door, he kicked it open and jerked to the side, spinning out of the line of fire as another machine gun chattered at him and sent steel-jacketed death sizzling through the air of the stairwell. Ford dived through the opening, staying as low as he could, and spotted the gunner about halfway along the corridor that stretched out in front of him. The 9mm in Ford's hand barked twice.

Both slugs tore into the machine gunner's body on rising angles. One came out his back in a spray of blood. The other hit a rib and bounced around crazily, pulping everything in its path. The gunner jerked and shuddered and sprawled back against the wall for a second before pitching forward on his face.

The intensive care unit where Brad Parker was being taken care of lay on the left-hand side of the corridor, beyond the point where the machine gunner now lay with a spreading pool of blood under him. The elevator was at the far end of the corridor. Its door stood open, and Ford could see why. A body lay across the threshold, stopping the door every time it tried to close. The man wore the uniform of a Pakistani soldier; he had been on guard in the elevator, his job to keep any suspicious characters from reaching the third floor.

Clearly, he had failed. Even from this distance, Ford could see the soldier's wide, emptily staring eyes. The man's face was already starting to turn purple from the blood trapped in his head by the wire garrote that was dug deeply into the flesh of his neck.

From behind the double, swinging doors of the ICU came more gunshots. Ford scrambled to his feet and ran toward them. Parker had had two guards with him. Ford could only hope that those guys were holding out somehow against the assassins who had come to the hospital to make sure that Parker never revealed what he knew about Hizb ut-Tahrir's plans.

It came as no surprise to Ford that there was a leak at the embassy. That had to be how the terrorists had found out about Parker and knew where to look for him. No embassy in the world could be a hundred percent secure, because no embassy was a hundred percent self-sufficient. You *had* to rely on the locals for a few things. That opened the door to potential leaks.

If he had been here to supervise things personally, Ford thought bitterly, instead of dealing with that stuffed shirt Keyne, the would-be killers never would have gotten this close.

Too late to worry about that now. Instead, he had to stop them from shutting Parker up permanently, if it wasn't already too late for *that*.

And if it was . . . God help the folks back in the States who found themselves sitting on this year's Ground Zero.

CHAPTER 26

The woman doing the yelling was heavyset, middle-aged, and black. Her right hand clutched the hand of a little boy; the left pointed, finger jabbing forward as she shouted, "Stop him, stop him!"

Hurrying toward Burke at a pace halfway between a walk and a run was a man in his early twenties, one of those skinny Goth kids dressed all in baggy black clothes, the lank hair falling around his face dyed an unnatural shade of black to match his garb. All that darkness made the doughy pallor of his face even more pronounced. His frantic eyes locked for a second with Burke's, and in that second Burke saw the multiple studs in both ears and the one right below the guy's mouth. His tongue was probably pierced, too, but Burke couldn't see that.

He saw the woman's purse that the guy was trying to stuff under his bulky jacket, though.

What sort of dumb-ass would try to snatch a woman's purse in the middle of a huge crowd like this? That was Burke's first thought. But maybe it wasn't such a stupid move after all. Nobody was trying to stop the guy, despite the black woman's screams. Burke figured the purse belonged to her. The crowd was so thick that if nobody did anything, within moments the thief would be swallowed up by the mob. Yeah, he was pretty distinctive-looking, but surely he wasn't the only Goth kid here this morning, and if he passed the purse off to a more normal-looking confederate, there wouldn't be any way to prove that he'd done anything wrong. All it took to pull off something like this was steady nerves and a certain amount of slick daring.

And a bunch of sheep who didn't give a damn, didn't want to be involved, just wanted to get in the store and turn over more of their money to a modern-day robber baron like Hiram Stackhouse.

Well, it was somebody else's lookout, thought Burke, not his.

Then some hot, soccer-mom blonde had to go and step in front of the purse snatcher and say in a loud, clear voice, "Hold it! What do you think you're doing?" She reached for the purse and tried to drag it out from under the thief's leather jacket.

"Hey, lady!" he yelled. He gave the blonde a hard shove. "Bug off!"

A pretty, brown-haired teenager got in the guy's face. "Leave my mom alone!" she told him as she shoved him right back.

Crazy rednecks, Burke thought. Always looking for a fight.

Then the guy popped the teenager with a backhand, grabbed the hot blond mom and slung her out of the way, and tried to force his way into the crowd again.

That put him right in Burke's face. Burke didn't think about what he was doing. He just drew back his right fist at his side and planted it in the thief's midsection as hard as he could.

The guy's eyes widened and bulged out in surprise and pain. One of his eyebrows was pierced, too. Idiot. Burke hit him again, putting the second shot right where the first one had landed. These were the first punches he had thrown since grade school. His parents had been firm believers in nonviolence and had taken little Ellis along to all of their protests and sit-ins, making sure he was raised to know how important it was to fight the Man, but to do it peacefully.

Nobody had ever told him how good it would feel to hit some scuzzball in the belly.

The thief whined a little and dropped to his knees. The blonde and her daughter both started walloping him from behind, driving him the rest of the way to the asphalt. He curled up in a ball and put his arms over his head, even though nobody was trying to kick him. In fact, the crowd stepped back and gave him some room. Burke leaned down and took the stolen purse from him. As he was straightening, a couple of uniformed security guards shouldered through the press of people.

"Hey!" one of them shouted at Burke. "Drop that purse, mister!"

"He's not the thief," the blonde said. She pointed to the Goth kid. "There's the one who stole the purse."

"That's right, officer," Burke said as other people began to nod in support of the blonde's statement. "I'm an attorney. I was just recovering the stolen property."

"He stopped that man," the black woman said excitedly as she came up, dragging the little boy with her. "Just hauled off and gave him what for."

"You apprehended the thief, sir?" one of the rent-a-cops asked Burke.

He shrugged and nodded toward the blonde and her daughter. "It was really more these ladies—"

"No," the mom said, "I'm afraid he would have gotten away from us. He would have gotten away with that purse if you hadn't stopped him."

Burke didn't mind being the center of attention in a courtroom; in fact, he'd always liked that. But he didn't care for the feeling of having a whole horde of Texas yahoos staring at him in admiration like he was Chuck Norris or the Lone frickin' Ranger, stepping in to stop the bad guy. He wasn't even sure why he had done what he did. It hadn't been any of his business.

And now he just wanted to get on into the store and buy the damn toy for his daughter and get the hell out of here.

With that in mind, he turned to the black woman and held the purse out to her, saying, "Here you go, ma'am. No need to thank me—"

"That's not my purse," she said.

Burke frowned. "It's not? But I thought—"

"I just started hollerin' when I saw that man grab it away from another woman. Looked like it hurt her, too, the way her arm got jerked around by the strap. That ugly fella wasn't just about to let it go, though."

The security guards had lifted the thief to his feet and were ready to haul him into the store. That was one way to get in ahead of everybody else, Burke thought fleetingly as looked at the black woman.

"But if the purse isn't yours," he said, "then who does it belong to?"

"It's mine," a voice said from behind him. He turned and saw the prettiest woman he had run across in a long time, standing there with her hand out for the purse.

Well, Burke thought, maybe it was a good thing he

had intervened after all, instead of letting the thief scurry on past him. After all, he was an officer of the court. It was his civic duty to uphold the law.

Especially when that included making the acquaintance of a beautiful—and grateful—young woman.

CHAPTER 27

Allison had been taken totally by surprise when she felt the hard tug on the purse strap that wrenched her arm around behind her back. She had cried out, a short, sharp exclamation that hadn't carried very far in the hubbub of the throng moving slowly into the UltraMegaMart. She made a desperate grab at the strap, but she was too late.

The purse was gone, and with it the money she had saved for her son's Christmas.

A mixture of despair and outrage had exploded in Allison's brain at that moment of realization. It was so powerful that it froze her in place for a second.

But only for a second. Then she began fighting to push her way through the crowd after the thief. She yelled for help, but nobody seemed to hear her. At least, nobody tried to stop the man who'd stolen her purse.

Then the black woman who had witnessed the theft added her voice to the outcry, and it carried a lot better than Allison's did. A couple of women got in the thief's way and slowed him down, and then a man hit him, knocking him to the ground. Because of the crowd, Allison couldn't see the man that well at first . . .

Now she was standing in front of him as he held the purse out toward her, and she saw that he was considerably older than her, around forty, she guessed. He was better dressed than most of the people waiting to get into the UltraMegaMart, in a conservative dark suit, a white shirt, and what Allison guessed was called a power tie; she wasn't sure about that. He wasn't fat, just big and solidly built, with some streaks of gray in his dark hair and the slightly flushed face of a man who liked to take a drink—or three or four—on a fairly regular basis. She reminded Allison of her dad.

The look in his eyes as he smiled at her wasn't particularly paternal, though, or even avuncular. He said, "Here's your purse, miss. Are you all right? Did he hurt you when he grabbed it?"

Allison took the purse and then rubbed her arm. "No, he just jerked me around a little. I thought the way I had the purse strap wrapped around my arm that nobody could get it loose, but obviously I was wrong."

"Well, if you're injured, you can file suit against the guy. I'd be glad to represent you. We'd win, I guarantee it." He grinned as the security guards led the thief off through the crowd. "I'm not sure you'd ever be able to collect any judgment, though. Not unless you were willing to accept nose rings and eyebrow rings in lieu of cash."

Allison had to laugh. This man was older than her, old enough to be . . . well, her older brother anyway . . . and from what he'd just said he was a lawyer to boot. Allison wasn't too fond of lawyers, having had a crappy one during her divorce. But at least this one seemed to have a sense of humor.

"I'm Ellis Burke," by the way," he said.

"Allison Sawyer," she replied. She took the hand he held out to her and shook it, letting go quickly so that his grip couldn't linger. She was used to guys hitting on her, especially once they found out she was divorced, and while she was grateful to Ellis Burke for helping her, she didn't want him getting any ideas. Keeping her voice brisk but polite, she said, "Thank you, Mr. Burke."

"Please, call me Ellis. Ellis, Allison . . . kind of goes together, don't you think?"

Before she could respond to that blatant come-on, the older blond woman who had also helped stop the thief introduced herself. "I'm Terry McCabe," she said, "and this is my daughter Ronnie."

Allison smiled at them. "I'm pleased to meet both of you." Her gaze took in the two women and Burke. "I'd offer you a reward for helping me, but all I have is the money I've saved up for my son's Christmas presents—"

"A reward?" Burke broke in. "Nonsense! You don't owe us a thing."

"Really, we were happy to help," Terry McCabe said. "I'm just glad we were able to stop that man, so your son's Christmas won't be ruined."

Allison nodded. "You and me both, Mrs. McCabe."

"So," Burke said, "how old is your son? And do you and your husband have any more children?"

Allison knew what he was angling for, but she didn't see any way out of providing the information without being rude. She didn't want to do that. After all, Burke *had* stopped the thief and saved her money.

"Nate's eight years old," she said, "and he's my only child." There. She had neatly avoided having to tell Burke that she was divorced, she thought.

But she could tell he hadn't missed the fact that she wasn't wearing a wedding ring, so that must have emboldened him. "I know it's very difficult being a single mother these days," he said. "It's hard to make ends

meet and still devote enough time to raising your child.
I see it all the time in my practice."

"You're a divorce lawyer?" Terry McCabe asked.

"Personal injury." Burke laughed. "That's right, I'm
one of those ambulance-chasing shysters. There, I've
said what we're all thinking, so we don't have to worry
about it anymore, do we?"

The uproar over the attempted purse-snatching had
subsided. The lines were moving toward the doors again,
and people's attention had returned to the thing that had
brought them here: the desire to grab up as many bargains as possible during the grand opening of the Ultra-
MegaMart.

The press of the crowd kept Allison from thanking
Burke again and moving on. She was sort of stuck there
with him and Terry and Ronnie McCabe, as well as the
black woman, who introduced herself as Judy Winston.
The little boy was her son Darius.

To make small talk, Allison said to Burke, "What
brings you here before dawn on a chilly morning, Mr.
Burke? Shouldn't you be getting ready for court?"

"The courts are all in recess until after the Thanksgiving weekend," he told her. "No judge would dare interfere with the biggest shopping day of the year. And I
guess I'm here for the same reason you are . . . because
of my kid."

"Boy or girl?"

"A little girl. She's twelve." Burke supplied the information about his daughter's age before Allison could
ask the standard question.

She turned the tables on him, though, by asking, "Do
you and your wife have any other children?"

"No, just the one. But she's not my wife anymore.
I'm divorced."

He didn't seem to mind saying it. Allison still had a little bit of a hard time with that sometimes.

"I'm sorry."

"Don't be. It was for the best. If someone doesn't want to be with a certain person anymore, than no amount of rationalizing or denial will ever make them happy again. Once whatever it was between two people that drew them together is gone, they're both better off moving on."

"That's sort of a cynical way to look at it, isn't it? If there's something wrong with a marriage, isn't it better to try to fix it?"

"Did you try to fix yours before you and your husband split up?"

Allison wanted to tell him that was none of his business, but instead she said, "As a matter of fact, I did. I couldn't do it by myself, though. He wasn't willing to stop drinking or cheating on me."

"Then he was a damned fool. And the fewer damned fools in your life, the better. That's the law. Burke's law." Then he laughed.

Allison didn't see what was funny.

He must have seen the puzzled look on her face, because he said, "It was a TV show. *Burke's Law.* About this millionaire who was a cop . . . Never mind, you're too young."

Allison felt slightly offended at that, but tried not to show it. She changed the subject, sort of, by saying, "That's all right, by the time we actually get into the store I'm going to be old."

Burke laughed, and so did Terry and Ronnie McCabe. "Let's just hope that when we get in there, it was worth waiting for," the lawyer said.

CHAPTER 28

At first Hamed had felt panic shoot through him when the shouting started near his position in line. Even though he knew the two Heckler & Koch machine pistols he carried were well concealed under the bulky fatigue jacket he wore, for a second he thought that someone had somehow spotted the weapons. It was enough of a drawback that the Americans were nearly all suspicious of every Middle Eastern–looking man that they saw. The infidels' paranoia was one of the main dangers to the plan laid out by Sheikh al-Mukhari.

And, of course, in this case the unbelieving dogs would have been right to be paranoid. Scattered through the huge crowd jammed in front of the store were twenty fighters for Islamic freedom, all of them carrying weapons and explosives. Sheikh al-Mukhari was there, too, carrying the briefcase that contained the dirty bomb Hizb ut-Tahrir had purchased from a supplier in the former Soviet Union. This bomb had, in fact, once belonged to Saddam Hussein before he had disposed of it, along with his other nuclear, chemical, and biological weapons, by either smuggling them out of Iraq to sympathetic parties, or in some cases simply selling them back—at a loss, of course—to the dealers who had supplied them in the first place, getting rid of them before the American invasion. Without enough such weapons to actually stop the infidels, Saddam had opted to try to get world opinion on his side by appearing to be the helpless victim of American aggression.

Part of that plan had worked. Always eager to believe the worst of everything their nation did, a significant number of foolish Americans had accepted without any trouble the notion that simply because Iraq had no weapons of mass destruction at the time of the invasion, it followed that Iraq had *never* had any such weapons and that the American President had lied, lied, lied. The Europeans had been quick to jump on that bandwagon.

While that strategy had worked for Saddam on a global public relations level, it hadn't done a thing for him personally, as he found out at the wrong end of a rope. Ever since, the always-worried-about-their-image Americans had tried not to rush to judgment about anything, and of course they would never do anything on an official level as sane and reasonable as racial profiling, since such a thing was heinous in their eyes.

But that didn't stop the everyday Americans from being at least a little suspicious of every dark-skinned, dark-eyed, dark-haired man between the ages of eighteen and fifty, especially if he had a beard. Hamed had grown accustomed to their wary stares, which was why he thought for a harrowing moment that he had been discovered.

But it was just a petty crime going on, he realized within moments, the attempted theft of a purse from an American slut, with her tight jeans and her bright, fair hair uncovered. There was a brief outbreak of violence, during which bystanders prevented the thief from fleeing. A pair of security guards arrived to take him away.

The ridiculous-looking young man would be arrested, probably fined and given a suspended sentence, and would be committing crimes again with barely a break in his routine. If Americans were more sensible, they would realize that a thief with his hands chopped off would have a much more difficult time stealing in the future.

Hamed was glad the incident had occurred. It had given him a chance to observe the security guards in action, and he saw nothing in their manner or their behavior to cause him any worry. Both uniformed men were out of shape and lackadaisical.

Even if the Americans somehow received advance warning of the plan—and that seemed unlikely to Hamed, since no one knew of it except loyal members of Hizb ut-Tahrir—events were already in motion.

Before this day was over, infidel blood would be spilled by the gallon, and it was too late for the foolish Americans to do anything about it.

CHAPTER 29

Ford hit the doors of the ICU in the hospital in Islamabad at a dead run. It was a dumb thing to do and he knew it, but he didn't have time to scope out the situation first. Sometimes you just had to bust in with all guns a-blazin' and hope for the best.

Sometimes that got you in deep shit, too.

Like now.

He hit the floor and rolled as bullets chewed up a cart full of medical equipment right beside him. The ICU was relatively small, with a nurses' station to the left and a row of curtained alcoves, each with a bed in it, to the right. There were half a dozen of the alcoves, and Brad Parker was in the one at the far end, the farthest away from the door. At least he had been when Ford left the hospital earlier, and Ford assumed he still was because the assassins who had invaded the hospital were directing their gunfire in that direction—except for the one who was doing his damnedest to kill Ford.

The analytical part of Ford's brain took in all the details of the scene, processing them quickly and efficiently. Four men, two wearing white doctors' coats, two in turbans. All of them armed with automatic weapons. Ford didn't see any grenades, but that didn't mean they didn't have some. The alcoves were separated by solid partitions that ended about a foot from the ceiling; the fronts had curtains over them that could be drawn for privacy. One of Parker's guards was firing around the corner of that partition, while the other man was down, sprawled at the foot of Parker's bed while blood leaked from the wounds that had turned him into a sieve. The killers must have gotten him with a couple of bursts of automatic fire, but the other guard had managed to get behind some cover and try to hold them off.

Ford's arrival changed the odds, but he and the guard were still outnumbered two to one. Ford grabbed the bullet-riddled cart and shoved it at the nearest assassin, the one who had turned and opened up on him when he burst into the ICU. The cart's wheels still worked. It crashed into the gunner, causing him to stumble to the side, and that gave Ford a chance to center the pistol's sights on the man and send two rounds sizzling into his chest. The guy howled in pain, spun around, got tangled up with the cart, and fell to the floor with a loud clatter as the cart overturned on top of him.

Ford rolled into the nearest alcove. It wouldn't give him much cover, but in a firefight any cover was better than none. From the corner of his eye he saw that an old woman lay in the bed in the alcove, surrounded by tubes and beeping equipment and worried relatives. Ford wished he could reassure them that everything would be all right, but he didn't have time and anyway he didn't know that was true.

Everything might still go all to hell.

Events took another turn for the better, though, when the surviving guard put a pair of slugs into the belly of one of the assassins. The killer doubled over with a groan, dropping his gun. He went to his knees and then toppled over on his face. The odds were even now.

And guys like these didn't care for a fair fight. Cowards at heart, like all terrorists, the sick bastards preferred to send others to do their killing for them, usually women and kids with several pounds of explosives strapped to their bodies, poor deluded fools who could be persuaded that they should die for the glory of Allah. Ford's lips drew back from his teeth in a grimace of outrage and disgust as he surged out of the alcove and fired again and again and again at the shocked assassins, riddling them with lead. The bullets threw them back against the counter of the nurses' station. They hung there for a second and then slowly slid down to the floor as the life died in their eyes.

They wouldn't be waking up in paradise, Ford thought as his heart pounded wildly in his chest and he lowered the gun. They would be shaking hands with the Devil in hell instead . . . and he wasn't sure but what even *that* was too good for the sons of bitches.

"M-Mister Ford?" The voice came from the surviving guard, a Pakistani security officer named Sharezz. In the echoing silence that followed the fury of battle, it sounded strange to Ford's ears. "You are all right, sir?"

Ford glanced down at his light-colored suit, which was rumpled and dirty from rolling around on the floor, but didn't seem to have any bloodstains on it. "Yeah," he said. "Yeah, Sharezz, I'm okay. What about Parker?"

Ford started in the direction of the alcove, but before he could get there a nurse hurried past him. Even here in the hospital, the women wore the baggy dresses and the head coverings, but the tunic this woman wore over her dress had the crescent symbol on it that denoted medical personnel. Ford supposed that she had been huddled behind the counter of the nurses' station while the shooting went on.

At the last second as she darted into the alcove, Ford spotted her hand coming out from under her garments with a knife in it. She wasn't going to check on the patient after all. She was hurrying to kill him while she still had the chance.

"Sharezz, look out!" Ford yelled as he lunged toward the alcove. The warning came too late. He heard a grunt of pain, then a thin, gurgling cry. As Ford reached the partition he saw Sharezz slumping backward, pawing futilely at his throat while crimson flooded from the gaping wound where the knife had slashed it open. The blade was held high in the woman's hand now, poised to swoop down into Brad Parker's chest as he lay there unconscious on the bed.

Ford shot her in the back of the head. Wasn't time to do anything else. If he'd made a grab for the knife, he would have been too late. A body shot might have left the woman conscious enough to finish the killing stroke. He had to put her down, fast.

The knife dropped from suddenly nerveless fingers as blood and brains sprayed over the bed and the medical equipment around it, as well as the patient lying there. The woman fell against the side of the bed and sprawled on the floor, next to Sharezz, who had collapsed in the corner and now sat in a pool of blood as his head drooped forward over his ruined neck. Ford knew he was dead.

So was the female assassin, the nurse who was undoubtedly working with Hizb ut-Tahrir, if she wasn't a full-fledged member of the group.

But Brad Parker was still alive, as the steady beeping of the monitor hooked up to him indicated. His pallid face was speckled with blood from the woman. And as Ford stood there, shaken from all the violence, drawing the back of his hand across his mouth in a gesture of revulsion for all the killing, necessary though it had been . . .

The machine started beeping faster.

Ford's eyes widened. He had a rudimentary knowledge of medical gizmos like this, and the readouts and graphs on the machine told him that Parker's pulse, respiration, and blood pressure were increasing. He stepped around the corpse to get closer to the bed and leaned over the injured man. "Parker?" he said. "Brad, you hear me, old buddy? Parker?"

With a weak flickering of the eyelids, Brad Parker's eyes opened. They didn't focus at first, but then they locked in on Ford and he husked through dry lips, "F-Fargo? That you? Wh-what's goin' . . . on here? Sounded like . . . thunder . . ."

"Nothing to worry about, pal," Ford assured him. Just an ICU full of dead bodies. Ford's fingers were working automatically now, sliding a fresh clip of ammunition into the pistol in case more would-be killers showed up. He went on. "I know you just woke up, Brad, but we've gotta talk. You were telling me about what Hizb ut-Tahrir is going to pull in the States. You said there was gonna be a terrorist attack, but you didn't say where. You've got to tell me where, Brad."

Parker might pass out again at any second. Ford had to get that vital intel from him while he could. They were already out of time—

"D-Day after Thank . . . Thanksgiving," Parker rasped.

Ford grimaced. It was already Friday morning in the United States, anywhere from 10:30 to 7:30, depending on the time zone involved. Although Parker hadn't been able to reveal the exact time of the terrorist attack, they already knew the day. Now they needed the location, so they could start to prevent it if there was still time.

"Where, Brad?" Ford asked in a desperate half-whisper. "Where?"

"T-Texas," Parker got out with a struggle. "Mega . . . Mart . . . Ultra . . . Mega . . . Mart . . ."

With a sigh, his eyes closed again. He was still alive, the machines testified to that, but he was unconscious again.

And Ford was left standing there saying to himself, "UltraMegaMart? What the hell?"

He knew what MegaMart was, of course, but he'd never heard of an UltraMegaMart. Somebody in Washington would know, though, or could find out, as soon as Ford got back to the embassy and sent a radio message bouncing off a satellite.

He just hoped the warning would come in time for those folks in Texas, who had no idea of the threat looming over their heads.

CHAPTER 30

McCabe had arrived at the giant MegaMart distribution center at Alliance Airport about ten minutes before eight o'clock. The sprawling complex of warehouses wasn't actually on airport property but adjoining it; everybody talked about the distribution center as if it were part of the airport anyway, since they were next-door neighbors, so to speak.

Even though McCabe had been looking forward to the time off, this unexpected job wasn't a big deal. He didn't think it would take more than thirty minutes or so, start to finish. He just drove, he didn't load or unload. Hiram Stackhouse paid other people to handle those jobs.

Somebody else could bring the empty truck back to the distribution center, too. As soon as somebody at the UltraMegaMart signed for it, McCabe was done. He would call Terry on her cell phone and find out where he was supposed to meet her and Ronnie, and then he planned to enjoy spending an hour or two shopping with his wife and daughter.

Surely an hour or two was all it would take for them to finish their shopping, he told himself. After all, they had gotten up a long time before the chickens and had planned to be at the store when it opened. They would have more than a two-hour head start on him. Once they were done, they could run him back up to the distribution center, where he would get his pickup and head home to spend the rest of the weekend doing some serious vegetating.

That was the plan anyway.

But as happens so often with plans, things began to go wrong with it almost right away.

The trailer he was supposed to take wasn't loaded when he got there. "Sorry, McCabe," the warehouse supervisor told him without really sounding very apologetic about it. "We've been workin' pretty much around the clock for weeks now, tryin' to get that damn store stocked. You wouldn't think it could hold so much. But we'll have you loaded and ready to go as soon as we can."

"How long are we talking about?" McCabe asked.

The supervisor shrugged. "Half hour, maybe less."

That wasn't enough time to go and do anything and then come back, McCabe decided. "I'll just hang around here and wait then," he said.

"Use my office," the supervisor suggested. "Pour yourself some coffee and read the paper. We'll let you know when you're ready to roll."

McCabe nodded his thanks and headed for the row of offices along one side of the vast, noisy warehouse. The walls of the office wouldn't keep all the racket out, but at least it wouldn't be quite so loud in there.

He poured that cup of coffee the supervisor had mentioned and sat down on an old, cracked leather sofa to glance over the front page of the newspaper that was scattered on the sofa as well. At home he had brought in the paper but hadn't even glanced at it. He knew what was going to be on the front page. Tensions in the Middle East, with both sides rattling their sabers . . . and if you read between the lines, somehow all the trouble would be America's fault.

Sure enough, that was what he found, along with a story about continued Iranian protests over the presence of American warships in the Persian Gulf. McCabe was a little surprised that the President had sent the fleet to keep the Strait of Hormuz open. It wasn't like her to do anything except back down from every potential confrontation. He supposed it was because any disruption in the flow of oil would cause gasoline prices to skyrocket again. No politician wanted that, especially a President who would be facing an election in less than a year.

McCabe tossed the front page aside in disgust. He had put in his time in the front lines of the shadow war, and like most veterans of that conflict, he felt an immense love for his country but an instinctive distrust—and often disgust—for the politicians who ran it. Most of them had no idea what was really going on behind the scenes.

And if they knew the truth, knew how close the country had come to utter disaster on numerous occasions, most of them would shit their pants.

McCabe picked up the sports section instead, and started reading about how the Cowboys had beaten the Redskins in the Thanksgiving Day game the day before. Now *that* was interesting.

Engrossed in the story, he didn't really notice how much time was passing until he happened to glance at the clock on the wall of the supervisor's office and saw that it was nearly nine o'clock. He grimaced. That half-hour wait had almost doubled.

McCabe tossed the paper aside and was about to get

up and go looking for the supervisor to ask him what the holdup was, when the door of the office opened and the man himself came in, a smile on his face.

"Got you loaded and ready to go, Jack," he said. "Sorry for the delay."

McCabe shrugged. "I guess it couldn't be helped."

"That's right. The Old Man wants this to be the best store ever. Not just the best MegaMart, mind you. But the best store, period."

McCabe had no trouble believing that. Hiram Stackhouse was larger than life and wasn't going to settle for second-best in anything. He liked media attention, too, and in McCabe's opinion, Stackhouse carefully cultivated the colorful, eccentric image he presented to the world.

The old guy wasn't all hat and no cattle, though. He had plenty of guts, and had proven it a couple of years earlier by getting himself right in the middle of a dangerous ruckus out in Arizona, when a small town near the border had found itself overrun by a criminal gang from Mexico. The bastards had shot up a MegaMart there and drawn the wrath of Stackhouse down on their heads. During the final showdown between the town and the gang, the Old Man had shown up with his security forces, using them like a private army as he stepped in to fight on the side of the good citizens of Little Tucson. Stackhouse had risked his own turkey neck, too, driving into the besieged town in his fancy car with the longhorns mounted on the front, his old-fashioned ivory-handled six-gun blazing.

What a character. McCabe had met Stackhouse several times and wouldn't mind seeing the Old Man again. Stackhouse was supposed to be at the grand opening of the UltraMegaMart today, but McCabe wasn't sure exactly when he was going to show up. If McCabe missed him, that would be too bad, but he wasn't going to lose any sleep over it.

He left the office, walking through the warehouse and out the huge doors at the far end to the loading docks. The trailer he was supposed to take was waiting for him there, with the back door still rolled up. McCabe glanced in at the cargo. He never drove without making sure the truck was loaded properly. A load that shifted while he was on the road could cause some definite problems.

Satisfied, McCabe nodded to the warehousemen, who rolled the door down and dogged it closed. He gave them a wave, then walked to the cab of the eighteen-wheeler and climbed into it, settling himself in the comfortable driver's seat. He had taken this truck out before, so he was familiar with it. He ran through a mental checklist, sort of like an airplane pilot getting ready to take off, he thought. The dashboard of the truck wasn't as complicated as the control panel of an airliner, but there were things to check as he fired up the engine.

Of course, the biggest difference was that if his engine died, it wouldn't be at thirty thousand feet. He could just pull over onto the shoulder. McCabe hated flying. He hated jumping out of a perfectly good airplane into pitch darkness where enemies were waiting to kill you even more, but he had done that on numerous occasions. Surviving things like that made it easier not to sweat the small stuff of everyday life, like having to work for a while on a day when you thought you would be off from work.

The time was a few minutes after nine o'clock when McCabe drove out of the distribution center. The sun was shining, and it was a chilly but beautiful autumn day. He thought about calling Terry to let her know that he was on his way, but he didn't really see any point in doing that and decided not to. Calling her could wait until he was at the store and had delivered his load. Then he would be through with work and ready to spend the rest of the day with his family.

The UltraMegaMart was less than five miles from the distribution center and it should have taken only a few minutes to drive there. McCabe suppressed a groan as he reached the interstate and saw that that wasn't going to be the case today. Traffic was at a near-standstill on the highway, both lanes just inching along in a sea of brake lights. McCabe knew why it was that way, too.

Everybody wanted to go shopping.

His mind worked quickly, trying to figure out an alternate route. Unfortunately, there just wasn't one, he admitted to himself a few moments later. He could circle around on some back roads and come up toward the store from the south, but the traffic from that direction would be just as bad, if not worse. Like it or not, McCabe thought, he was just going to have to be patient and fight his way through the traffic jam.

It took him five minutes just to get through the entrance ramp and onto the highway itself. He bulled his way into the line of vehicles. He knew people resented truckers for doing things like that, but it wasn't his fault that what he was driving was ten times bigger than what they were driving. Let them try to maneuver one of these behemoths and see how they liked it.

Once on the highway, McCabe tuned the cab's radio to a local sports talk station and listened to the hosts and callers rehashing the Cowboys' victory the day before. Winning any game was sweet, of course; winning the annual Thanksgiving Day game was sweeter still. But beating the Redskins on Thanksgiving . . . well, short of playoff victories, it didn't get much better than that.

The traffic's pace picked up a little, and when McCabe checked the speedometer he saw that he was going ten miles per hour. At that blazing rate, he'd reach the Ultra-MegaMart in thirty minutes or so. He looked at the clock on the dash. Nine twenty. He ought to be there by ten. He wasn't running that awful late.

Shouldn't be any big deal.

CHAPTER 31

At nine twenty-five, a dark-haired man pulled into the parking lot of a bank in one of the suburbs just north of Fort Worth and brought his late-model car to a stop in a place right next to the sidewalk, less than fifteen feet from the front door. The bank wasn't very busy yet this morning. The man got out of the car and walked to a strip shopping center about fifty yards away, as if he intended to run a few errands first and then return to the bank to finish up his business.

But as soon as he was in the shopping center parking lot, another car pulled up beside him. He opened the passenger door and got in. This second car drove away, and the first one was left at the bank, with no one paying any attention to it.

At a post office a few miles away, another dark-haired man parked in a handicapped spot right next to the door. A bright blue handicapped parking hanger dangled from the rearview mirror of the van that the man drove. He got out, not appearing to be disabled, but of course it was possible that he had heart trouble or some breathing difficulty or some other medical condition that wasn't readily apparent. Certainly, none of the people going in and out of the post office challenged his right to park where he did.

Once inside the building, he didn't go to the busy counter, but remained in the lobby area instead, where several alcoves full of post office boxes were located, along with coin-operated stamp machines. He went to one of the machines and studied it for long moments as if he were trying to make up his mind exactly what he needed to buy. Finally reaching a decision, he fed coins into the machine, pushed the appropriate buttons, and took a book of stamps from the trough at the bottom where they had been dispensed. He slipped the stamps into his pocket and walked out of the post office.

A car pulled up at the curb. The man climbed into it and the driver drove away. The van with the handicapped hanger on the mirror was still parked beside the post office's front door.

A few miles from the post office, the morning rush was over at the Little Friends Day Care Center. A few moms who were on later schedules would be dropping off kids throughout the morning, but for the most part the children were already there. None of them were supposed to be picked up until nearly lunchtime. The center wasn't as full today as it usually was, since some of the parents had the entire Thanksgiving weekend off from work and had kept their kids at home today or taken them with them on short trips, but still, there were about sixty children inside the building, along with five workers.

None of them noticed the man who pulled his car up

at the end of the building at nine thirty-five and then got out and walked away quickly, leaving the vehicle there. There were no windows in that end of the building. If anyone had been inside the enclosed playground at the rear of the center, they might have noticed the man or the car, but the playground was empty at the moment. The kids would come out later, once the temperature had warmed up some.

At least, that was the plan.

At nine forty-one, yet another man pulled into the parking lot of a drugstore across the street from a Fort Worth Police Department substation in a busy retail and residential area not far from Loop 820. The car being driven by this man was the only one involved in the plan that would not be left behind and triggered by remote control. He knew the American police were dolts, but even they might become suspicious of a vehicle parked in front of their building and then quickly abandoned. The chance of that happening, slim though it might be, could not be taken.

And so the driver's life was now numbered in mere minutes. Four . . . no, three.

Three minutes from paradise. Three minutes from a reward so glorious that he could barely conceive of it. And he would die, too, with the knowledge that he was striking a blow for Allah as a soldier in the holiest of wars. The trunk and the backseat of the car were packed with enough explosives to level the entire building. All the infidels inside would die. All he had to do to accomplish this was to drive the car right at the entrance to the police station, crash through the glass doors and on into the lobby, and trigger the detonator that he held in his right hand. He pushed down the button with his thumb and set the switch, so that now all he had to do to cause the massive explosion was release the button. If he was injured in the crash, or if the police managed somehow to shoot him, it wouldn't matter.

Allah's will would still be done. *Allahu akbar!*

Less than two minutes now. With his left hand the driver wiped away the sweat that had sprung up on his brow. Even though he was willing to die . . . no, *anxious* to die . . . ending one's own life was a hard step. He knew that Allah would give him the strength he needed to carry out his mission, though. He hadn't turned off the car's engine. Now he put it back in gear and drove carefully to the exit from the drugstore parking lot. He looked both ways along the four-lane street that ran between the drugstore and the police station, waiting for the traffic to clear. This was a busy boulevard, and the driver grew impatient as he waited for a clear enough opening in the oncoming cars. He had to build up some speed before he hit the entrance doors, which were probably more reinforced than they looked.

Where were all these damned Americans going? he asked himself. It was nine forty-five on a Friday morning. The road shouldn't have been this busy. Even though the explosion wasn't timed to the second since he was going to detonate it manually, he was eager to get on with it. The dashboard clock in the car now read nine forty-five. The other three bombs would be going off now. He had to do his part. He couldn't fail, he just couldn't.

There were virgins waiting for him in paradise!

Sweat drenched his face. His lips pulled back from his teeth. His desperate eyes spotted a gap in the traffic. With a muttered prayer, he jammed his foot down on the accelerator.

He never saw the cement truck coming from the other direction. It had just pulled out from a side road and hadn't been there the last time the driver looked that way. The truck hadn't built up much speed, but it was moving fast enough. The terrorist heard brakes screaming and started to turn his head in that direction, but even as he did a terrible impact smashed into him and engulfed him in more pain than he would have dreamed was possible. In his last coherent moment he was aware of his thumb slipping off the detonator button; then there was a blinding flash and he knew that it heralded his arrival in paradise.

But if that was true, where were the virgins? Why did everything still hurt so bad? Why did his body blaze as if it were burning with a never-ending fire?

No one heard his scream. The explosion that disintegrated car and driver and flung the massive cement truck into the air as if it were a child's toy drowned out everything else.

CHAPTER 32

"When was Dad gonna call us?" Ronnie McCabe asked as she and her mother made their way along a crowded aisle in the craft section. Terry was looking for some needlework that she could use as a spare present if she needed one. You never knew when somebody extra, a visiting aunt or somebody like that, was going to show up at a Christmas party.

"He said he'd call and find out where to meet us when he gets through making that delivery," Terry said. She glanced at her watch. "It's nine forty-five already? He should have been here by now."

"Yeah, that's what I was thinking."

"Well," Terry said with a shrug, "he must've been delayed for some reason. You saw how terrible the traffic was earlier. It's probably worse now. He may be sitting out there on the highway in his truck, not even able to get into the parking lot yet."

"So we just wait for him to call?"

Terry smiled. "We haven't even gone through half the store yet. I think we still have enough shopping to keep us busy for a while."

That was certainly the truth. Once you were inside the cavernous store, it seemed endless, as if you could wander around in here for days and still not see everything there was to see.

"Hey, there's Allison," Ronnie said a few minutes later. "Oh, look, that lawyer guy is still hanging around her."

Terry looked where her daughter was pointing and saw Allison Sawyer making her way toward the shoe department, which was next to crafts. Ellis Burke was still with the younger woman, smiling and talking to her. Terry thought that Allison looked a little distracted and annoyed, but she was trying not to show it.

Earlier, when they first made it through the doors into the store, Allison had attempted to go her own way, thanking Burke with a finality in her tone that made it clear that despite the gratitude she felt toward the attorney for his help in recovering her purse, that was the end of whatever relationship they had.

Burke had been oblivious, though. Or rather, thought Terry, he had *chosen* to be oblivious. He was going to continue his single-minded flirting with Allison no matter what she said or did.

It was at that moment Terry had decided that she and Ronnie would stay with Allison, too, in hopes that Burke would get tired, give up, and leave them alone. Things hadn't worked out that way, however. The UltraMegaMart was so crowded that Terry and Ronnie had gotten separated from Allison and Burke in the press of people. It was all they could do to keep up with each other in that mob.

"Let's go see if we can give her a hand," Terry said now that they had run across Allison and Burke again.

Ronnie nodded in agreement. "Yeah. I guess Mr. Burke's a nice enough guy, but the way he's following her around and all but drooling is a little creepy."

They slid along the aisle, winding their way around customers' baskets, and intercepted Allison and Burke. "Hello again," Terry said to Allison with a bright smile.

"Hi," Allison said, looking relieved.

"Hello, ladies," Burke added, a smug grin on his face.

Terry nodded to him. "Mr. Burke. Did you find what you were looking for, for your daughter?"

"No, not yet," Burke replied. "I've been busy helping Allison here with her shopping." He hefted the armload of toys and clothes he was carrying.

"Yes, Mr. Burke's been very helpful," Allison said.

"Ellis. I told you, call me Ellis."

Allison forced a smile. "All right. I don't know what I would have done without your help today, Ellis."

He beamed, obviously pleased, and said, "Well, I'm just glad I was here to lend a hand when I was needed. First with stopping that purse-snatcher and now being your pack mule."

"Ronnie and I could help Allison carry her things," Terry offered. "That way you could get on with your own shopping, Mr. Burke." She reached for the merchandise he was holding.

"No, no, that's not necessary," he said as he turned to put the stuff out of Terry's reach. "It's no bother at all, I assure you. I'm in no hurry. I have all day."

"But what if that toy sells out that your daughter wanted?" Terry asked.

For a second, a worried frown crossed Burke's face. Clearly, he hadn't considered that possibility. But then he shook it off, saying, "If that happens, I'll just get it somewhere else. I might have to pay more for it, but that's all right. I can afford it. I'm a lawyer, you know."

"Yes, of course," Allison said, and Terry thought she was trying hard not to grit her teeth.

"You know, there's a restaurant in the back of the store," Terry said. "Why don't we go sit down and get a cup of coffee or something? I wouldn't mind getting off my feet and out of this mob for a while."

"Sitting down sounds good," Allison agreed, "but I don't think we'll get away from the mob. I'll bet the restaurant is just as crowded as the rest of the store."

Terry laughed. "You're probably right. Let's go find out."

The four of them started toward the rear of the store, and as they did, Terry's cell phone rang in her jacket pocket. Ronnie said, "That's probably Dad."

"If it is, I'll tell him to meet us at the restaurant," Terry said as she reached for the phone. "That'll be a good place to rendezvous."

Before she could open the phone and answer the call, though, someone began to shout nearby. Terry turned her head, recognizing the sounds of shock and fear, and knew instinctively that something was very, very wrong.

CHAPTER 33

The traffic surprised McCabe by continuing to move fairly well. Not fast, but at least the mass of cars and trucks wasn't at a dead stop anymore.

Telling himself to be patient, he turned the radio off when he got tired of sports talk and drove in silence, thinking about the leftover-turkey-and-dressing sandwiches that Terry would make for supper tonight. Sometimes, McCabe thought that the leftovers from Thanksgiving dinner were better than the dinner itself.

It was nine fifty when he pulled around the rear corner of the UltraMegaMart and drove along the back of the store toward the loading docks and the service entrance. He'd planned to pull right up to the entrance, but two trucks were already backed up to the docks, where they were being unloaded.

McCabe found a place to park and climbed down from the cab. With his hands in the pockets of his jacket, he walked over to the stairs that led up to the docks and the service entrance. "Got another one for you," he called to the guy who seemed to be bossing the unloading operation.

The man rolled his eyes. "Lord, is it ever gonna stop?" He consulted the little handheld computer he carried and checked some numbers he saw there with the numbers on McCabe's truck. "Okay, I got you here. We'll get to you as fast as we can, but it's gonna be an hour at least before we get that truck unloaded."

"Doesn't matter to me how long it takes," McCabe said with a shrug. "I'm done for the day. My boss is sending somebody else to pick up the truck later."

The loading dock supervisor grunted. "Lucky man. I'm not sure I'll even get time off to fart today, let alone go home and see my family. Hang on, lemme print out some paperwork for you."

McCabe followed the man through the service entrance into the huge stockroom at the rear of the store. The man printed up a delivery ticket from another computer, signed it, and handed it to McCabe.

"There you go, pal. It's our worry now, not yours."

McCabe nodded and tucked the paperwork inside his jacket. As of now, he didn't have any worries. "Good luck," he said as he lifted a hand in farewell and walked toward one of the sets of swinging doors that led into the store itself.

Just before he got there, the doors swung inward and a man walked quickly into the stockroom. He wasn't wearing a MegaMart vest, which struck McCabe as strange since only employees were allowed back here, but maybe he was a customer who had gotten turned around and was looking for a restroom. Things like that happened all the time. McCabe brushed past him and shouldered through the doors without giving the man another thought. He took the cell phone from the clip on his belt, opened it, and thumbed the speed-dial button that would connect him with Terry's phone.

Just as he heard the ringing on the other end, people started to yell nearby. He wasn't far from the electronics area, and as people started to run in that direction, McCabe swung his gaze after them and saw that the two dozen or so television sets lined up in display rows on shelves were all tuned to the same thing.

The screens, including several large high-definition plasma units, all showed flames and a cloud of smoke, shot from a high angle that told McCabe the video feed came from a news chopper. His jaw tightened. Something bad had happened. Really bad.

Terry hadn't answered her phone. McCabe closed his. Still holding it, he reached out with his other hand and grasped the arm of a man who was hurrying past him, away from the display of TV sets.

"What's going on?" McCabe asked.

The man had a frantic look on his face. "Explosions all over the north side of Fort Worth," he said. "Some sort of terrorist attack. They said on TV that a bank had been blown up. My wife works in a bank! I've gotta call her!"

McCabe let the man go. Poor bastard was scared out of his wits, and McCabe couldn't blame him. Obviously, this news story had just broken, and there wouldn't be many details available yet. Chances were the guy's wife was all right—there were dozens of banks in the area, maybe more than a hundred—but right now he couldn't be sure of that.

Screams and sobs came from the people gathering in front of the TV sets. McCabe forced his way through the crowd, getting close enough so that he could see the crawl going along the bottom of the screen on one of the big plasma units, under the footage of a burning building with a debris field around it that looked like something from a war zone. McCabe stiffened and sickness punched into his gut as he read that there were reports of a post office and a day-care center being bombed, too, as well as the bank. There had also been a fourth explosion near a police station.

McCabe's jaw was tight with anger and horror. He had spent long years of his life fighting the bastards who did this sort of thing, but ever since 9/11 they had kept their cowardly acts on their own turf. Now they had brought their madness back to American soil.

Of course, there was always a chance that the terror was domestic, not foreign. McCabe hadn't forgotten Oklahoma City. But every instinct in his body, all of them honed by his experiences in the shadow wars, told him that these atrocities were the work of Islamic terrorists. The multiple strikes, timed to go off together, the choice of soft civilian targets . . . those were the hallmarks of an attack planned by Al Qaeda or one of the other Islamic groups. McCabe had been out of the loop long enough so that he wasn't sure which bunch of psychotic bastards represented the biggest threat to the United States these days.

And it didn't really matter who had done it. What was important was that they had hit us again, McCabe thought, feeling like he wanted to puke. What would we do about it this time? That was the question. Would the liberal politicians and the mainstream media get out of the way and stay out of the way while the people who were trained and equipped to deal with threats like this did their job?

McCabe doubted it. Based on the evidence of the past decade or so, the country had lost its will to stomp the snakes that needed stomping—and knowing that made McCabe almost as sick as the thought of all the innocent lives that had been snuffed out this morning in a burst of insane hatred.

The phone he still clutched in his hand vibrated. He lifted it, looked at the display. Terry. Thank God. Right now, in this time of tragedy, he wanted more than ever to be with his wife and daughter.

McCabe opened the phone, put it to his ear, and said, "Hey, babe, where are you?"

But instead of his wife's voice, McCabe heard a horrible, familiar sound, one that he knew all too well.

The deadly chatter of automatic-weapons fire, followed by terrified screams.

CHAPTER 34

Burke didn't know what was going on. One minute he had been trying to think of a way to get Terry McCabe and her daughter to buzz off and leave him alone with Allison—well, as alone as you could get when the two of you were surrounded by hundreds of yokels and yahoos anyway—and the next people were carrying on like something terrible had happened.

Burke supposed that was true, that something terrible *had* happened. He heard somebody talking about an explosion, and had a bad moment when he thought that something had blown up here in the store. Maybe the place was on fire, and he would either burn to death or get trampled in the redneck stampede.

Then he realized that they were talking about something they had seen on the television sets in the electronics department, which was a good third of the way across the store from where he, Allison, and the McCabe women were. Bad news traveled fast.

Allison turned and clutched at his arm. Burke had been hoping all morning that sooner or later she would touch him, but grabbing him in panic wasn't exactly what he'd had in mind. Anything was better than nothing, though, he told himself.

"My God, did you hear that?" she asked frantically. "Did somebody say something about a day-care center being blown up?"

Burke felt a stab of genuine worry. "Your little boy," he said. "Is he—"

Allison was shaking her head before he could finish asking the question. "No, thank God," she said. "My neighbor babysits him. He doesn't go to day care."

"Then he's all right," Burke said.

"Yes, but all those other children—! It's horrible, just horrible."

Burke agreed, of course, but whatever tragedy had happened, there was nothing he could do about it. And his daughter didn't go to day care either, so he didn't see how it could affect him personally. Still, he started to put his arms around Allison to comfort her. He would have, too, if Terry McCabe hadn't swooped in like a hawk and embraced her first, turning her away from Burke.

"It'll be all right," Terry said, patting Allison on the back.

But it wouldn't be for a lot of families, Burke thought. He heard people saying that explosions had occurred in other places, too, like a bank and a post office. A lot of people must have been killed in those blasts. Banks and post offices were busy places, and of course, so were day-care centers. The death toll might reach into the hundreds. It was a sobering thought.

And a chilling thought went right along with it. Multiple explosions didn't happen at the same time by accident, especially directed at specific targets like that. This was terrorism, pure and simple, Burke realized.

He wasn't the only one to come to that conclusion.

Nearby, a man shouted, "By God, we need to go over there and nuke ever'one o' them Ay-rab countries back to the Stone Age!"

"Hell, I'll sign up to go right now!" another man said. "I'd rather kill those damn camel-jockeys up close and personal, though!"

A wave of revulsion went through Burke at the sound of those racist, hate-filled rants. He heard himself saying, "Hold on, hold on, we don't know who did this. We don't know yet who's responsible."

"Y'all know it had to be the Muslims," a woman snapped at him. "Just like on 9/11."

"What about Timothy McVeigh?" Burke said. "After Oklahoma City I heard people saying the same sort of things about Muslims, and it turned out they didn't have a thing to do with that."

"This is different," a third man insisted. "Al Qaeda did this, sure as hell."

"Or one of those other terrorist groups," yet another man chimed in.

They were all ignorant bumpkins, jumping to the easiest, most hateful conclusion, Burke told himself. Typical red-state behavior. As far as he was concerned, reactions like that were more dangerous to the country than all the Islamic terrorists combined. He hated to think about what was going to happen over the next few days. Mosques would be vandalized. Peaceful, innocent Muslim Americans would be harassed—or worse. The way most Americans acted at times like this, Burke could understand why the rest of the world hated us. *We deserve it,* he thought. *We deserve whatever they do to us.*

He was so incensed and morally outraged over the unfairness of it all that for the moment he had forgotten about Allison Sawyer and the hopes he'd had of talking her into having lunch with him. Then he remembered her and looked around, fearing that she might have slipped away in the crowd.

He saw to his relief that she was still there. She had settled down a little and didn't look quite so panic-stricken and upset now. She was talking to Ronnie McCabe, who looked around as Terry lifted her cell phone and said, "I'm going to try to call your father back. Maybe he's somewhere here in the store."

Burke was trying to figure out a way to ease Allison away from the McCabes when he looked over Terry's shoulder and saw something that, for a second, his brain refused to comprehend or even admit that he was really seeing. Then, with a shake of his head, he realized it was real. A tall, dark-complected man with black hair and a neatly trimmed beard had opened his long, bulky jacket and was reaching for a couple of guns strapped to his body. Burke recognized the weapons vaguely from action movies he had seen as some sort of machine pistols. They had to be toys of some sort, he thought. Yeah, that was it. Toys the guy was trying to shoplift for his kids. Poor bastard was probably out of a job because the heartless corporation he'd worked for had downsized and outsourced all its personnel. Corporate executives were the real terrorists—

Then Burke screamed as the guy pointed the guns at the ceiling and squeezed off two quick bursts as he shouted, "Everyone down! On the floor now, or I'll kill you! Everyone down!"

BOOK TWO

"We interrupt regular programming to bring you this special news bulletin. In a story datelined today, November 4th, at 4:22 PM Eastern Standard Time, from Dallas, Texas, the Associated Press reports that a series of explosions has rocked the suburbs north of Fort Worth. We're told that these were powerful blasts and that several buildings have been destroyed, including a bank, a post office, and a day-care center. It's expected that the death toll from these explosions will be considerable.

"At this point we have no information on what caused these blasts, whether they were tragic accidents or deliberate acts of violence. No group has stepped forward to claim responsibility for them. The government is said to be monitoring the Web sites of suspicious organizations, both foreign and domestic, but so far there has been no mention of these explosions. However, best estimates say that the blasts occurred approximately fifteen minutes ago, so more information may be forthcoming at any time.

"The President has not issued any statements, and neither has the Governor of Texas.

"What's that? . . . We have a correspondent from our network affiliate in Dallas on the line for an update on this situation . . . Hello? Can you hear me? Can you tell us what's happened down there?"

"It . . . it's all gone . . . it's like the day-care center was never there, it's just a crater in the ground . . . Oh, God . . . Oh, God . . . all those children—!"

"We'll get back to that report in a moment. Right now we have some raw video footage from the Fort Worth area . . . I would warn our viewers that the images in this footage may be graphic. You may see things you don't want to see. . . ."

CHAPTER 35

The President wanted to put her hands over her face and shut out the sight of what she was seeing on the television in the Oval Office. If she couldn't see it, maybe it wasn't really there.

This couldn't be happening on her watch. It just couldn't.

But of course it was, and no amount of denial would make it go away. Covering her eyes wouldn't do a damned bit of good.

"We shouldn't have let the Israelis do it," she whispered. "And once they did, we shouldn't have sided with them."

The National Security Advisor had already arrived. She had been in the White House when word of the explosions in Texas had started to spread. She was there because of the terror alert based on the intel from Pakistan. Fresh intel had just arrived, pinpointing the location of the attacks.

But it had come too late to save any of the people in the bank, the post office, and the day-care center that had been leveled.

"This is all my fault," the President moaned. She and the NSA were the only ones in the Oval Office at the moment.

"Nonsense," the NSA said in her usual cool, brisk voice. "The Iranians didn't do this."

The President looked around at her. "Do we know who did?"

"Hizb ut-Tahrir."

"Who's that?" the President asked with a puzzled frown.

The NSA couldn't keep from sighing in disgust. The President had a reputation for being extremely intelligent, the sort of policy wonk who knew everything about everything. But that only held true for subjects she was interested in, like social policies. Foreign policy and defense meant little to her other than as areas she could manipulate if she had to in order to line up more support for her reelection campaign, which had begun about ten seconds after she took her hand off the Chief Justice's Bible and finished swearing to the oath of office during her inauguration to her first term.

"Hizb ut-Tahrir is a pan-Islamic terror group similar to Al Qaeda," the NSA explained. "They've always kept a lower profile until recently. Now, though, they're poised to take the lead in the terror campaign against the West. Their goal is to eventually unite all the Muslim nations and do away with the individual governments, leading to the rise of what they refer to as the Caliphate, a Muslim super state that will dominate the entire world."

"But . . . but that's insane," the President said.

The NSA shrugged. "Everybody's gotta start somewhere."

The President looked at the TV again. "You're *sure* these people are behind what's happening in Texas?"

"Positive. The CIA just received an encrypted transmission from one of its agents in Islamabad. Another operative discovered the plans that were drawn up for this strike during a raid on a Hizb ut-Tahrir training facility on the border between Pakistan and Afghanistan."

The President glanced sharply at her. "We're still conducting covert missions in that area? I thought I made it clear that America was no longer going to wage war in the shadows." She slapped a hand down on her desk. "Everything has to be clean and open and above-board."

Now *that* was a recipe for certain disaster, the NSA thought, and she was glad that certain people in government—including the Vice President and the President's husband—realized it. Without some careful skirting of certain executive orders, the country might be conducting its official business in Arabic by now.

The NSA knew that. The President didn't.

But the President probably slept better at night. At least . . . until now. Until all hell had broken loose in Texas.

The NSA ignored the other woman's sanctimonious glare and got back to the subject at hand by saying, "I repeat, the Iranians didn't do this. Hizb ut-Tahrir may be planning on using the heightened tensions in the Middle East as the excuse for this new terror offensive, but they would have done it sooner or later anyway. They've been biding their time, but they believe that now is the moment to begin the rise of the Caliphate."

"What can we do to stop them?"

That was a question that should have been asked—and answered—long before now. But the NSA just smiled thinly and said, "We can try to get ahead of them, so that something like this doesn't happen again."

The President gestured toward the TV screen. "But . . . but what about Texas?"

The NSA shook her head. "It's too late for us to stop whatever is happening there. Whatever is going on . . . the only ones who can do anything about it are the ones on the scene."

The sound was muted on the TV set, but the President suddenly grabbed the remote and raised the volume as a news anchor said excitedly, "We're now receiving reports of shots being fired in the UltraMegaMart just north of Fort Worth, in the same general area as the explosions that occurred a short time ago. This UltraMega-Mart, billed as the largest discount store in the world, is having its grand opening today, and reportedly thousands of shoppers were on hand for it. It's unknown at this time what exactly is happening inside the store—"

The President turned the sound off again. This time she gave in to the urge and covered her face with her hands.

And groaned in despair.

CHAPTER 36

Walt Graham was on the phone with the Director of the FBI when Eileen Bastrop hurried into his office and put a note on his desk. "Yes, sir," Graham said into the phone. "I'll give you a direct report on the situation just as soon as I can. I'm on my way out of the office right now. I'll be on the scene shortly."

Graham looked at the note. It read, *The press is here.* The burly SAC made a face. He hung up the phone and said to Bastrop, "Back door?"

"They're probably there, too," she said. "Damn buzzards."

"Shouldn't talk that way about the intrepid guardians of our freedom."

"I thought the people who guarded our freedom were the ones on the front lines."

"Shows how little you know." Graham grinned, but there was no real humor on his face. His eyes were hard and bleak.

He had gotten the encrypted transmission from Langley, too, since he was the SAC of the FBI office closest to the terrorists' target. The Company's covert-ops guy in

Pakistan had identified the UltraMegaMart as the place where the scumbags intended to strike, but even as Graham had been about to send a desperate warning to local law enforcement, bulletins had started to come in about the devastating car bombings in the suburbs just north of Fort Worth. The CIA agent in Pakistan hadn't mentioned anything about *them*. Either there had been some miscommunication somewhere, or the source of the intel just hadn't known about the other bombings. Or the business about the UltraMegaMart being the target was just false intel, a deliberate decoy. Graham had run all those scenarios through his head.

Then, hard on the heels of the reports about the bombings came the news that shots had been fired inside the big discount store, and Graham knew the truth. The bombings were nothing but a prelude to the main attack, just something to get the attention of the government and the news media and let them know that the terrorists were serious about their demands.

And there *would* be demands, Graham thought. There always were in hostage situations. Even without being on the scene yet, he knew that was what was developing at the UltraMegaMart north of Fort Worth.

He motioned for Bastrop to follow him, and left the office through a rear door that led to a corridor through a service area, ending up outside where extra cars that belonged to the Bureau were parked. As Graham and Bastrop emerged into the sunny but chilly day, Graham was relieved to see that the reporters and camera crews hadn't made their way back here yet. The sound of a helicopter made him glance up, though, and he saw a news chopper circling overhead. Within seconds the pilot would be radioing down to his associates on the ground that somebody was slipping out of the FBI office by the back door.

Sure enough, a camera crew charged around the corner of the federal building a moment later, but by that time Graham and Bastrop were in one of the spare cars. Graham was behind the wheel. He drove out fast, leaving the newshounds behind. He didn't know if they had gotten close enough to recognize him and Bastrop. If they had, they would probably follow.

Didn't really matter, he told himself. He and the assistant SAC were on their way to the scene, and there would already be dozens of media people there. The grand opening of the UltraMegaMart was a big story all by itself.

If bloodthirsty terrorists had already taken the place over, then it would soon be the biggest story of the century so far.

CHAPTER 37

Hamed's heart pounded wildly in his chest. He had never felt such exultation as that which coursed through him at the sight of all those terrified infidel faces as he fired his machine pistols into the ceiling. Fluorescent light fixtures burst under the assault of lead like fireworks, showering the crowd with fine bits of plastic.

As Hamed lowered the weapons, more people screamed and went diving for the floor. Nearly everyone in the crowd around him obeyed his shouted orders. One woman, a lean blonde about forty years old, glared at him and stayed on her feet longer than the others, but then a younger woman with her reached up, grabbed her arm, and dragged her down to the floor, saying urgently, "Do what he says, Mom, do what he says!"

Near that pair, a man in a business suit stared for a second as if he couldn't comprehend what he was seeing, but as Hamed started to swing the barrel of his right-hand gun toward the man, the infidel's beefy face paled and he dived to the floor next to a fair-haired young woman. The man put his arms over his head—as if that would protect him from a storm of bullets if Hamed chose to unleash one! The only thing the infidels possessed in greater quantity than arrogance was stupidity.

"No one move!" Hamed shouted. "Everyone stay down! Eyes on the floor!" He heard similar orders being shouted in other parts of the store.

It would have been better if their numbers were larger, of course; they were a mere twenty believers against a horde of infidels, twenty-two if you counted Sheikh al-Mukhari and Shalla Sahi, who had made good on her insistence that she participate in their holy mission.

But those twenty-two were warriors in a holy cause, and they were opposed by American sheep who were too cowardly to fight back. If the events of the past decade had demonstrated anything, it was that American resolve was weak and would crumble at the first sign of danger or difficulty. That was why the minions of the Great Satan were destined to lose every conflict.

Not only were the Americans godless, they were cowards. They had proven it again and again.

A few among them were aberrations, however . . . like the man who suddenly rushed toward Hamed from behind. The fool moved like a water buffalo, and courage was not enough to protect him. Hamed heard him coming in plenty of time to swing halfway around, heft his left-hand gun, and send a burst of lead ripping into the man's body.

The American shrieked in agony as the steel-jacketed slugs punched into him and stopped his charge. He went over backward instead, blood spraying from a dozen wounds as he fell. His bullet-riddled body landed on several people who were trying frantically to get out of the way. They started screaming louder and even more hysterically as the infidel's corpse crashed down on top of them.

"You see what will happen if anyone tries to oppose us!" Hamed cried. The Americans were disoriented; now it was time to demoralize them even more than they already were. "Anyone who disobeys will die! *Allahu akbar!*"

Now Hamed heard something even more satisfying than screams of fear—weeping. Despair was spreading among the captives. That meant most of the battle was won, at least in this section of the store. The Americans were giving up in hopes that their pathetic lives would be spared.

They had no idea that they were all doomed. Hamed, Mukhari, Shalla . . . they all knew they would never leave the UltraMegaMart alive. In the end, it would not even matter whether the American President agreed to Hizb ut-Tahrir's demands.

No, the real victory would come in a moment of searing nuclear bliss that would take the lives of hundreds of Americans and leave a gaping, radioactive crater in the North Texas prairie as an eternal monument to the ultimate fate of all infidels.

That would be the final legacy of this day, the death and destruction that would haunt the Americans for all time.

And there was nothing they could do to prevent it, Hamed told himself triumphantly. Nothing . . .

CHAPTER 38

McCabe pressed his back against the wall of the cavernous, high-ceilinged stockroom that ran along the rear of the UltraMegaMart from one end of the store to the other. His knees were bent, so that he hunkered low behind a stack of big-screen televisions in their thick cardboard cartons.

The terrorist machine-gunner had missed him in the initial sweep through the stockroom, as the guy herded all the employees who were back here into the far end, so he could keep them contained. The terrorist had no idea McCabe was here.

McCabe intended to keep it that way—for now at least.

He had to take stock of the situation. Gather some intel. Figure out just how bad things were.

Decide what to do about them.

His mind began replaying everything that had happened in the past few minutes, the interminably long time since he'd first heard the gunfire through the cell phone. His first reaction had been that of a husband, fear for his wife's safety. He didn't know where Terry was, only that she was somewhere in the store. He wanted to hurry to her side and make sure she was all right.

But he couldn't do that because he had no idea of her location, and after a second the connection had been broken, as if she'd snapped the phone shut.

McCabe hadn't needed the phone to hear the shots then. They were sounding all over the store, along with shouted commands and cries of fear. His training and years of experience had kicked in as he listened to that unholy racket. He knew what he was hearing. Gunmen were taking over the store, taking everyone in here hostage.

The automatic-weapons fire came in short bursts designed to terrify and force compliance, not the continuous, unholy roar of a massacre in progress. McCabe was moving even as that realization came into his mind. Here in the electronics section, nobody was shooting yet, so he still had time to act. Probably just a matter of seconds, though.

As everybody else who had been watching the horrible news on TV began shouting frightened questions and milling around, McCabe moved toward the wall and slid along the display of television sets until he reached a small door.

Even though he had never been inside this store until today, he had been around enough MegaMarts to know that the door would lead to a short corridor running back to the stockroom. Large merchandise such as the TVs themselves had to be brought out through one of the sets of swinging double doors between the main room and the stockroom, but smaller items could be retrieved by this access hallway.

Nobody saw him duck through the door, and it had barely swung closed behind him when he heard shots on the other side of it, not far away. Whoever had been assigned to take over this part of the store had been just a little slow getting into action. Maybe the guns the bastard had hidden under his coat had snagged or something. The reason didn't matter.

What was important was that McCabe wasn't a prisoner—yet. He had to stay free as long as he could.

Otherwise, he couldn't do anything to save his wife and daughter and all the other innocent people in the store.

The civilian, the truck driver, was gone now, vanished in those bursts of gunfire. Jackknife was back.

People thought that was just his nickname, because his name was Jack and he drove a truck. Jackknife was also his handle. Only a handful of people—Terry and the surviving members of his unit, the men he had worked with for so long—knew that it was also his call sign, the only name he had used when he and the team were operating behind enemy lines, in dangerous situations.

The first step in beating the enemy was to think like the enemy. If he was a terrorist, how would he go about taking over a store as big as the UltraMegaMart? How many people would he need, and how would they be armed?

He knew he had heard automatic-weapons fire, so that gave him a partial answer. If they were homegrown terrorists, which was possible even though the fringe militia and white-supremacist movements had died down in recent years, chances were all they had were the guns.

But if they were Islamic, they probably had bombs, too, maybe even strapped to their bodies. Islamic terrorists loved it when stuff blew up real good, McCabe recalled. He wasn't sure what that said about them psychologically.

He didn't give a crap either, except as for how their psychology related to their mission—and his. Islamic terrorists would be much more likely to go to any lengths to achieve their goals, even to the point of blowing themselves up. That fanaticism made them more dangerous, but sometimes it could also be turned against them.

McCabe put the question of their identity aside for a moment as he tried to figure the odds. Even a well-trained group, operating with military precision, would require quite a few members to take over a target as big as this store. Say, two dozen, give or take, McCabe decided. More would be better, but they might have to make do with what they had.

Sleeper agents, he thought. Possibly smuggled into the United States illegally, although it was certainly possible that some of them had legal work or student visas. Despite its best efforts, a free country couldn't keep all of its enemies out—although that effort had been anything but the best these past few years.

So he was looking at odds of twenty to one, at a bare minimum, McCabe decided. Not good, but if he could whittle them down a little . . .

If he could, they might get to the point where they were simply ridiculous, rather than utterly overwhelming.

But what choice did he have except to try? Terry and Ronnie were in here somewhere, probably scared out of their wits. Not to mention hundreds of other innocent folks who had gotten up from their beds today with nothing more on their minds than doing some shopping at the grand opening of the new UltraMegaMart.

All those thoughts had gone through his head in the mere seconds that it took him to reach the door at the other end of the corridor. Instead of grasping the knob, he pressed his ear against the steel panel and listened intently.

He had hoped that the terrorists hadn't gotten back here yet, so he'd maybe have a chance to organize some resistance among the guys working in the stockroom.

But he heard shouting in faintly accented voices, followed by the rattling rumble of the big doors on the back of the store going down, and he knew he was too late for that. Shots rang out, a machine pistol firing with the sound of heavy cloth ripping. The shouting moved off to McCabe's left.

At least one of the terrorists had gotten into the stockroom somehow and now was rounding up the workers. McCabe remembered the guy he had passed as he was leaving the stockroom a few minutes earlier. At the time, McCabe hadn't paid much attention to him, but now his memory was able to bring up the man's image in his mind.

Stocky, a little below medium height, with a broad, swarthy face, dark curly hair, and a mustache. Hispanic? Middle Eastern?

Definitely Middle Eastern, McCabe decided. Not as common in this part of the country as someone of Hispanic origin, but certainly not uncommon. Some of them belonged to families that had been in this country for generations, while others were more recent immigrants. But many were naturalized citizens and were honest, hardworking, law-abiding Americans.

But not that particular guy, McCabe was willing to wager. He had even been wearing a thick, fairly long jacket, just the sort of garment that weapons could be hidden underneath.

What were you gonna do? Set up metal detectors at every entrance? Pat down all the shoppers as they came in? Yeah, that would be really good for business.

Running risks was part of being free. McCabe knew

that. At this moment, though, he wished something could have been done to stop those sons of bitches before they ever got in here. He was sure the guy he had seen had hung around back in the stockroom for a few minutes, stalling for time by asking dumb questions of the supervisor or something, until the terrorists inside the main store made their move.

Since the shouts were all coming from the far end of the stockroom now, McCabe eased the door open an inch or so and peered out. Nobody was moving in his line of sight. He saw heavy metal shelves with stacks of boxed DVD players, boom boxes, and other electronics gear. He opened the door a little wider and saw stacks of boxed-up big-screen TVs. There was a small gap between the crates and the wall. McCabe slipped into it, intending to move along the space until he might be able to get a look at the terrorist and the hostages.

Then he heard a footstep nearby and slid down into the deeper shadow that obscured part of this narrow gap. One of the boxes hadn't been shoved over completely against the one next to it, so he was able to peer through that tiny opening.

He saw a man walk past, a machine pistol in each hand. McCabe didn't get a good look at his face, just enough to see the short, dark beard and the piercing black eyes.

"We have them all," the guy called toward the other end of the stockroom. "I did not see anyone else."

It took McCabe a second to realize that the man had spoken in Arabic. His mind had translated the words automatically.

Well, that settled the question of the terrorists' identity. He was dealing with Islamic fanatics, the sort of men who would go to any lengths to get what they wanted, because they had been sold a bill of goods by the crazed sheikhs and mullahs and ayatollahs who led them. They believed they were doing the will of their god and were willing, even eager, to die as martyrs for their cause.

In a true war, such single-minded devotion to duty was admirable, even on the part of the enemy. But these so-called "freedom fighters" didn't make war on other soldiers. They made war on women and children and the elderly. They targeted the most helpless in society.

McCabe recalled the news bulletin he had seen a few minutes earlier—God, only a few minutes? It seemed longer—about the bombing of the day-care center. That was a perfect example of the evil perpetuated by these monsters. That was why they had to be stopped—

McCabe's instinct warned him and he turned, twisting in the narrow space, trying to get some room somehow to fight, but he was too late. Too rusty from the years of soft living.

Even in the dim light, he saw that he was staring into the barrel of a gun.

CHAPTER 39

Terry felt her daughter trembling as she lay on the floor next to her with an arm around Ronnie. The maternal instinct to protect her child was irresistible even though Terry knew that her arm wouldn't shield Ronnie if that madman decided to shoot them.

Her mind was half-stunned by the shocking, sudden developments inside the UltraMegaMart. Like most Americans in these perilous times, Terry McCabe had thought about what it might be like if she was caught in the middle of a terrorist attack.

But even so, also like most Americans, she hadn't really expected that it would ever happen. She was lulled by the knowledge that she was in her own homeland and that it had been attacked only on rare occasions in the past.

So she had been taken by surprise and was still struggling to cope with what had happened, to accept the terrible, dangerous situation in which she and Ronnie found themselves, along with hundreds, maybe even thousands, of other innocent shoppers.

The part of her brain that *wasn't* stunned was filled

with anger. As she listened to the whimpering of the people who lay there with the bloody corpse sprawled on top of them, she thought, *How dare that man come in here and start waving guns around and shooting? What gives him the right?*

His own twisted, fanatic beliefs gave him that right in his diseased mind, Terry realized. What the terrorists were doing made perfect sense to them.

That was why you couldn't negotiate with people like them. They lived in a universe that was stuck in a primitive, millennia-old barbarism. They had no common frame of reference with normal, rational people. They might as well have lived in a world where the sky was a different color, like green or purple.

So if you couldn't talk to them, couldn't reason with them, couldn't even communicate with them, really, what did that leave?

Terry knew the answer to that, and if she'd had a gun right now, she would have given it loud and clear. She had learned how to shoot when she was a girl, and long sessions with Jack at the firing range had just improved her skill. Put a gun in her hand and she could plant a bullet right between that bastard's eyes, no problem.

That is, if she could bring herself to pull the trigger, knowing that to do so would end another human being's life. She thankfully had never been put in the position to have to make that decision.

So as she lay there on the cool tiles of the floor, she took a second to consider the question. *Could* she kill in order to save her daughter, herself, or any of those other innocent folks?

Damn right she could.

There was not an ounce of doubt in Terry McCabe's mind.

But she didn't have a gun, and she couldn't fight the guy bare-handed, not while he had those two machine pistols. She'd worked out enough on self-defense moves with Jack—he had taught her a lot of what he had learned from his Special Forces training—so that she figured she would stand a good chance against the terrorist in a hand-to-hand fight. But only if he was unarmed.

So, how was she going to get those pistols out of his hands?

"Mom," Ronnie whispered, "what are we gonna do?"

Terry heard the ragged strain in her daughter's voice and tried to keep her own voice calm and level as she replied, "Right now we'll just do what that man says and wait to see what happens."

"Do you think Dad's all right?"

Terry was about to answer when the terrorist swung one of the guns toward them. "No talking!" he shouted.

Terry swallowed and tightened her arm around Ronnie. She gave the man a curt nod to show that she understood the command and would follow it.

Ronnie's question had started more wheels clicking over in Terry's brain, though. Since she hadn't gotten to talk to Jack during their brief phone connection, she didn't know if he was inside the store somewhere or still outside.

If he was outside, he was probably aware by now of what was happening, and he would be going crazy knowing that she and Ronnie were in here and in danger. He would want to get in, but surely the authorities would prevent him from doing so.

But if he was inside, if he had been taken hostage, too, then it was only a matter of time before he did something to try to turn the tables on his captors. She knew her husband. She knew him better than anyone else on the face of the earth.

There was no way that Jackknife McCabe would allow himself to be held prisoner by a bunch of terrorists for very long. He would fight back.

And then he would probably get killed.

Terry closed her eyes for a second and told herself not to think like that. As she did, yet another possibility occurred to her.

What if Jack was inside the store—but *hadn't* been taken prisoner?

If he was loose and had somehow managed to escape the terrorists' notice, then he would be a wild card in their plans. A *big* wild card, because he had spent years of his life battling their kind. He knew how to beat them. He knew how to kill them. Because he had done it, time and again—

"Everyone together!" the man with the machine pistols ordered. He waved the automatic weapons to emphasize the command. "Crawl over to each other. Huddle together as closely as you can."

He didn't want them spread out, Terry realized. He wanted them grouped so that it would be easier for him to watch them. It must have occurred to him that if they charged him from several directions at once, he wouldn't be able to stop all of them. Many of the hostages would die, but in the end he would be overwhelmed.

Nobody wanted to be one of the ones who died, though, so the prisoners slowly began to cooperate, crawling together in one of the main aisles. The terrorist stalked along, checking the aisles in shoes and crafts, herding the hostages together like sheep.

Terry, Ronnie, Allison Sawyer, and Ellis Burke were already in the main aisle, so they didn't have to move.

As they lay there, Terry muttered, "We shouldn't be doing this. We shouldn't be cooperating."

"Then what should we do?" Burke asked, keeping his voice barely above a whisper. "He'll kill us if we don't go along with what he says. You know that."

"If we all rushed him at once—"

"He'd kill half of us," Burke snapped. "Do you want your daughter to die, Mrs. McCabe?"

Terry just glared at him and didn't say anything.

"Anyway," Burke went on, "you heard the shooting in the other parts of the store. This guy isn't alone. Even if we got him, the others would get us. He's probably got a bomb strapped to him, too, so if we jump him he'll just set it off and blow us all to kingdom come!"

"A . . . a bomb?" Allison said.

Burke had his arm around her. He tightened it and said, "Don't worry. We'll get out of this all right. We'll just play along with that maniac and his friends, and eventually they'll let us go."

"How do you know that?" Terry asked.

Even in this situation, the lawyer managed to smirk. "Because I know how negotiations work. They'll ask for something. They're bound to want *something,* or they wouldn't be doing this. When they get it, they'll let us go."

"How do you know the authorities will give them what they want?"

"Please. Nobody's going to risk the lives of the hostages. This isn't Israel, you know."

No, thought Terry, it certainly wasn't. Since the blame-America-first crowd had taken over the government, with the willing assistance of the mainstream media, it was entirely possible that the administration would try to appease the terrorists and give them whatever they wanted. But Terry didn't believe for a second that giving in would save the lives of the hostages. Above all else, terrorists wanted to make a point. They valued symbolism over substance. You would have thought that the liberals would understand that, since they felt the exact same way themselves, but that wasn't the case. They prided themselves on being so rational—even though they really weren't—and thought that everyone else should be like that, too. That was why they believed that talking could solve any problem.

Talking solved nothing when you were dealing with lunatics. Terry understood that. That was why she knew that Burke was wrong.

The authorities, from the local level all the way up to the White House, could give the terrorists everything they wanted—and the sick bastards would still be capable of killing everyone in the UltraMegaMart, including themselves. There was only one way to ensure that the innocent people in here lived to see another day.

And that was to kill the sick bastards first.

She knew her husband would be thinking the exact same thing.

"Jack," she whispered, so low that no one else could hear it, even Ronnie, "be careful."

CHAPTER 40

"Who the hell are you, mister? Are you one o' them?"

Relief went through McCabe as he realized that the only accent in the voice behind the gun pointing at him was pure Texan. There was something familiar about it, too.

"No, sir," he said.

The stranger who crouched in the shadows alongside him grunted as he lowered his gun. "Can't see all that well back here, but I didn't think you was one o' them camel-humpers. I can tell by your voice that you ain't. What's your name?"

"Jack McCabe. I'm a truck driver for MegaMart." McCabe didn't say anything about being ex-Special Forces.

"One o' my boys, eh?"

"Your boys?" McCabe repeated, even though he had already figured out who the man with the gun was.

"Yeah. I'm Hiram Stackhouse."

McCabe grinned in the shadows. "Yes, sir, I know. We've met a few times."

"What'd you say your name was?"

"Jack McCabe."

"Good Lord. I remember you now. I tried to hire you for my security force, but you wasn't havin' none of it. Said you just wanted to drive a truck."

The conversation was being carried out in low whispers, inaudible to the terrorists who were still shouting orders at their prisoners at the far end of the stockroom.

"What're you doin' here?" Stackhouse went on.

McCabe was about to answer when there was a sudden commotion at the far end of the stockroom. They couldn't see what was going on, but they heard yelling in a foreign language that McCabe recognized as Arabic, followed by a scuffling sound, a heavy thud, and a muffled groan that abruptly turned into a gurgling cry. That noise trailed off into nothingness with a sigh.

McCabe's jaw tightened. He knew what that last sound meant. He had heard it often enough, back in the day. He had *caused* it more than a few times during his career as an operator.

It was the sound of some poor bastard dying from a slashed throat.

"What—" Stackhouse started to say, but McCabe stopped the older man with a hand on his arm.

In English now, one of the terrorists shouted, "You see what will happen if you do not cooperate! If you fight back, or if you disobey orders, you will die like this dog of an infidel!"

Stackhouse whispered in a shocked voice, "Bastards killed one o' my boys."

McCabe gave him a grim nod. One of the workers who had been rounded up must have tried to jump the terrorists and had been murdered for his efforts. Even though McCabe hadn't seen what happened, he had been able to follow the sequence of events from the sounds. The MegaMart employee had struggled with his captors, been hit on the head, slumped half-conscious to the floor of the stockroom . . .

Then his head had been jerked up, probably by the hair, and a knife drawn across his throat, slicing deep into the flesh. McCabe closed his eyes for a second, but it didn't help. In his mind, he saw the sudden spurt of blood from the jugular, a crimson fountain that quickly formed a coppery-smelling pool around the dead man.

Once seen, images like that were never forgotten. McCabe knew he would never forget the ones he had witnessed. They were part of him, like his DNA.

But he had planned to spend the rest of his life without ever having to see anything like that again.

That would teach him to make plans. All too often, life had other ideas.

McCabe was sorry for the man who had just died, but he and Stackhouse—and all the other captives—had their own problems. He forced his mind back to that and leaned closer to the billionaire entrepreneur.

"We can't stay here," he whispered. "If they conduct a better search, they'll find us." He nodded toward the near end of the stockroom, where a wall had been erected, behind which were offices. "Let's see if we can get in there. They've done a sweep of the offices already, so maybe they won't check them again for a while."

Stackhouse nodded. On hands and knees, they crawled along the narrow space behind the mountain of crated-up TV sets.

They only had to cover fifty yards or so, but it was a *long* fifty yards, McCabe thought. About halfway there, they had to cross a twelve-foot-wide opening where two of the double swinging doors opened out into the main store. The doors were closed at the moment, but each of them had a large Plexiglas window set into it. If one of the terrorists happened to be on the other side of those doors and happened to glance through the clear Plexiglas at the wrong time . . . Well, it was an unlikely possibility but a possibility nonetheless.

"Don't waste any time getting across there," McCabe told Stackhouse. "And stay low." He was struck by the irony of him giving orders to the man who paid his salary, a man who was worth so much more than McCabe was that the difference seemed astronomical.

Stackhouse didn't seem to think anything of it, though. He nodded and did as McCabe told him, crouching to stay below the windows in the swinging doors and darting across to the point where the narrow aisle continued along the wall, behind shelves and stacks of assorted merchandise.

McCabe waited until Stackhouse was safely concealed back there again, then hurried across himself. Luckily, the terrorists were still making noise at the other end of the vast stockroom, blustering and threatening and generally lording it over their prisoners.

McCabe wished he could do something to help those guys, but for now they would have to wait. He and Stackhouse needed to get somewhere safe, so they could catch their breath and start putting together a plan for dealing with this threat.

Stackhouse had a revolver of some sort; McCabe had seen it, had stared down the barrel of it, in fact. The only weapon McCabe had was a pocketknife.

So there were two of them, armed with one gun and one knife, against a couple of dozen terrorists with automatic weapons and, for all McCabe knew, bombs.

Shouldn't be that difficult, he thought wryly.

The terrorists had left the door open into the stockroom

supervisor's office. The upper half of the wall that looked out into the stockroom was glass, but the bottom half was solid. McCabe and Stackhouse went to their hands and knees to crawl in there. To reach the door they had to come out into the open. A central aisle that had been left in the piles of merchandise ran all the way from one end of the stockroom to the other, so if the terrorists turned around and looked, they would be able to see the two men slipping into the office.

From the shouting that was still going on down at the other end, McCabe figured the terrorists were still haranguing the hostages. He slid past Stackhouse and ventured a look. Both men, who wore jeans and thick jackets, had their backs turned. Without taking his eyes off them, McCabe flipped a hand at Stackhouse and said quietly, "Go."

Stackhouse went, scurrying through the door into the office without wasting any time or making a sound. McCabe was right behind him. He turned to his left as soon as he was through the door and sat with his back pressed against the half-wall under the window. Stackhouse was beside him.

McCabe breathed a little easier now, even though the overall situation was as perilous as ever. As long as he and Stackhouse stayed low, the terrorists couldn't see them without walking all the way down here from the other end of the stockroom. If they did that, McCabe and Stackhouse would hear them coming, because footsteps echoed in the cavernous room whenever somebody wasn't trying to be careful and not make any noise.

"Well," Stackhouse said, "we're in quite a fix, ain't we, McCabe?"

"Yeah, you could say that."

"Those boys are Ay-rab terrorists, aren't they?"

"They're Islamic, all right," McCabe agreed, "but they may not be Arabs. Hard to say. They were speaking Arabic, but that doesn't mean much. Nearly all the terrorist groups have members who speak Arabic."

"Sounds like you know somethin' about this sort o' shit. Used to be a spy, didn't you?"

McCabe grunted. "I was in Special Forces. I didn't work for the Company. And how the hell do you remember anything about me? You probably have hundreds of thousands of people on your payroll."

"Yeah, just about," Stackhouse agreed. "But I pay special attention to fellas with security backgrounds. Fella who's worth as much money as I am needs to have good people around him. People who're loyal. Hardasses, too. I figured you'd qualify . . . if you hadn't been so damn stubborn about wantin' to drive a truck."

"I was retired from the other stuff," McCabe said, even though he didn't really think he owed Stackhouse any explanations.

"Well, you ain't anymore," the older man said. "I reckon you're right back in that line o' work."

McCabe was afraid that Stackhouse was right. There was probably no one else inside the UltraMegaMart who was as qualified as he was to fight back against the fanatics who had taken over the store.

To satisfy his curiosity, he asked Stackhouse, "What are you doing here anyway? I thought you weren't supposed to be on hand for the celebration until later in the day."

Stackhouse chuckled. "I like to show up early. Helps me weed out employees who don't like to work anytime except when the boss is around. That keeps ever'body on their toes."

McCabe looked over at him. Stackhouse didn't give the appearance of a man worth billions of dollars, a man who was in charge of the biggest retail organization in the world, a man whose business contributed more to the country's economy than any other private enterprise in history.

No, in boots, jeans, and a long-sleeved cowboy shirt with pearl snaps, Hiram Stackhouse looked more like a farmer or rancher than an entrepreneur. He was in his seventies but still healthy and vital, with a ruddy face and a shock of silver hair. He could be brusque and domineering, but he also had a folksy charm that made people like him even when they didn't always agree with everything he did. And not one penny of his fortune had been inherited. He had built his business empire himself, from the ground up.

"Where are your security people right now?" McCabe asked. A man like Stackhouse wouldn't travel without a complement of bodyguards.

Stackhouse grimaced as he jerked a thumb over his shoulder toward the far end of the stockroom. "They got rounded up out there with the others," he said. "I think I'm payin' those boys too much."

"How come the terrorists didn't get you, too?"

"I was back in the can, takin' care o' business."

"They didn't check the bathroom?"

"They did," Stackhouse said, "but not before I'd climbed up on one o' the walls around the stall, pushed up a ceilin' tile, and climbed into the crawl space."

"How did you know to do that?"

"I heard the shootin' and the yellin' and knew something was mighty wrong. I just figured it was another kidnappin' attempt. My bodyguards have fought off a couple o' those over the years." Stackhouse shook his head. "Turned out to be even worse, though. I'd barely got that ceilin' tile back in place when I heard somebody come in, and then a couple of seconds later he hollered somethin' in some language I couldn't understand. That Arab lingo you were talkin' about, I imagine. I knew then the shit'd really hit the fan. I stayed where I was for a few minutes and then climbed down, figured I'd take a look and see just how bad things really are. I was workin' my way down to the other end o' the stockroom when I came across you."

"What were you gonna do, take on a whole gang of terrorists with one revolver?"

"Well, I hadn't quite figured it out yet. I tell you one thing, though—it really chaps my ass to see them towel-heads runnin' around givin' orders and hurtin' my people."

McCabe didn't like it either. He gestured toward the gun that Stackhouse had tucked behind his belt and said, "Why are you carrying that anyway? Because of those kidnappers you mentioned?"

"Yeah." The old man grinned. "And because I like packin' heat."

McCabe couldn't help but chuckle. He had always figured that Stackhouse's colorful personality was largely a put-on, a show for reporters and news cameras, but clearly, what you saw was what you got with Hiram Stackhouse.

McCabe wouldn't have mind having a whole bunch of Stackhouse's private army here right about now. Then things might have been different.

Or maybe not, if the terrorists had explosives. That would put a whole new angle on things.

"What're we gonna do?"

McCabe raised his eyebrows. "You're asking me? You're the billionaire here."

"Son, I know about makin' money and sellin' folks what they need for lower prices than just about anybody.

I don't know diddly-squat about fightin' terrorists. That's *your* department."

"Well, I don't know yet," McCabe said. "I haven't figured it out."

"I wouldn't spend too much time thinkin' about it. The rest o' the world knows by now what's goin' on in here. A jillion cops'll be stormin' the place soon, and then all hell's gonna break loose."

McCabe shook his head. "Nobody's going to storm the place, not with a thousand or more hostages inside. Not until they've found out what the terrorists want and have stalled for as much time as possible."

"What *do* those bastards want?"

McCabe shook his head. "I have no idea. We may be the last to know. But I'm sure they'll be telling the world very soon, if they haven't already."

CHAPTER 41

Shalla Sahi held up the cell phone, angling it so that its camera lens caught the lean, bearded image of Sheikh al-Mukhari. The sheikh said, "They are seeing this at the television station now?"

"They are," Shalla replied with a nod. "I spoke to their news director just a moment ago. He can see and hear you, and your message is being recorded."

Mukhari smiled thinly. "Thank you, my dear." He looked directly into the lens and said, "I am Sheikh Mushaff al-Mukhari. I am a proud member of Hizb ut-Tahrir, the Party of Liberation. I am speaking to all of you out there in the godless nation of America. Today we have struck a blow for the glory of Allah and the cause of Islam. Today you have felt only a small sample of the pain that my people have felt for decades because of Western and Zionist aggression and imperialism. The new crusade launched against my people by the infidels must now come to an end. My fellow freedom fighters and I are in control of this . . . this satanic monstrosity you call an UltraMegaMart. Everyone in here is now our hostage, and if our demands are not met, they will all die."

The sheikh paused and cleared his throat. He and Shalla stood near the front of the store, at the end of a seemingly endless row of checkout stands that were now empty of clerks and shoppers.

The sheikh nodded, and Shalla turned, moving the cell phone slowly and steadily so that the camera lens caught the scene. She paused on a group of a dozen men and women, some of them shoppers, the others Mega-Mart employees. They were on their knees on the floor, their hands clasped behind their heads. Behind them stood one of the terrorists, a machine pistol in his hand. He wore no mask. His dark, bearded face was exposed for the world to see.

Shalla moved the phone again so that it showed one of the main entrances of the store, just a few feet from where she and Mukhari stood. Another half-dozen hostages sat there cross-legged, their arms pulled behind their backs uncomfortably and their wrists tied together. Directly in front of them was a small but powerful bomb, the components of which had been smuggled into the store under the jackets of several of the terrorists and assembled only after they had taken over the place.

Mukhari cleared his throat again and Shalla turned the phone back toward him.

"You have seen for yourselves that I speak the truth. I would warn the authorities that the bombs placed at every entrance are armed and equipped with motion sensors that will detonate them if anyone approaches them too closely. Such a blast will instantly kill the hostages placed near them." The sheikh smiled. "So storm the place if you will, but know that if you do, you will be killing your own people."

Mukhari grew more solemn. "Now, as to what we want . . . it is quite simple really. The United States must immediately withdraw its warships from the Persian Gulf and cease its unlawful interference with the affairs of the sovereign state of Iran. In addition, all U.S. military forces must be withdrawn from Saudi Arabia and all other Muslim countries. There must be no American boots on Islamic soil. Also, Americans engaged in business in Muslim countries will depart immediately, and all American business interests in those countries will be turned over to the Caliphate established by Hizb ut-Tahrir. These demands also apply to the military and business interests of all other Western nations, not just America. The Caliphate, the new Islamic order, must be completely free of the taint of Western corruption and godlessness." Mukhari smiled again. "It is a new day, the first day of the holy Caliphate that will rule over all of Islam and, in time, the world, forever erasing the stench of the godless. Meet our demands with no delay, or else all the hostages in this place will die and it will be destroyed in cleansing fire. *Allahu akbar!*"

Shalla closed the phone, ending the transmission.

"Do you think they got all that?" the sheikh asked.

Shalla nodded. "They got it. Now, what will they do about it?"

CHAPTER 42

The Oval Office was crowded again. The President sat in her chair, watching the TV monitor that had been wheeled in front of the big desk. In chairs that had been arranged in wings that curved away from the desk were the usual suspects: the Vice President, Secretary of State, Secretary of Defense, Chairman of the Joint Chiefs of Staff, National Security Advisor, Attorney General, Director of the FBI, Director of the CIA, Secretary of Homeland Security, White House Chief of Staff, and White House Press Secretary. Everybody who was anybody in the decision-making process, in other words.

A council of war, although the President would not have wanted to hear it described as such, given her antiwar background.

The President's husband slouched in his usual chair in the corner, eyes heavy-lidded with apparent weariness, but actually alert and taking in everything. From where he was he could see the TV screen.

As the image of Sheikh Mushaff al-Mukhari faded, only to be replaced by a grim-faced network anchor, the President muted the sound and waited. Every head in the room swung toward her, but no one spoke. Clearly, they were all waiting for her to take the lead.

"Well?" she said after a moment, unable to keep the slight tremor out of her voice. "Ideas?"

Again, a strained silence filled the Oval Office, broken at last by the Secretary of Defense saying, "We can't withdraw all of our forces from the Middle East. We just can't."

"Can't," the President repeated, "or just choose not to?" She looked at the Chairman of the JCS. "How long would such a withdrawal take?"

The man shook his head. "Days at best," he said. "More likely weeks. Maybe as long as a month."

"Those terrorists aren't going to squat in that store for a month!" the Vice President said.

"I agree," the President said. "But maybe if we began the process of withdrawing our forces, that would be enough of a show of good faith to convince them to re- lease the hostages. Some of them anyway. Do we know how many there are?"

"It's impossible to get an accurate count," the FBI Di- rector told her. "But estimates place the number upward of a thousand shoppers. Counting the employees, there could be as many as fifteen hundred innocent people being held prisoner in there."

The Secretary of Homeland Security added, "And by the time they get through counting the bodies at the sites of those bombings, the death toll from them will prob- ably be over a hundred."

"Then even if we lose the store, it won't be as many people as died on 9/11," the President mused. "It won't be as bad as what happened on Bush's watch."

The President's husband grimaced. Nobody in the room said anything about the callousness of the

President's comment, or the political tunnel vision that had prompted it, but he knew that some of them were thinking it anyway.

He'd have to have a talk with her before she went on the air to issue a statement. If she got in front of the network news cameras and said, *Yeah, this is bad, but what happened when the other guy was President was worse,* the country would turn against her.

"This isn't the first controversy you've had to face, ma'am," the Press Secretary pointed out. "Our polls took quite a bruising over that John Howard Stark business, then all the trouble in Little Tucson, the mass kidnapping in Del Rio, and then that whole Alamo mess was the worst yet." He swallowed as she glared at him, and went on. "I'm sorry, ma'am, but it has to be said. A lot of the American people don't think that you're really on our side. They believe that you'd rather side with our enemies."

"That's absurd," she snapped. "I always do what I think is best for America."

"Of course. But a lot of people don't agree with what you think is best anymore."

The fella didn't lack for guts, the President's husband thought. Talking to her like that . . . telling her the truth when she didn't want to hear it . . . was a good way of getting taken to the woodshed.

"The people elected me, didn't they?"

"Yes, ma'am. But the poll numbers don't look good for your reelection."

She shook her head. "I can't worry about that now. I have to deal with *this* problem *today.*"

That was unusually nonpolitical of her, her husband thought. Ever since she had taken office, everything had been about getting reelected and hanging on to power.

He knew her well enough to know that power was like food and drink to her. She couldn't live without it.

"What about the business angle?" she asked. "Can we convince American companies that have holdings in the Middle East to divest themselves of them? Maybe that would be enough to satisfy the terrorists without the military withdrawal."

"You'll never get them to go along with it," the Vice President said. "You're talking about billions and billions of dollars at stake."

"Can we force them to comply? Maybe issue an executive order—"

The President's husband had to risk speaking up. He did a lot of traveling and fund-raising, and he knew the CEOs of all the top companies in the United States on a first-name basis. He said, "If you do that you'll have a real crisis on your hands. You can't force an American company to turn over its holdings to a bunch of terrorists."

"American companies have been nationalized by foreign countries before," she replied.

"Yeah, and in those cases it was a foreign government doin' the nationalizing, and we didn't like it. What you're talking about would be *us* doing it to our own people. They won't stand for it."

"They stand for having to work more than half the year just to pay all their taxes," the President pointed out.

"But it took more than forty years to reach that point. The process was slow enough so that people just shrugged and went along with it, when they noticed at all."

The President fidgeted with a pencil on the desk. "Then if we can't give the terrorists what they want, how can we convince them to release the hostages? Would it do any good to promise them amnesty? Perhaps provide them with a safe way out of the country?"

"What about a reprimand or even sanctions against Israel for that raid on Iran?" suggested the Vice President. "That would certainly show our good faith—"

"What the *hell* is wrong with you people?" The sharp voice of the National Security Advisor cut through the room. "You're sitting around here trying to figure out the best way to let those terrorist bastards win!"

The President glowered at her and said stiffly, "We have the lives of all those hostages to consider."

"Then with all due respect, ma'am, you should be trying to figure out a way to rescue them and kill the criminals who have taken over that store, instead of asking yourselves how bad a screwing do we have to take in order to convince them to play nice."

"You are *out . . . of . . . line,*" the President grated.

"No, ma'am, the thinking in this country is out of line," the NSA snapped back. "No sooner had we gone into Iraq than the press and a certain segment of politicians began carping about what our exit strategy should be. There's only one acceptable exit strategy in a war. *Win the damned thing!* Let the losers worry about exit strategies!"

The President was on her feet, shouting. "You think we shouldn't have pulled out of Iraq?"

"I think we shouldn't have gone in unless we were prepared to win! But once we were there, retreating just turned the country over to the bad guys and made them stronger than ever. The previous administration made the rest of the world mad at us, yes. But your administration, ma'am, has made the rest of the world sneer at us in contempt." The NSA crossed her arms and matched the President's icy glare for icy glare. "I'd rather have the rest of the world mad at us rather than contemptuous of us.

And I'd sure as hell rather have our enemies afraid of us instead of scornful of us, knowing that we don't have the stomach to put up a real fight anymore." She blew her breath out through her nose in a frustrated sigh. "Of course, that appears to be the truth . . . at least in this room."

"You're fired," the President whispered.

The NSA reached for her briefcase. "No, ma'am. I quit the minute you started talking about how we could best go about giving in to the terrorists' demands. You just didn't know it yet, you prissy little bitch."

With that she turned and stalked out of the Oval Office, leaving a stunned silence in her wake.

Finally, the President slumped back in her chair. She took several deep breaths, visibly struggling to bring herself under control. When she had, she said, "All right, now that we're all on the same page again, let's find an answer to this problem. Options?"

No one answered.

"For God's sake, somebody has to have an idea!"

The director of the CIA spoke up for the first time. "Madame President, I don't have any suggestions regarding how you should handle this crisis, but a thought did occur to me while we were watching the tape of the sheikh's statement."

"What's that?"

"He told you his name and showed you his face. The other terrorist we saw wasn't disguised in any way either. We should be able to figure out who he is without any trouble."

"So?" the President snapped.

"Even when they're operating in their own countries," the top spook said, "terrorists will usually wear hoods or masks of some sort, to conceal their identities. These guys don't care if we know who they are."

"And what does that mean?"

The President's husband answered before the director of the CIA could, because the same thought had occurred to him. "It means they're not planning on coming out of there," he said. "Whether you give them what they want or not . . . this is a suicide mission and always was, right from the start. They *want* to be martyrs. They want to die for the cause of jihad."

"My God," the President breathed. "How can you negotiate with people like that?"

No one said anything, but they all knew the answer to her question.

CHAPTER 43

"Talk to me, Captain," Walt Graham said.

Captain Jarrod Huckaby of the Texas Rangers said, "Well, sir, we've taken control of the situation at the request of the Tarrant County Sheriff's Department and the Fort Worth Police Department, who share jurisdiction up here. We have Department of Public Safety SWAT teams and Texas Rangers surrounding the place. We have our hostage negotiators on hand, but so far those fellas in there aren't answering any of the phone lines we've tried."

"Those bastards aren't interested in negotiating," Graham said. "There's not any compromise in them."

"Well, sir," the stocky Ranger captain said, "I think they'll find that there's not much back-up in *us* either."

Graham managed not to grin. This wasn't the time or place for it. But he knew exactly what Huckaby meant. Graham was a Fed, but he had been a Texan long before he went to work for Uncle Sam. To the type of man Graham had always been, that meant a lot.

They were in the Rangers' mobile command center, a long black motor home packed to the gills with high-tech equipment and the men and women to operate it.

On a monitor next to where Graham and Huckaby were standing, a video image had been frozen. It showed a gun-wielding terrorist standing behind a line of hostages on their knees, with their hands clasped behind their heads. Graham reached over and tapped the screen.

"You know what that means, don't you?"

"They don't care if we identify them," Huckaby said.

"Exactly. They plan on dying. Doesn't matter what we do, they're not coming out peacefully."

Huckaby's broad shoulders rose and fell in a shrug. "Then we might as well go on in and root 'em out," he said. "Can't be more'n a few dozen of 'em."

"They'll start killing the hostages," Graham warned.

Again Huckaby shrugged. "Gonna kill some of 'em anyway. Might as well minimize the casualties."

The look in the Ranger's eyes told Graham that Huckaby wasn't as resigned to those deaths as he was trying to sound. He just couldn't think of anything else.

And a part of him was probably afraid that the Feebs were going to waltz in here and take over. After all, the SAC from the Dallas office of the FBI was already on the scene. Sure, so far all that Graham had done was ask for a sitrep, but how long could that last? The Feebs weren't known for their restraint.

"What about the explosives at the entrances?" Graham asked. "They're supposed to have motion detectors on them that will trigger them if anyone comes too close."

"The bomb squad guys think that might be a bluff. They've been studying the apparatus through binoculars, and they don't think the bombs are really that sophisticated."

Graham frowned. "It doesn't strike me as likely that those men would be bluffing under these circumstances."

"We can find out easy enough."

"How?"

"Robot," Huckaby said. "Roll one of those little suckers right up to a bomb and see if it goes off."

"And what happens to the hostages who are sitting nearby?"

Huckaby shook his head. "Won't be enough of 'em left to scrape up with a spoon. But we'd know whether the terrorists are bluffing or not."

Graham's eyes narrowed. "I hope you're just speaking hypothetically, Captain."

"For God's sake!" Huckaby exploded. "You really think I'd blow up those folks? We're just brainstormin' here, Agent Graham."

"That's what I was hoping you'd say. Let's come up with something else."

Both men drew a blank, though, as they stood there amid the glow from a dozen monitors and the low-pitched chatter of the Rangers working in the command center. One of the doors opened, letting in a slice of pale, autumn sunlight before it quickly closed again behind Agent Eileen Bastrop.

"Anything new to report?" Graham asked her.

Bastrop shook her head. "Negative, sir. Hasn't been another peep out of them, and they're staying away from the entrances. None of the snipers have been able to spot anybody except the hostages who were placed near the explosive devices."

"What about around back?"

"We can't see through the service doors because they're solid, but heat sensors detect the presence of a dozen or so individuals right behind each door. They probably have bombs with them, too, and if we roll the doors up, the devices will detonate."

"But that's just a guess," Graham said.

It was Bastrop's turn to shrug. "But an educated one."

Graham clenched one big hand into a fist and smacked it into the palm of the other hand. "Damn it! The hostages probably outnumber their captors fifty to one. Why don't they just . . ."

"Just overpower them? If the terrorists are all armed with automatic weapons, they might be able to kill a couple of hundred hostages before they went down. Nobody wants to be one of the unlucky ones who dies. Sooner or later it may come to that, but right now everybody's still hoping they'll get out of this alive somehow."

Graham looked over at Huckaby again. "Any chance of putting together a list of the people who were in there?"

"We're working on that already," the Ranger said with a nod. "All we have to go by, though, are citizens who call in and say that their friends or loved ones planned to go to the UltraMegaMart today and they want to know if they're all right. We're assuming that the ones we can't locate are still in there."

The wheels of Graham's brain were still clicking over. "Carry permits?"

"We'll cross-reference the names on the list we come up with. There are bound to be some customers in there who are carrying handguns. But I imagine the terrorists are familiar with the laws here, and one of the first things they would've done was make a sweep for weapons and get everybody they could to give up their guns."

"Maybe some people managed to hide their weapons. If they did . . ."

"If they did, then sooner or later we're gonna have a gunfight in there," Huckaby said, finishing the thought.

CHAPTER 44

Allison still couldn't believe this was happening to her. *Nate,* her brain cried out to her. She wanted to be with her son. She wanted to go home.

Burke must have felt the shudder that went through her. His arm tightened around her shoulders, and he said quietly, "Don't worry. I'm sure it's just a matter of time until they get everything worked out and let us out of here."

Was he just trying to comfort her, Allison wondered, or was he really that stupid? Those men were killers. They weren't going to let anybody go.

She was never going to see Nate again.

Tears began to roll down her face.

"Go ahead and cry," Burke told her. "I'm right here for you."

At least they were sitting on the floor now instead of lying on it on their bellies. That was a little more comfortable. The terrorists had forced men to work at gunpoint, clearing merchandise away in certain areas to create open spaces where large numbers of hostages could sit. She suspected that there were at least a dozen of these enclaves—she remembered that word from one of her college courses and thought it fit here—in the store, with ninety to a hundred hostages in each one.

Terry McCabe sat on Allison's other side. She muttered, "We should have jumped them when some of the men were already on their feet. Our chances would have been better that way."

Burke had heard her. He gave a skeptical grunt and said, "Chances of what? Getting killed? The only smart thing to do is cooperate with them. They probably want to get out of here every bit as much as we do."

Allison doubted that. The man who was primarily responsible for guarding them didn't look like he cared one way or the other. His dark eyes burned with the fanaticism of a man to whom life and death were the same thing. He never put down either of the two machine pistols he carried, and he looked like he would enjoy nothing better than to squeeze the triggers of both weapons and send leaden death spewing into the crowd of prisoners.

A man who was sitting in the row behind them leaned forward and whispered to Terry, "Ma'am, you sound to me like you got the right idea. You reckon you could distract that fella?"

Terry looked back over her shoulder. So did Allison. "Why?" Terry asked.

"Because I got a .38 I managed to hide on one o' the shelves when they come around yellin' for us to give up our guns. Got my hands on it again while we were movin' stuff."

"You've got it now?" Terry asked from the side of her mouth.

"Damn right, pardon my French. If you can get that fella lookin' somewhere else, I think I can draw a bead on him and put him down."

Terry hesitated. Allison didn't know what she wanted

the older woman to say. She hated their captors and wished all of them were dead, but if that hostage with the gun tried to shoot the man with the machine pistols and missed, there might be a bloodbath right here and now.

"You'll probably just get one shot," Terry breathed.

"I know. I won't miss."

The man sounded confident—but scared. Allison couldn't blame him for that. Even if she had known anything about shooting a gun, she was too shaky now to have any hope of hitting anything she shot at.

Burke had been listening, too, and now he turned his head to hiss, "You're crazy! You're both crazy to even be thinking about such a thing! And you're going to get us all killed!"

"You got a better idea, mister?"

"Yes. Cooperate. I'm sure the authorities are working on a solution to get us out of here right now."

"Trust in the government, eh? If those ol' boys who were holed up in the Alamo last spring had done that, they'd all be dead now, wiped out by that rogue Mexican army general. The government can't help us. It's up to us to save our own lives."

"I think you're right," Terry said. "He has two machine pistols. If we can get our hands on those, we can all scatter and hide. It's a big store. They can't track all of us down. Whoever gets the guns can put up a fight, maybe take down some more of them, get more guns . . ."

"Mom." Ronnie was shaking her head, a terrified look on her face. "Mom, you can't. You'll get killed."

Terry managed to come up with a smile. "I won't get hurt, honey. I'm just the distraction. I'll hit the floor before the shooting ever starts."

"What about the rest of us?" Burke asked in a savage

whisper. "You're talking about throwing all of our lives away, and by God, I won't let you do it!"

Allison started to say, "What are you talking about?" But she only got the first couple of words out before Burke put a hand on the floor and started to lever himself out of his sitting position.

"Hey!" he said. "Hey, Omar, or whatever your name is! Get over here. I need to talk to you."

CHAPTER 45

It was night now in Pakistan. Lawrence "Fargo" Ford was in the embassy's communications center, the most heavily shielded and most often swept room in the entire place. He was as certain as you ever could be that it was secure from any electronics eavesdropping. He had been here all evening, in constant touch with CIA Headquarters back in Langley, Virginia, getting reports on the situation in Texas.

Ford had overruled all the doctors and practically hijacked an ambulance, bringing Brad Parker back to the embassy with him. Parker shouldn't represent a threat to Hizb ut-Tahrir anymore, since he had already regained consciousness and passed along all the intel he had, but you never knew what those turban-wearing crazies might do. Parker seemed to have made the trip without suffering any further setbacks, and at least here at the embassy he would be safe from any more assassination attempts.

Anyway, the plan hatched by the sheikhs who led Hizb ut-Tahrir was already under way. A series of vehicle bombings in Texas had wreaked havoc and death. That news had been flashed worldwide, followed by even more startling reports that terrorists had taken over a huge discount store called the UltraMegaMart.

Ford remembered shopping in regular MegaMarts the last time he was Stateside, but he didn't recall any Ultra-MegaMarts. Must be a new thing, he had thought when he heard the name.

Sure enough, more intel kept coming in during the evening, indicating that today had been the store's grand opening. It was packed full of holiday shoppers when the goons came in and started shooting.

So now the authorities in Texas had a full-blown hostage situation on their hands, with hundreds of hostages, maybe even more. An UltraMegaHostage Situation, Ford caught himself thinking at one point. A bleak chuckle came from him.

It wasn't funny, of course, and he knew that. Lots of people had already died, including children. The terrorists had aimed directly at America's heart—and hit it. Ford's brief attempt at humor was just a case of trying to laugh instead of crying.

The worst of it was that there wasn't a damned thing Ford could do to help. All he could do was sit and monitor the situation at extreme long distance. To that end, he had established a secure computer link with Langley and networked it so that everything that came in from the field showed up here in Islamabad, too.

Ford didn't recall when he had eaten last, but he didn't care. He didn't feel the hunger. He sat there in front of a bank of computer screens and video monitors, coat and tie off, sleeves rolled up, his eyes behind the black-framed glasses always moving, flicking from report to report, from satellite feeds of U.S. network news broadcasts to intel from military and CIA surveillance satellites. The supercomputers at Langley were trawling through trillions and trillions of bytes from the Web, searching for anything that might be helpful to the people in Texas who were trying to come up with a way to get those hostages out of there safely.

A list of names scrolled by on one of the monitors. A line of type at the top of the screen told Ford that these people were employees of MegaMart who had been scheduled to work today at the UltraMegaMart at the time of the attack. No telling if all of them were actually in there or not, but most of them probably were.

The Company must have gotten a massive info dump from MegaMart's computers, because information on store inventory began to scroll past Ford's bleary eyes, along with a restocking list and a delivery schedule. Documents blinked into view for a second and then were gone. Ford reached up, about to take his glasses off and rub his eyes in weariness.

He stopped short as a name on one of the documents jumped out at him. Then it was gone and he couldn't call it back. The flood of info kept rolling along.

Ford knew what he had seen, though. He sat forward in his chair, pulled a keyboard over in front of him, and began typing furiously as he got an encrypted e-mail ready to go through a seemingly endless series of secure servers to Langley. He had to confirm the information he had glimpsed so briefly.

That took about twenty minutes, and when Ford was sure, he switched to radio transmission and talked to his bosses at Langley for another five minutes before they agreed to find out the cell phone number he wanted and patch him through to it.

Ford didn't know if this was going to do any good or not, but he figured that the odds in favor of the hostages had just gone up a little.

CHAPTER 46

"Sporting goods," McCabe said.

Stackhouse's eyes lit up. "Oh, hell, yeah. Plenty o' guns and ammunition there."

"Is there an access door, like the one in electronics?"

Stackhouse frowned in thought. "It ain't like I know every inch o' every store," he said. "But I remember signin' off on the plans for this one . . . and I don't recall there bein' one."

McCabe nodded. "That'll make it a little harder then. But not impossible. If we can take out the two terrorists back here in the stockroom, then all of us can make a rush for sporting goods and arm ourselves before the rest of those bastards can cut us off. It's not that far."

"Sounds like you're comin' up with a plan after all, McCabe," Stackhouse said with a chuckle. "How we gonna get rid o' those two fellas?"

"I'm still working on that," McCabe admitted.

Before he could think about anything else, he felt a familiar vibration in his shirt pocket. His eyes widened in surprise. He had forgotten all about his cell phone.

And now it was about to ring.

He and Stackhouse had left the door of the office open so they could hear if the terrorists started coming in this direction. Now that precaution was about to backfire on them. McCabe didn't know if the sound of the cell phone's ring would reach all the way to the other end of the stockroom, but he couldn't take the chance that it would.

He grabbed desperately for the phone, which was set to vibrate a couple of times before ringing. If he could just get it open in time—

He didn't have a chance to look at the display and see who was calling. He flipped the phone open just as the first note of the ring tone sounded and jammed it to his ear. "What?" he asked savagely, through gritted teeth.

"Hey, Jackknife, old buddy. Hope I didn't call at a bad time."

The shock of recognition jolted McCabe. Of all the voices he might have heard coming from his phone, this was just about the last one he would have expected.

"Fargo?" he said.

"That's right, pal. Where are you?"

"In a world of shit," McCabe answered. "I'm inside the UltraMegaMart here in Texas. Turn on your TV," he added dryly. "I'm sure you'll see something about it."

"Oh, I know what's going on, don't worry about that. I assume since you answered your phone that you're not a prisoner. Our towel-headed friends would have taken it away already if you were."

"That's right," McCabe said. "Where are you, Fargo?"

"Islamabad," Ford said. "Pakistan."

"I know where Islamabad is." McCabe gave a grim chuckle. "I was hoping you were somewhere closer, like right outside this damned store."

"No such luck. I wish I wasn't halfway around the

world, too, so I could give you a hand. Got time for a sitrep?"

McCabe had given situation reports to Lawrence "Fargo" Ford on numerous occasions in the past. Special Forces and the Company had an alliance that was uneasy at times, but for the most part they worked together without much trouble. Ford had functioned as the CIA liaison on several missions that McCabe and his team had carried out in several different Third World hot spots.

Given their familiarity with each other, McCabe was able to fill Ford in very quickly on what he knew about the situation, which was admittedly not much.

"If you've been monitoring U.S. news broadcasts," McCabe concluded, "I'm sure you know more about what's going on here than I do."

"You know about the bombings in Fort Worth?"

"Yeah."

"Those were just to get our attention. You're right in the middle of the main part of the attack. It was planned and carried out by a sleeper cell of Hizb ut-Tahrir agents, led by Sheikh Mushaff al-Mukhari."

McCabe recalled attending briefings on Hizb ut-Tahrir while he was still an operator. The group hadn't been a major player back then. Obviously, it had grown in power. He didn't remember any mention of Mukhari, but he was sure the guy was your typical Islamic fundamentalist maniac.

"Mukhari is on the scene, leading the attack in person," Ford continued. "He and his friends sent out a video of their demands via a cell phone camera."

"Mukhari told you who he is?"

"Yeah," Ford said, "and one of the guys with him showed his face, too."

McCabe closed his eyes for a second and rubbed his forehead. That bit of news was bad, really bad.

"All right," he went on. "Do you know how many of them are in here?"

"Best guess is around two dozen."

"How are they armed?"

"Machine pistols are all that we've seen, except for the bombs at each entrance into the store."

"Bombs?"

"Yeah, armed with motion sensors so they'll detonate if anybody comes too close, and they have hostages sitting practically on top of them, too. There won't be any SWAT teams rushing the doors, Jackknife. Nobody wants footage of hostages being blown up on the six o'clock news tonight."

McCabe thought about Terry and Ronnie. It was possible they were some of the hostages who had been placed near one of those bombs . . .

He shoved those thoughts out of his head. He couldn't afford to dwell on the danger that his wife and daughter might be in, because then fear for them might paralyze him. He had learned during many hazardous years to keep all his attention focused on whatever task lay in front of him next. Deal with one problem before worrying about the next one.

"What do the terrorists want?"

"More than they'll ever get. All U.S. military off Muslim soil and all Western business interests in the Middle East turned over to the Caliphate, a new Islamic superstate they're trying to put together. It's impossible."

"Even if it wasn't, it doesn't matter," McCabe said.

"Yeah. What they really want is to hurt us even more than they already have."

Something else occurred to McCabe. "How did you know I was mixed up in this?"

"Saw your name on some intel I was monitoring. MegaMart's let Langley into their computers, and I'm hooked into the network."

"Why? Because the plan came out of your part of the world?"

"Yeah. In fact, it was hatched at a Hizb ut-Tahrir training facility in the mountains along the Pakistan-Afghanistan border. One of our guys led a raid on the place and discovered the intel. You probably remember him. Brad Parker."

McCabe remembered him, all right. Parker was a good man. A little bit of a cowboy sometimes maybe, but still a good man.

"Is he all right?"

"Bunged up some, but he'll be fine." Ford paused. "Listen, Jackknife, I'm sorry we didn't get the word out in time to keep this from happening."

"Yeah, so am I," McCabe said. "My wife and daughter are somewhere in the store, too."

"Oh, Lord. I'm sorry, Jack. If there was anything I could do—"

"You'd be right here doing it. I know. I may call on you for intel later."

"Sure. What are you going to do? You *do* have a plan, don't you?"

"Sort of," McCabe said. "There are only two of the guys back here in the rear of the store. We're going to take them out, free the prisoners in the stockroom, then see if we can reach the sporting-goods section."

"Guns and ammo," Ford said, realizing what McCabe was getting at. "Better be careful. The bastards are liable to have explosives strapped to their bodies."

A grim smile touched McCabe's mouth. "Head shots," he said. "That'll solve that problem."

"Yeah. Good luck, my friend."

"We'll need it," McCabe said. He closed the phone, breaking the connection between North Texas and Pakistan.

"Who in blazes was that?" Stackhouse asked as McCabe slipped the phone back into his pocket—*after* turning off the ringer completely.

"An old friend."

"And he calls you at a time like this to catch up on old times?"

"He works for the CIA," McCabe explained. "He found out that I was in here and thought he ought to touch base with me, so he could pass along any intel we didn't already have." He told Stackhouse about the bombs at the store entrances and the demands that the terrorists had made.

"The gov'ment's liable to cave in, too," Stackhouse snapped. "I never saw such a bunch o' gutless folks as we got in Washington now."

McCabe gave a weary shake of his head. "It doesn't matter what they do. The terrorists plan on going out in what they consider a blaze of glory. Otherwise, they wouldn't have been so casual about revealing their identities."

"You mean they're gonna kill everybody in here and themselves, too."

"More than likely," McCabe said.

"That means a big bomb."

McCabe nodded. "Yep."

Stackhouse scrubbed a gnarled hand over his face. "Then we got our work cut out for us, and we ain't got a lot of time neither."

"That's right. I'm going out there, behind those shelves full of baby formula. Wait until I get in position, then make some sort of racket. One of them will have to come down here to investigate."

"Then you'll jump him and get his gun."

"That's the plan," McCabe said.

"Then once we're both armed, we go get the other fella."

"Right."

Stackhouse hefted his gun. "Why don't I just shoot the sumbitch when he comes down here?"

"Because that would warn his partner and we wouldn't be able to get him, too." McCabe suppressed a feeling of exasperation. "Just do like I say, all right, Mr. Stackhouse?"

"Sure, sure," the billionaire said. "You're the boss, son."

But McCabe wasn't so sure about that as he began crawling out of the office. If anybody ever fit the description of a loose cannon, it was Hiram Stackhouse.

And in this case, if that cannon went off, it could wind up killing hundreds of people.

CHAPTER 47

Hamed's breath hissed between his teeth and he lifted both machine pistols as the infidel stood up and shouted at him. He came close to sending a burst from each weapon into the red-faced man's chest, but at the last second he held off on the triggers.

The man didn't seem to realize how close he had just come to dying. He said, "Yeah, I'm talking to you, Omar. You gotta listen to me."

The man started forward, stepping around some of the other hostages, as he ignored both blond women, the older one and the younger, who reached out to stop him.

Hamed thrust the guns at the man and shouted, "Do not move! Come any closer and I will shoot!"

The infidel stopped and raised both hands. "Take it easy, Omar," he said. "I'm just trying to keep everything peaceful here, okay?"

"My name is Hamed." Sheikh al-Mukhari had told all of them that it didn't matter if the Americans found out who they were. Hamed understood the reasoning behind that decision perfectly well. "Do not call me Omar again!"

The American kept his hands up. "Sure, sure, whatever you say. All I wanted to tell you—"

"Burke, shut up." That came from the lean blonde, the older one.

Hamed swung his left-hand pistol toward her. "Be quiet," he ordered harshly. Then he looked at the red-faced infidel again. "What is it you wanted?"

That was when the other blonde spoke up. "Mr. Burke . . . Ellis . . . please don't."

Now the infidel hesitated. Obviously, the words of the younger woman meant more to him than those of the older one. That meant the woman herself was more important to him.

Hamed knew what to do.

"Back!" he shouted, gesturing with the machine pistols. "Back, all of you!"

The hostages began scooting backward on the floor.

"Except you!" Hamed stepped forward quickly and trained the right-hand pistol on the young blond woman. "Stay where you are!"

She froze, her blue eyes widening.

"Hey!" The startled exclamation came from the red-faced man called Burke. "Hey, there's no need for that, Om—I mean, Hamed. We're cooperating here. I understand why you and your people are so angry with us. We've been jacking around with you for years, always taking the side of the Israelis, starting wars for oil—"

"Stop lying, American," Hamed said, his voice cold with hatred. "I know you do not truly feel this way. Do you think I haven't been around the likes of you long enough to know when you are lying?" He looked back at the blonde. "On your feet."

"There's no need for that, I tell you!" Burke moved as

if he were going to try to get between Hamed and the woman. "I'm trying to make you understand—"

"Get back, damn you!" Hamed slashed at Burke's face with the left-hand gun. The weapon thudded heavily against flesh and bone, and Burke fell back with a startled cry of pain as the sight ripped a gash in his cheek.

At that second, while Hamed's back was half-turned, one of the other men leaped to his feet. Hamed just caught a glimpse of the movement from the corner of his eye and started twisting in that direction. The sight of the gun in the second man's hand jolted him.

Flame spurted from the little revolver's muzzle as the man fired. Hamed felt the impact on his upper left arm. He was already turning toward the man, and the bullet finished the job of jerking him around. His left arm and hand suddenly didn't want to work anymore, but his right functioned just fine.

He triggered the machine pistol in that hand.

The burst of lead ripped into the man with the pistol, stitching wounds across his body and driving him backward. He dropped the gun as he started to fold up.

Not all the bullets found their intended target. A teenage boy sitting near the man jerked and grunted as a black hole appeared in the center of his forehead. He sat there for a second as blood trickled from the wound and formed a red trail down his face.

Then he toppled over into the lap of the girl sitting next to him, who started to scream hysterically. Hamed's already taut nerves began to fray at the sound.

"Make her be quiet!" he ordered. "Or I will kill her, too!"

Several people grabbed the girl. They surrounded her, as if to form a human shield. A man clapped his hand over her mouth to muffle her cries.

Hamed turned back to Burke, who had started this whole thing. He gestured again to the young blond woman and said, "You. On your feet. Stand next to him."

She climbed unsteadily to her feet and shuffled over until she was next to Burke, where Hamed could cut down both of them with ease if he needed to.

"Now," Hamed said to Burke. "Tell me what you wanted to tell me. But no tricks! If you lie to me, I will kill you and the woman both!"

Burke's face was still flushed, but a terrified pallor had spread beneath the red. He swallowed hard as he looked at the bodies of the two people Hamed had just killed. Then he looked at the woman beside him for a second before looking back at Hamed, who knew that he would now tell the truth.

He was too frightened to even consider doing otherwise, Hamed thought.

Burke swallowed again. "I . . . I just . . . I just wanted to tell you . . . I'm, uh, a lawyer. An attorney-at-law." He started to reach toward his coat, as if to delve into a pocket. "I can give you a card—"

Hamed jerked the barrel of the right-hand gun and shook his head.

Burke stopped the motion and went on. "That's fine, that's fine. I was just gonna say, I'm a lawyer, and when you guys get out of here, I think you're going to need representation." His voice was stronger now, as if he were on firmer ground. "I mean, there are bound to be some court cases arising from this whole thing, and you won't find a better lawyer to handle them than me. I'd be glad to tell you about some of the cases I've handled and the judgments I've won—"

Hamed had listened in growing disbelief to what was Burke was saying. He knew the man was being truthful, but he had a hard time accepting the idea that anyone could be so venal and greedy, even a godless American infidel.

But Burke *was* a lawyer, Hamed reminded himself.

"Shut up!" Hamed screeched at him. "Sit down, you fool! Your courts, your whole American legal system, mean nothing! Nothing! There will be no trials!"

Burke held up his hands, palms out. "I'm sorry, I just don't like to see anyone acting without legal counsel—"

"Shut up! Sit down!"

The blond woman was tugging on Burke's arm by now. He allowed her to lead him back to where they had been sitting before, with the older blond woman and the teenage girl. They sat down. Burke looked vaguely confused and ashamed of himself. More confused than anything, though.

Hamed could not believe how crazy some of these Americans were. Had the lawyer really believed that he could—what was the expression—drum up some business in the middle of a hostage situation?

The distraction had almost proved fatal. Hamed's arm throbbed where the other man's bullet had struck it.

Had that been Burke's aim all along? To distract Hamed so that the other man could shoot him?

Hamed's eyes narrowed as that thought occurred to him. He considered killing Burke, just on the off chance that he was right about the lawyer.

But he didn't think that was the case. Burke wasn't that smart. He probably hadn't even known that the other man had a gun.

"Hamed!"

That was Shalla Sahi's voice. Hamed looked around and saw the young woman hurrying toward him, trailed by Sheikh al-Mukhari. Both had worried looks on their faces.

"We heard shooting," Mukhari said. "Are you all right?"

"Of course he's not all right," Shalla said. "There's blood on his arm. Let me take a look at it."

Hamed knew she had taken nursing courses at the university in Arlington. She was as close to a doctor as they had among them. So he allowed Mukhari to take his left-hand machine pistol while Shalla pulled back his jacket and the sleeve of his shirt to reveal a raw gash in his upper arm.

"The bullet just creased you," she told him. "I'll get a first-aid kit from the sporting-goods section and clean and bandage the wound."

Hamed shook his head. "No need to waste your time."

Why bother to tend to a minor wound when they would all be perishing soon in the cleansing flame of nuclear fire?

Shalla blinked, then nodded in understanding. "It should be bound up anyway, so that you can use the arm better."

Hamed considered the suggestion, then said, "In that case, go ahead."

"I'll be right back," she said.

When she had gone toward the sporting-goods section, Sheikh al-Mukhari asked Hamed, "What happened here?"

"Nothing important. One of the infidels had a gun." Hamed nodded toward the man and the boy he had killed.

"You missed it when you disarmed them," Mukhari said with a stern look on his face. He looked and sounded like a professor chiding a wayward student.

"A thousand pardons," Hamed said.

"Seek not my pardon, but that of Allah."

Hamed bowed his head humbly.

He thought the sheikh was overreacting a bit, though. They were talking about only one gun, and one American. How dangerous could that be?

CHAPTER 48

McCabe heard the shouts and the shooting from inside the store as he crouched behind the shelf full of cartons of baby food. A pang of worry throbbed through him. He couldn't help it.

Terry and Ronnie were out there somewhere.

He forced his mind back onto the task at hand. He looked at the door of the office, saw Hiram Stackhouse peering around the jamb, and nodded to the elderly billionaire.

Stackhouse returned the nod. He drew back his arm and flung the heavy stapler that he held toward the rear of the stockroom.

The stapler hit a shelf with a loud metallic *clang!* then hit the floor and bounced several more yards with a clatter. McCabe thought the noises sounded like somebody had run into something and knocked it over.

That was just about perfect. The racket was loud enough that the terrorists must have heard it, and they would have to investigate. One man would come down here to the other end of the stockroom while the other remained where he was, guarding the hostages.

That was the plan anyway.

McCabe heard startled talking from the two gunmen. Breathing shallowly, he waited and listened for one of them to approach.

Stackhouse had withdrawn back into the office. If the terrorist got past McCabe, Stackhouse would be waiting with his revolver. A shot would warn the other bastard, but at least the odds would be cut down a little.

In the long run, though, killing one of the terrorists wouldn't do any good, and McCabe knew it.

He had to get *all* of them, and before they could trigger any explosives they might have with them.

That was a tall order. But like all journeys, it started with a single step.

Like the one he heard as shoe leather brushed against the concrete floor somewhere close by.

The terrorists must have figured that one of the Americans was hiding in the office. That was really the only feasible explanation for the noise they had heard. The man who moved past the shelves where McCabe was hidden had his machine pistol trained on the partially open door, and his tense attitude told McCabe that he was ready, even eager, to pull the trigger.

McCabe had already taken off his belt and formed it into a loop. He had it in his left hand. His right held the pocketknife. Moving silently, he dropped the belt around the guy's neck and yanked him backward.

At the same time, McCabe's right hand flashed up and then drove down. He kept the pocketknife's blade razor-sharp, and it went into the back of the terrorist's neck without much trouble. McCabe put plenty of force behind the strike to make sure of that.

The terrorist spasmed as McCabe felt the blade grate against bone. He had hit the spine, just as he intended.

It all happened so fast that the bastard didn't even have time to jerk the trigger on the machine pistol before his spinal cord was severed. The weapon slipped out of suddenly nerveless fingers and thudded to the floor.

McCabe pulled the knife out and reached around the terrorist's body. The guy was deadweight now, but he wasn't actually dead yet.

That changed a second later when McCabe thrust the knife under his chin and into his throat, angling the blade up so that it went through the soft tissue and into the base of the brain. The terrorist's body gave one more spasm as he died.

McCabe lowered the corpse to the concrete. Killing the terrorist had taken approximately three seconds, and except for the noise of the gun hitting the floor, it had been carried out in complete silence. McCabe checked under the guy's jacket for explosives. Finding none, he wiped the blood from the pocketknife onto the garment.

Then he folded the knife's blade and put it away. He picked up the machine pistol and checked it. It was a Heckler & Koch model with which he was intimately familiar. The clip was full. McCabe looked in the pockets of the dead guy's jacket and found two more full clips. He stowed them in his own jacket.

Stackhouse was looking around the doorjamb again. McCabe smiled faintly and nodded to him. Stackhouse stood up and slipped out of the office and cat-footed over to join McCabe.

"Now what?" Stackhouse asked in a whisper.

"Now we to get the other guy."

The second terrorist had quite a dilemma on his hands, McCabe thought over the next couple of minutes as he and Stackhouse worked their way silently along the narrow passage next to the wall. That time had to seem even longer to the killer at the other end of the stockroom.

The man called out in Arabic, asking Achmed what was going on down there. So the dead terrorist was named Achmed, McCabe told himself. *Enjoy your stay in hell, Achmed. It's just what you deserve.*

Meanwhile, Achmed's partner had to be going nuts with worry. He couldn't leave the prisoners and come down here to see what had happened to Achmed. If he turned his back on the MegaMart employees, they would either jump him or make a break for freedom.

So all he could do was get more and more nervous.

What if he had a radio? McCabe suddenly wondered. Then he could call some of the other terrorists for help. That would ruin everything. He needed to move a little quicker.

He left Stackhouse at a tiny opening between some stacks of crates, after whispering, "Give me to the count of thirty, then squeeze through there and step out where the guy can see you."

"Puttin' a target on me, eh?"

"I'll move fast enough he won't have a chance to do anything."

Stackhouse grinned. "See that you do, son, or I'm liable to dock your pay next month."

McCabe returned the grin and gave the old billionaire a nod. He slid along the wall, closer and closer to a large opening near the spot where the remaining terrorist was holding the hostages.

The numbers were running in his head. He was counting them down as Stackhouse was counting them up. Just as McCabe reached zero, he heard the terrorist's startled exclamation, followed by a shouted order in heavily accented English.

"Do not move, or I kill!"

Stackhouse had stepped into the open, McCabe knew.

Even as the terrorist was yelling at the old man, McCabe came around a pile of cardboard cartons containing jugs of antifreeze. The gunman was half-turned away from him, but the man was alert enough to spot McCabe's movement.

Just not fast enough to avoid the side-hand strike that McCabe smashed against his throat, crushing the windpipe. As the man's eyes widened in shock and pain and he struggled to gasp for the next breath he would never draw, McCabe hit him again.

The force of the killing blow made the guy's arms and legs flail around like he was doing an old-fashioned jitterbug. A sharp stench suddenly filled the chilly air as he shit himself. He folded up to lie in a stinking heap on the floor.

McCabe reached down and picked up the machine pistol the terrorist had dropped. As he straightened, he smiled at the group of MegaMart employees, who were staring at him in a mixture of shock and disbelief, obviously struggling to comprehend what they had just witnessed.

"Y'all ready to go kick some terrorist ass?" McCabe asked.

CHAPTER 49

Every sort of high-tech surveillance equipment available to the FBI and the Texas Rangers was pointed toward the UltraMegaMart, so when more shooting erupted inside the store, the people outside knew about it. They heard it on their supersensitive sound pickups, and they saw the bursts of heat imagery on the feed from the spy satellite that had been moved into a geosynchronous orbit overhead.

The shooting didn't last long, but it caused a considerable amount of interest and excitement while it was going on, especially in the mobile command center parked about a hundred yards in front of the main entrance to the store. All the cars in the parking lot between the command center and the entrance had been towed away, giving the cameras and microphones a straight shot into the store.

After a few seconds, the technician at the console where the satellite feed was coming in looked up at Walt Graham and said, "They seemed to have stopped shooting, sir." The listeners at the audio posts confirmed that.

"Do you think they've started executing the hostages, sir?" Eileen Bastrop asked her boss.

Graham pondered the question, but not for very long, before shaking his head. "I think if they were going to do something that dramatic, they would have boasted about it first and made sure we knew what they were doing. No, that sounded to me more like somebody tried to jump one of them and got shot down for his trouble."

"Then they *did* kill a hostage, you think."

"Maybe, in a struggle. I suppose the guy could have been just wounded."

"But whoever it was, they weren't able to overpower any of the terrorists," Bastrop said.

"Yeah," Graham agreed. "If they had, the fighting would still be going on."

"TV networks have picked up on it," one of the agents at a monitor reported.

"Of course they have," Graham said, unable to keep the frustration and disgust out of his voice. The media people always knew what was going on almost before the authorities did. Sometimes they *did* know before.

Graham's cell phone buzzed. He took it out of his pocket, opened it, and identified himself. A look of surprise appeared on his normally impassive face. A lot of things were going on today to give his self-control some trouble.

"Madame President, this isn't a secure line," he said after a moment, causing Bastrop's perfectly plucked eyebrows to rise. "Yes, ma'am, we're aware of it," Graham went on. "We don't know what happened in there, but our best guess is that there was some sort of brief struggle between the terrorists and the hostages . . . Yes, ma'am, it appears to be over now . . . We don't know yet what it means, and at this point I wouldn't want to speculate . . ."

He shook his head at Bastrop, who understood the gesture to mean that her boss damn sure wasn't about to tell the President of the United States that they thought some Americans might have just been killed in there.

One of the techs swiveled away from his console and held out a headset toward Graham, who shook his head again and held up a finger to tell the man to wait. Whatever the guy had, it couldn't be as important as talking to the President.

"Yes, ma'am, we're on top of it," he assured her. "We have our top hostage negotiating team here, and as soon as the terrorists contact us again, we'll attempt to establish some lines of communication . . . No, we won't do anything rash, you can count on that . . . We want a peaceful solution to the crisis just as much as you do, ma'am . . . Of course. We'll let you know right away if anything changes . . . Thank you, Madame President."

Graham closed the phone and grimaced.

"What did she want?" Bastrop asked. Her chilly tone of voice made it clear what she thought of the current occupant of the White House.

"She saw the reports on TV about the most recent shooting inside," Graham said. "She's worried that this is going to end badly."

"So am I. I think we should move this command center back another hundred yards or so."

Graham smiled humorlessly. "If they've got a pocket nuke or something like that in there, another hundred yards won't make any difference, Eileen."

"I know, but what about conventional explosives?"

"Too big and bulky. The terrorists couldn't have smuggled them into the store if they were posing as shoppers, like they must have. It would take a truck bomb or something like that, and the whole parking lot has been swept. We're dealing something small but nasty."

"Sort of like the Presi—"

Graham held up a hand to forestall the rest of the comment.

"Sir?"

Graham looked around at the tech who had been trying to get his attention earlier. "What is it, son?"

The man held out the headset again. "I've got radio contact here with someone at the American embassy in Islamabad, Pakistan."

Graham's forehead creased in a frown. "Pakistan?"

"Yes, sir?"

"Who's on the line?"

"An undersecretary named Ford?" The tech's voice rose as if he were asking a question instead of stating a fact.

Graham didn't know the name, but he could think of only one reason a seemingly minor diplomat would be calling him from Pakistan on today of all days.

He took the headset, settled it so that the buds were in his ears, and moved the mike in front of his mouth. "Special Agent in Charge Graham here," he barked. "Talk to me, Mr. Ford. I assume you really work for our friends at Langley, rather than the State Department."

"That's right, Agent Graham," a voice drawled in his ear, sounding like the speaker was less than a mile away, rather than on the other side of the world. "My name is Lawrence Ford. It was one of my associates who discovered the terrorist plan aimed at the United States. Unfortunately, he wasn't able to deliver the information in time to prevent the attack."

"Well, if you've called to apologize, I appreciate it, but I'm a little busy right now."

"No, the reason I called is to pass along some more intel that might prove useful to you." Ford's tone of voice was crisper now. "You have an asset inside the Ultra-MegaMart that you probably don't know about."

Graham cocked an eyebrow at a clearly puzzled Bastrop and said, "Oh? What might that be?"

"A man," Lawrence Ford said. "He used to work with me. His call sign is Jackknife . . ."

CHAPTER 50

Burke started shaking a few minutes after the shooting in which the man who'd had the .38 and the boy next to him had been killed. Terry wasn't surprised. She had seen delayed reactions like that hit people before, when they had been involved in sudden, unexpected violence.

Of course, in this case the violence wasn't all that unexpected, Terry thought. After all, they were dealing with lunatics.

But Burke had looked surprised that the terrorist named Hamed had killed two people so brutally, and without any sign of remorse. As hard as it was for Terry to believe, the lawyer seemed genuinely shocked that anyone would do such a thing.

She would have been willing to bet that Burke's parents had been antiwar protestors during the Sixties. The apple, as the old saying went, didn't fall far from the tree.

At least Burke had had sense enough to fall back on his ambulance-chasing shyster persona and hadn't told Hamed the truth about why he got to his feet. If the terrorist knew that the hostages had been plotting against him, he might have killed even more of them, just as an object lesson.

Burke sat with his head down, seeming to stare at his hands, which he held in his lap. His hands were trembling, Terry saw. Burke was taking deep breaths, almost like he was trying to hyperventilate.

He was about to lose it, she sensed. She didn't want that to happen. It couldn't help anything.

She put a hand on Burke's arm and said in a low voice, "Take it easy. It's all over now. No need to get upset."

"It's not," he replied, his voice shaking just as much as his hands. "It's not over. He . . . he killed those people."

"That's what he does," Terry pointed out. "He's a terrorist. Anyway, he killed a man earlier. Didn't that tell you what sort of monster he is?"

"It's different," Burke insisted. "I . . . I saw his eyes. He was thinking about . . . about killing Allison and me. All he had to do was squeeze a trigger, and he came so close . . . so close . . ."

Terry remembered the old joke about how a liberal was just a conservative who hadn't been mugged yet. There was a lot of truth to that, and Ellis Burke was a classic case of it. He was beginning to realize that he had been making excuses for a bunch of animals.

Worse than animals really. Only man was capable of as much wanton cruelty as these terrorists exhibited.

"Listen to me," Terry said. "You're alive. Allison's alive. We can't give up hope. You know the sort of people we're dealing with now. You won't make the same mistake again. They're the enemy, Mr. Burke. They *want* us dead. All of us. And you can't reason with them."

Burke's gaze was bleak as he raised his head. "But . . . if we can't reason with them . . . how can we hope to get out of here alive?"

She knew he wouldn't want to hear the real answer.

Kill all of them before they can kill all of us.

So she told him, "You just said it. We can hope."

Hope . . . and wait for another chance to strike back.

There were fourteen guys in the stockroom who had been held prisoner by the two terrorists who were now dead. The dock foreman McCabe had spoken with earlier, when he arrived with his truck, was dead, too, his throat cut just as McCabe had supposed. The other fourteen men were alive and healthy, though.

McCabe had had to stop them from stampeding toward the service doors at the rear of the stockroom. He had spotted small backpacks sitting in front of each of the large, roll-up doors, and knew from his conversation with Fargo Ford that those were probably bombs equipped with motion-sensitive detonators. McCabe had explained quickly to the men that they couldn't take a chance on setting them off.

There was no way out except through the store.

Counting himself and Stackhouse, McCabe had sixteen men to deal with the threat of the terrorists. The odds were almost even.

Except for the fact that the terrorists were heavily armed, of course.

McCabe intended to do something about that.

"We're going to try to make it to sporting goods," he explained to the men he and Stackhouse had liberated from captivity. "There are rifles and shotguns there, along with ammunition. Better stay away from the shotguns, though, with so many hostages around. We don't want buckshot spreading and taking out innocent people."

"How are we gonna get from here to there without some of those bastards spottin' us?" one of the men asked.

"I don't know yet," McCabe answered honestly. "That's why I'm going to have a look first and see if I can get the enemy located, especially the ones right around this part of the store."

"They're liable to be spread out all over the place," Stackhouse commented.

McCabe nodded. "Yeah, and that's going to work against them. They took too many hostages. All they were thinking about was the maximum number of people they could kill. They didn't stop to consider that they have to *watch* all those prisoners, and there are too many to pack them into a compact area."

"You sound like you know something about things like this," one of the other men said.

"A little," McCabe admitted.

Stackhouse snorted. "No need to be modest, son. Boys, McCabe here used to be Special Forces. He's fought them terrorist sons o' bitches before, on their home ground."

That revelation made the men look at him a little differently. McCabe didn't care about that, except for the fact that knowing his background might make them more likely to follow his orders quickly and without question.

"All right, we can't afford to waste any time," he said. "Some of the other terrorists may be coming back here to check in with these two. Lay low here while I have a look around." He nodded to the man who held the second H&K machine pistol. "If any of them come back here, try to stay out of sight . . . but if you can't, kill the bastards."

The man gave McCabe a grim nod. "Damn right."

McCabe went to the double swinging doors and crouched so that he was below the level of the Plexiglas windows. He raised his head enough so that he could take a quick look through one of the windows.

His line of sight ran up an aisle between the shoe department on his left and something else on his right. Crafts? He wasn't sure. He didn't know the layout of this store, although Stackhouse had given him a quick verbal sketch of it from memory. He was sure, though, that sporting goods was to his right as well, past several other sections.

From where he was, McCabe couldn't see all the way to the front of the store. Shelves full of merchandise cut off that view. But in the area he *could* see, no one was moving. He eased one of the swinging doors open about six inches and listened intently.

He heard talking, but it wasn't very close to his position. He couldn't make out the words. After taking a deep breath, he pushed the door open some more and stepped out of the stockroom into the main part of the store.

He gazed left and right, along the wall dividing the stockroom from the rest of the store. A narrow aisle ran along that wall, at the back of the shoe section to his left and crafts—he'd been right about that—to his right. Again he saw no movement.

The terrorists must have herded the hostages into groups in central locations, probably in the main aisles of the store. They would have swept their areas already to round up any stragglers. They probably felt like they had everyone under their guns by now.

Making no noise even in his thick-soled work boots, McCabe started to his right in a crouching, gliding pace, machine pistol held ready in his hand. He moved past shelves full of needlework and crochet kits, bins filled

with skeins of brightly colored yarn, packages of beads
and baby doll heads, hot glue guns, and paint-by-the-
numbers sets. Such things didn't mix too well with
terror and death, but they were here anyway . . .

The crafts section turned into bedding—sheets, pillow-
cases, blankets, and comforters—then a stretch of plastic
garbage cans, laundry baskets, ironing boards, plastic
storage tubs, and the like. McCabe cat-footed past them,
and suddenly he found himself at the rear of several aisles
full of camping equipment.

He had reached the edge of the sporting-goods section.
He looked ahead of him, past the fishing gear, and saw
the gleam of glass-fronted cabinets with rifles in them.

That was when the realization hit him that those cabinets would be locked up, as would the ammunition.
Employees who worked in this area would have the
keys—but those employees had all been taken hostage
and rounded up. McCabe could break the glass and get
to the guns that way, but the noise that would make was
bound to draw the attention of the terrorists.

He was pondering what to do about that problem
when a woman came around a display of exercise equipment a few feet away, started toward him, then stopped
short at the sight of him. Her eyes widened in shock, her
mouth opened to shout an alarm, and she jerked her
hand up to thrust the machine pistol in it at McCabe.

CHAPTER 51

McCabe was moving before the woman was. His senses were keenly alert, and his muscles were taut and ready for action. He knew that anybody he ran into moving around the UltraMegaMart would in all likelihood be an enemy. Even if he happened to encounter one of the hostages, he knew he would have to move quickly to prevent their surprise from giving him away to the terrorists.

So even as the woman's gun came level, McCabe reached her and clamped his left hand around the weapon, pinning the slide so that it couldn't fire. At the same time he drove his right fist into her jaw. He was holding the machine pistol he had taken from one of the dead terrorists in the stockroom, which just made the punch that much more potent.

The woman's knees buckled. Her eyes rolled up in their sockets, and McCabe knew she was out cold.

He got his right arm around her and kept her from collapsing to the floor. She let go of the machine pistol, so McCabe had no trouble taking it from her hand. He headed quickly for the counter behind which the gun cabinets were located, half-dragging, half-carrying the unconscious female terrorist.

No question she was one of them. She wore jeans and the same sort of thick jacket as the others McCabe had seen, plus her long, raven-black hair and olive skin testified to her Middle Eastern heritage. Of course, she could have been Italian or something like that, McCabe supposed . . . but the gun was kind of a dead giveaway, and so was the fact that her first instinct had been to try to shoot him.

All those things added up to the fact that she was one of the enemy.

Once they were behind the counter where they wouldn't be easily spotted, McCabe lowered her to the floor. Her eyelids were already fluttering. He knew she wouldn't be unconscious for very long.

The smart thing to do would be to cut her throat while he had the chance.

But McCabe wasn't made that way. Besides, she might come in handy. Not as a hostage, because the fanatics behind this attack wouldn't care whether she lived or died, but as a possible source of information.

He unbuckled her belt and pulled it out of the loops on her jeans, then used it to tie her wrists together. He pulled her knees up and lashed her ankles to her wrists, being none too gentle about it and not worrying about how uncomfortable she might be.

She groaned with returning awareness.

McCabe lifted her jacket, pulled her shirt loose from the jeans, and used his pocketknife to cut a strip from the bottom of it. Then he cut off another piece of material from the shirt, wadded it up, and jammed it into her mouth, tying it in place with the strip of cloth. His

movements were swift and efficient, and he had her
hog-tied and gagged in less than a minute.

She made noises and started trying to thrash around.
McCabe put the barrel of a machine pistol against the
back of her head. She must have recognized the feel of
it, because she got still in a hurry.

That wouldn't last long, though, and he knew it. She
would figure out that he couldn't afford to shoot her. So
he rolled her onto her side and let her see the razor-
sharp blade of the pocketknife. He held the index finger
of his other hand to his lips.

She lay still. He saw in her eyes the realization that he
would kill her if he had to, and she had to have figured
out by now that he could probably do it quietly, too.

McCabe leaned over her and put his mouth close to
one of her ears. "Here's the deal," he said. "I know
you're not afraid to die. I know you got up this morning
planning to die before the day was over. But I don't
think you really want to."

Hatred blazed from her eyes.

"You're coming with me, and you're not going to
struggle," McCabe went on. "If you do, I'll just knock
you out again. I can do it with one little pinch here." He
rested his fingers on her neck, at the spot where several vital nerves joined. "So cooperate with me, and
maybe you'll get your chance for Armageddon later."

Wrong word, he thought. Armageddon was a Jewish
thing. Jihad was probably closer. But he didn't waste
time correcting himself.

Instead, he picked her up and draped her over his
shoulder, aware as he did so that she was heavier than
she looked. Aware as well that he had an armful of
firmly packed female flesh, because even under these
dire circumstances he was still a guy. A happily married

guy, to be sure, which meant he wouldn't be grabbing a young woman like this unless it was in the line of duty—which this was, of course.

She cooperated. There wasn't much else she could do. McCabe got the feeling that she hadn't been highly trained in hand-to-hand combat or self-defense. Probably hadn't figured on needing any of that stuff. He retraced his steps to the swinging doors that led to the stockroom, again without seeing anyone else along the way, and shouldered through them.

He didn't see Stackhouse and the other men at first, but then they appeared, coming out of the places where they had been hiding behind stacks of merchandise. Stackhouse looked surprised at the sight of the woman, but then he grinned and asked, "Been doin' some shoppin', McCabe?"

"Yeah," McCabe grunted. "Maybe I was able to pick up a secret weapon for us."

Hamed knew something was wrong when he saw the worried look on Sheikh al-Mukhari's face.

"Have you seen Shalla?" the sheikh demanded.

"Why would I have seen her?" Hamed asked. "I thought she was with you."

Mukhari shook his head. "She was going around the store checking with all our men, making sure that everything is all right."

That didn't surprise Hamed. The woman had been serving as an extra pair of eyes and ears for the sheikh, running errands for him and delivering his orders to the other members of the group who were scattered around the sprawling store.

"Perhaps she, ah, needed to tend to personal business,"

Hamed suggested, embarrassed to be speaking even vaguely of such female things.

Mukhari nodded. "Perhaps. We should have had radios of some sort. I did not really think about how large this place is."

"There are probably walkie-talkies in the electronics area," Hamed said.

"An excellent idea—but it does not tell me what happened to Shalla."

"I'm sure she's around somewhere. Would you like for me to go and look for her? You could watch these infidels while I do."

The sheikh looked slightly offended that Hamed would suggest he lower himself to something as menial as guarding prisoners, and Hamed quickly backtracked from the idea, hoping as he did so that Allah would forgive him for speaking so to a holy man.

"I will find her," Mukhari snapped. "Continue to keep your eye on these godless ones."

"Of course," Hamed said.

He turned his attention back to the prisoners as the sheikh stalked off. The conversation had been carried out in Arabic, so of course the infidels had no idea what he and Mukhari had been talking about.

That was good, because Hamed didn't want them to get the idea that anything might be going wrong with the plan. He wanted them to continue being cowed and demoralized, because they weren't as much of a threat that way.

That older blond woman was watching him with keen interest, though, and Hamed didn't care for the look in her eyes. It seemed almost like she knew what he and Mukhari had been saying.

But that was impossible, of course. She was just a stupid American bitch. She knew nothing.

"Something's wrong," Terry whispered to her daughter, Allison Sawyer, and Ellis Burke.

"Of course something's wrong," Burke muttered. "We're being held prisoner by a bunch of bloodthirsty lunatics."

Terry was glad that the lawyer had finally come to understand that, but she said, "No, I mean they're upset about something. The older man was asking Hamed if he'd seen a woman named Shalla, or something like that."

Allison stared at her. "You understand that jabbering they were doing?"

"It's Arabic. My husband speaks it. He taught me a little of it." Terry shrugged. "I'm good with languages, and I enjoy learning new things."

Burke said, "Wait a minute. Your last name is McCabe. That's not an Arabic name, by any means. How come your husband knows . . . the language?"

"He speaks several different languages. He used to travel internationally a lot for his work."

That was putting it mildly. Terry couldn't think of many places that Jack hadn't been when he was an operator. Most of them had been backward corners of the world where he was always in danger.

But she wasn't sure he had ever been in any more peril than he was now, somewhere in this sprawling discount store less than fifteen miles from home.

She sure as hell hadn't been.

"So one of them has gone missing," Burke said. "What does that mean? And what good does it do for us?"

Terry tried to guard against the hope that had sprung up inside her. "It means something has happened to the woman," she explained, keeping her voice low enough so that Hamed couldn't overhear the conversation. The bearded terrorist was stalking back and forth, looking worried and glaring at the prisoners as he paced. "Maybe they didn't capture everyone in the store. Maybe some people are still free, and they grabbed the woman."

Allison caught her breath and then said, "If that's true, they could use *her* as a hostage to make the others release us."

"Never happen," Burke said with a shake of his head. "I know about trade-offs. You gotta have something the other guy really wants. These people all want to die. They won't care about one woman, even if she's one of them."

Terry knew that the lawyer was right, but she still dared to hope.

She hoped that Shalla's disappearance meant that Jack was somewhere in the store, loose and working to free the hostages. The odds against him would be overwhelming, of course . . .

But she clung to that hope anyway, because for the first time since this nightmare began, she began to feel that there was a real chance she and her daughter and the rest of the prisoners might get out of here alive.

CHAPTER 52

The woman tried to scream as soon as McCabe removed the gag, but once again he was too quick for her. His hand clamped over her mouth, stifling any outcry. He wasn't too gentle about it either.

Being a gentleman sort of went out the window when somebody wanted you and your loved ones and a bunch of other innocent folks dead.

She strained against the belt he had used to tie her. McCabe shook his head and said, "Might as well give that up. You're not getting loose."

The hatred he saw in her eyes would have curdled milk. He couldn't understand that. This woman didn't know him, didn't know anything about him.

How could she hate him so much?

He didn't hate her, or the men with her who were trying to carry out this great atrocity. He would kill them if he could, sure, but only to preserve innocent lives, not out of the sort of crazed fanaticism he saw in her eyes when she looked at him and the other men in the stockroom.

All any of them had done to make a deadly enemy

out of her and her kind was to live in America. Didn't even matter if they had been born here or just raised here.

"I'm going to take my hand away from your mouth," McCabe told her, "but don't try to yell. If I have to, I'll just knock you out again. Understand?"

The woman glared at him for a couple of seconds, but then her head moved in a grudging nod.

McCabe lifted his hand, ready to grab her again if she tried to make a peep. She just grimaced, turned her head to the side, and spat onto the concrete floor as if trying to get the taste of his hand out of her mouth.

She was propped up on some cardboard cartons that contained small microwave ovens. McCabe stood in front of her, and Stackhouse and the rest of the men formed a rough half circle around them.

"Go ahead," she said through clenched teeth. "Go ahead and rape me, you dogs! See if I care!"

McCabe shook his head. He showed her the pistol in his hand, which he had taken away from her, and said, "You've got it all wrong, miss. I'll put a bullet through your head if I have to, but nobody's going to rape you."

She didn't look like she believed him.

"All we want is information," McCabe went on.

She spat again. "You'll get nothing from me."

McCabe ignored her defiance and said in a quiet but determined voice, "How many of you are there?"

"Enough to make all of you infidels sorry."

"Do you have explosives?"

"Go to hell."

In Arabic, McCabe said, "You are a disgrace to Allah, uncovering your head and exposing your body. You should be taken back into the house of your father and beaten for your sins."

The woman's mouth sagged open in shock. McCabe knew what she was thinking: How was it that this godless American was speaking her language?

"Your mission is doomed because you do not truly serve the will of Allah," McCabe continued. "You bring shame and dishonor to the Prophet. You soil the holy cause of jihad with your iniquity. Speak now! How many misguided souls like yours have come to this place?"

For a second, he thought it was going to work. He saw the resolve in her gaze wavering.

But then her eyes hardened again and she said in English, "Go fuck yourself, American."

McCabe sighed. He knew he could break her if he devoted enough time to the effort.

But that was time he didn't have.

McCabe shoved the gag back into her mouth, despite her best efforts to bite his hand, and tied it into place.

"Reckon she told you, McCabe," Stackhouse said.

"Yeah," McCabe said with a nod. "We'll continue with the original plan. But somebody will have to stay back here and keep an eye on her to make sure she doesn't get loose and warn the others, and in case we need her later." He looked at the billionaire. "That'll be your job, Mr. Stackhouse."

Bushy white eyebrows lifting in surprise, Stackhouse said, "Why me? I was plannin' on goin' out there with you boys!"

"I know that, but I need somebody I can trust back here." McCabe hoped that explanation would mollify Stackhouse. There was some truth to it. He wanted somebody competent standing guard over the woman.

But mainly, he didn't want to risk the life of such an important man any more than he had to. Philosophically, each man's life was as important as any other man's. But realistically, the American economy could stand to lose a truck driver like McCabe a lot more easily than it could a billionaire entrepreneur like Hiram Stackhouse.

"Well, all right," Stackhouse agreed, although McCabe could tell that he was quite reluctant to do so. "If you need me, though, just holler and I'll come a-runnin'."

"Sure," McCabe said with a nod. He turned to the other men. "The rest of you follow me."

He had figured out what to do about the locked cabinets and cases in sporting goods that contained the guns and ammunition. What he needed was a distraction so that he could break them open while the terrorists were worried about something else. While thinking about that problem, he had remembered the smoke detectors and the sprinkler system that covered the entire store.

If he could start a small fire underneath one of the smoke detectors, and the smoke from the fire wasn't noticed by the terrorists until it reached the sensor, that would set off the sprinklers and all sorts of alarms. With that racket going on, the bastards wouldn't be able to hear the glass fronts of the cabinets being shattered, or the cases that contained ammo being wrenched open.

The plan would require a certain amount of luck, but McCabe thought it was workable.

He led the men to the swinging doors, checked through the Plexiglas windows, and saw that the coast was still clear. It might not stay that way for long, though.

The woman would be missed sooner or later, if she hadn't been already, and then the terrorists would start looking for her. McCabe wanted to put his plan into operation while the enemy was still fairly stationary, guarding the hostages.

"Once we get our hands on the guns, spread out," McCabe told the men in low tones as they crouched at the swinging doors. "Kill every terrorist you see. They may be wearing body armor, so take head shots if you can. But even if they're wearing armor, a slug from a high-powered rifle to the body ought to put them down and incapacitate them for a few seconds. That'll give you a chance to finish them off." He looked around at his "army." "Can you do it?"

All of them nodded, but he saw a lot of pale, frightened faces.

He knew that most of the men would come through despite their fear. They would rise to the occasion, as America's civilian soldiers had been doing for more than two centuries. As a country, the rot of liberalism and defeatism might have set in, but as individuals the people were still strong when they had to be. When they were backed into a corner and forced to fight for what was right. It was a shame that things had come to that, McCabe thought, but he still believed in his fellow Americans.

He still had hope.

"Let's go," he said with a nod as he pushed one of the doors open.

CHAPTER 53

At first, everything seemed to be going all right. The MegaMart employees moved fairly quietly for men who had never been trained to be stealthy. Several of them had stuffed wads of packing paper under their shirts that McCabe planned to use to start the fire. He had borrowed a cigarette lighter from one of the men. As he slipped along the narrow aisle that ran beside the rear wall of the store's retail area, he kept glancing up, looking for one of the smoke detectors attached to the ceiling.

He could have pulled a fire alarm and set off a racket that way, of course, but that wouldn't turn the sprinklers on. Smoke was required for that. McCabe thought the terrorists would be more disoriented with water pouring down on them, and that would make it more difficult for them to see as well.

He ran the risk of the bastards detonating a bomb, if they had one, at the first sign of trouble, but his hope was that they wouldn't do that. He was counting on their arrogance and their desire to milk this situation for all the drama it was worth. By now, the whole world would be watching.

McCabe and his men didn't run into any of the terrorists before they got to the sporting-goods section. McCabe spotted a smoke detector on the ceiling above the arts and crafts area. He paused and motioned for the men who had the packing paper to hand it over.

That was when everything went wrong.

McCabe suddenly heard glass shatter, and an American voice yelled, "Grab the guns! Hurry! Hurry!"

Instantly, McCabe's brain grasped the situation. Some of the other hostages had either gotten loose somehow, or had hidden from the terrorists and hadn't been rounded up in the first place. The idea of going for the guns in sporting goods had occurred to them, too.

But they were making a hurried grab, out in the open, with no distraction to keep the lunatics off their backs. It was a valiant try, but doomed to fail.

McCabe twisted around and motioned urgently to the men with him. "Down!" he ordered. "Get down and make yourselves as inconspicuous as possible!"

They hit the floor, crawled behind displays, plastered themselves against the bottom of shelves, did everything they could to make themselves difficult to see. McCabe bellied down and crawled along the aisle, past a long set of shelves to a place where he could see part of the sporting-goods area.

He saw half-a-dozen men breaking into the gun cabinets and the cases where the ammunition was kept. They were hurrying, fumbling with the weapons in an attempt to get them loaded, and McCabe knew they weren't going to make it in time because he also heard running footsteps and angry foreign voices.

Several of the terrorists skidded into view, carrying automatic weapons like the ones McCabe had taken off the men in the stockroom. One of the Americans behind the counter had finished loading the shotgun in his hands. He swung it up and fired. Even in the cavernous store, the blast was deafening. The charge of buckshot tore into one of the terrorists and flung him backward.

But then, before any of the other men could bring their guns into play or the shotgunner could pump the weapon and fire again, the killers opened up with their machine pistols.

Death spewed from the automatic weapons in a veritable storm of lead. The counter behind which the Americans crouched blew apart in a spray of splintered wood and glass. Bullets smashed into their bodies and drove them back against the gun cabinets they had broken into a few minutes earlier. They hung there, unable to fall because the devastating impact of the slugs held them up. Their faces disappeared in a crimson flood. When the guns finally fell silent and the Americans pitched forward, they barely resembled anything human.

McCabe slid backward along the shelf, pulling himself out of sight as the terrorists came forward to check and make sure the men they had shot were really dead. McCabe had no doubt of that. No one could have survived such a brutal, overpowering assault.

Even having witnessed the things he had during his life, he felt sick to his stomach. Not so much because good men had just died, although he felt a bone-deep grief for them.

It was the unholy glee on the faces of the terrorists as they massacred those men that sickened McCabe. He could never hate everyone of Middle Eastern descent, as the woman he'd captured hated all Americans just because they were Americans. He didn't hate all Muslims, not by any means.

But right now, he hated these particular sons of bitches. Damn straight he did.

He swallowed that hatred and the sickness that came with it and lay there, silent and unmoving. If the terrorists conducted a search of the area, he would fight, of course, but right now he wanted them to just be satisfied with the slaughter they had already carried out and go away.

The way the guy who'd been hit by the shotgun blast went down, McCabe knew he was either dead or badly wounded. That was one more of the enemy out of the fight. Trading six lives for one was unacceptable.

But at least those six men hadn't died completely for nothing.

McCabe listened as the terrorists talked excitedly among themselves, pleased by the murders they had just committed. Then they fell silent and after a moment, he heard what sounded like an older man's voice castigating the others for letting some of the Americans remain loose to start with.

How had they hoped to keep a thousand or more people corraled with only a couple of dozen men? True, the hostages were split up into smaller groups of forty or fifty apiece, and one man armed with automatic weapons and willing to kill was probably a match for that many unarmed civilians who just wanted to get out of here alive. When you broke it down like that, the whole thing didn't sound so unreasonable.

What they had really counted on, though, was the belief that the hostages wouldn't fight back because they were scared. Because in recent years America had pretty much taken whatever punishment its enemies wanted to dish out and hadn't done anything in response except some empty, futile saber-rattling.

Sure, the so-called "war on terror" had been victimized by some poor planning and worse execution, but at least the people in charge then had been trying to do *something* to stem the bloody tide of Islamofascism.

Even if those mistakes hadn't been made, McCabe knew, the effort had been doomed from the start because of the country's polarization and the stranglehold that the left had on the mainstream media, so that things would always look worse than they actually were. The rise to power of the liberal wing had just made the situation even more dire. Now our enemies around the world knew that they could do just about anything they wanted to and have nothing to fear except some harmless bluster and maybe a few economic and diplomatic sanctions.

Evil bastards like these terrorists just laughed at those hollow threats. Give them credit—they knew how to hate. They'd had centuries of practice. And they were never plagued by the self-doubt and self-recrimination that had paralyzed American willpower for close to fifty years.

No, what really gave the terrorists the upper hand, at least in their minds, was the utter confidence that Americans would throw up their hands and quit at the first sign of any tough sledding. They believed that Americans were gutless.

And when it came to most of the politicians and media figures, they were right.

That left any fighting that had to be done up to the common people . . . like the ones trapped in this Ultra-MegaMart.

McCabe heard the terrorists walking away. They were going the other direction, not toward him and the men with him. He closed his eyes for a second and breathed a sigh of relief.

They still had a fighting chance.

And now they could get to those weapons easier than they could have before, McCabe saw as he edged his head past the end of the shelves. The terrorists, in their arrogance, had walked off and left the rifles standing upright in the cabinets that were broken open. McCabe and his men would be able to get their hands on the guns, along with ammunition for them.

All they had to do was wade through the spilled blood of their countrymen and step over the bullet-riddled corpses of friends, neighbors, coworkers.

They could do it, McCabe thought. They could do it because they had to.

And using a small fire and the smoke detectors to set off the sprinkler system still wasn't a bad idea. Anything to make things more difficult for the terrorists worked to the hostages' advantage.

McCabe hissed, and when several of his men peeked out from their hiding places, he motioned them forward. With gestures, he asked for the paper he intended to use as kindling. He took it, being careful not to rattle it around too much. The terrorists might have left a man or two in the area, although McCabe didn't think that was the case.

He arranged the paper in a pile in one of the aisles in the crafts area, almost directly underneath the smoke detector on the ceiling high overhead. The store's heating system was running, which meant that air would be coming from the vents and moving around up there in currents, and McCabe didn't know exactly what that would do to the smoke. He hoped it would go almost straight up as it rose. If it didn't, he might have to start another fire, and he knew that it would be only a matter of time until some of the bastards spotted the smoke and came running to find out what was causing it.

But there was only one way to find out what was going to happen. *Here goes nothing,* he thought, and flicked the lighter into life.

CHAPTER 54

Terry's head jerked up when she heard glass break somewhere in the store, followed by shouts. The sounds weren't really close to where she, Ronnie, and the others were being held prisoner, but they weren't all that far away either.

Jack!

The thought went unbidden through her head. She still had no way of knowing for sure that her husband was even inside the store, but her gut told her that he was. That was how strong the bond between the two of them was.

"Mom, what's going on?" Ronnie asked as she huddled against Terry's side.

Terry put her arm around her daughter's shoulder and squeezed hard. "I don't know. But I'm going to hope it's something good."

"It's Daddy, isn't it? He's doing that—"

More yelling broke out, this time in Arabic. Terry recognized the language, although not the words in this case because they were being spouted so rapidly.

A second later, a heavy boom filled the air. That was

a shotgun, Terry thought. None of the terrorists had shotguns, did they?

But they had machine pistols, and that was the terrible racket that suddenly rolled through the store, a bull-fiddle roar of death maybe forty yards away, along the rear of the store.

Ronnie gave a short cry of fear. Terry tightened her arm around her. The rest of the hostages in this group looked frightened as well. Ellis Burke caught hold of Allison's hand, and she didn't pull away. Lucy Winston held her son Darius on her lap and bent her head over his as if to shield him from anything that was about to happen. Other parents clutched their children to them as the kids whimpered.

Terry kept an eye on Hamed. If he looked like he was going to get trigger-happy and start shooting, she would do her best to get to him and try to stop him before he could slaughter everyone. She knew she would likely die in the process, but that would be all right if she could stop him from killing everyone else.

But even though Hamed was wide-eyed with surprise, he appeared to be maintaining control. He glared at the hostages and swept the machine pistols back and forth menacingly, causing everyone to hunker even lower to the floor.

He didn't fire, though, and after a few moments the shooting from the other part of the store came to a stop. The sound of the shots echoed from the high ceiling and slowly died away, leaving a strained silence.

The older man who had been talking to Hamed earlier about the missing female terrorist came along the aisle a couple of minutes later. He looked angry, and when he spoke to Hamed the words came out fast and furious. Terry couldn't pick up all of them, but she understood enough to get the gist of what the older man was saying.

Several men had managed to elude capture by the terrorists and had hidden out until now. They had broken into the gun cabinets and ammunition cases in the sporting-goods department and tried to arm themselves.

Some of the terrorists had gotten there before they could do so, however, and killed the Americans—but not before one of the men had been able to fire a shotgun and kill one of the terrorists.

Terry felt a fierce surge of exultation when she heard that one of the bastards was dead. He'd had it coming, that was for sure.

But her heart sank when she thought about the Americans who had been massacred. Could one of them have been Jack? That sounded just like him, making an effort to get his hands on some weapons so that he could fight back against these heartless monsters.

She swallowed hard as she realized that her husband might be dead. Deep down, though, she couldn't make herself believe that was true. Jack would have been smarter than that, she told herself. He wouldn't have made such a clumsy effort to get to the guns. He would have done *something* to distract the terrorists first . . .

That was when she looked again toward the area where the shooting had taken place and spotted a tendril of grayish smoke curling its way upward toward the ceiling—and she knew in that moment that her husband *wasn't* dead.

Call it instinct, call it the bond between husband and wife . . . call it love . . . it didn't matter what you called it, Terry McCabe *knew* . . .

Just as she knew, looking at that smoke, that he was making his move.

"Jack," she whispered.

* * *

This standoff wasn't going to last much longer, Hamed thought as Sheikh al-Mukhari walked stiffly toward the front of the store. The sheikh was angry that Shalla was still missing, he was upset at the carelessness that had allowed some of the Americans to elude capture, and he was ready to put an end to everything.

By now, the cameras in the news helicopters circling the store at a safe distance would be sending out their signal to the entire world. The television sets in the electronics department were still on, although someone had muted the sound on them, and they all showed the same picture: the huge, boxy shape of the UltraMegaMart sitting in the middle of what was now a mostly deserted parking lot. Scores of emergency vehicles with flashing lights lined the access road and the farthest reaches of the parking lot, but there was nothing they could do to stop what was going to happen.

That same picture was being watched in Europe, Asia, Africa, India, and Australia, despite the time differences. This was the sort of high drama that could captivate the entire planet. Everyone would be waiting to see what was going to happen.

Hamed glanced at his watch. Not quite twelve o'clock. Hard to believe that he and his companions had been in the store for only a few hours. Harder still to accept that they had been in command of the place for less than two hours. It seemed much longer than that, more like days rather than mere hours.

Soon the drama would be drawing to an end. At noon perhaps. High noon, the Americans called it. They had a movie by that name. Hamed had never seen it, of course, because he didn't watch decadent American movies with all their unwholesome sex and violence, but he had heard of it.

That would certainly be fitting, and he wondered if Sheikh al-Mukhari had thought of it. At high noon, the UltraMegaMart would disappear in the blinding flash of a nuclear inferno, and the dirty bomb would render the entire area for miles around radioactive.

Hamed felt something go through him at the thought. A tingle of fear and regret?

No, he decided, it was a shiver of anticipation. He was ready to die for the cause of jihad. Ready to die for his god, and to take all these filthy unbelievers with him. He looked at them and smiled.

They didn't know how little time they truly had left in this world.

The thoughts continued to spool out in his mind. The Americans watching everything unfold on TV would be shocked to their cores when they saw the explosion. They wouldn't be able to believe that such a thing could happen.

In the Middle East, though, where everyone would be watching the coverage on Al Jazeera, wild celebrations would sweep the streets of Cairo and Damascus and Beirut, Baghdad and Tehran and Riyadh. The people there would know that a blow for freedom had been struck. This victory would be just the first step in the rise of the Caliphate and the ultimate doom of the sinful West. In time the Caliphate would rule the world, and through it Allah would reign supreme.

It was such a beautiful vision that Hamed almost wished he could be alive to see it.

But of course he couldn't, because he and everyone else here had to die to bring that vision about. To bring paradise to earth . . .

What was that smell?

He lifted his head and frowned as he sniffed at the air. Something burning?

"Hamed? Hamed, listen to me."

He looked around in surprise. One of the infidels was addressing him? It was that blond woman, he saw, the one who had bothered him all along with that look about her—a look that said she wasn't really afraid of him. She was climbing to her feet now, as she said, "Hamed, I really need to talk to you."

He jerked the barrel of his right-hand gun at her and barked, "Sit down! Sit down with the others or I will kill you."

She held her hands out toward him. "There's no need for that. Listen, if we can just talk for a minute—"

Hamed figured out then that she was trying to distract him, and the only possible reason she would be doing that was because she had noticed him trying to locate the origin of that smoke he had smelled. He had forgotten about it for a second, but now the realization that something was wrong came rushing back into his brain—and the blond woman was part of it.

She would pay for her treachery. "Infidel bitch!" he screamed as he leveled the right-hand gun to blast her into eternity.

Before he could pull the trigger, a wailing like that of crazed jinni filled his ears, and somehow—even though he was inside—the heavens opened up with a deluge.

CHAPTER 55

"—reports that more shots have been fired inside the UltraMegaMart just a short time ago! Our correspondents on the scene tell us that a considerable amount of gunfire was heard coming from inside the store. The shooting supposedly lasted for at least a minute, perhaps longer. As for what this latest outbreak of violence means for the safety of the hostages, we have no idea at this point."

"How long is this going to go on?" the President asked in despair.

"It's only been a couple of hours so far," her husband pointed out.

They had retreated to the family quarters on the second floor of the White House. Down below, the Oval Office was still crowded with all the subordinates who had been there earlier, except for the National Security Advisor.

That bitch was long gone.

The President knew that sooner or later she would have to call the NSA's top deputy and have him come to the White House, since he had inherited the job whether he knew it yet or not. For now, though, she couldn't stand people looking at her anymore, obviously waiting for her to make a decision.

That was why she had come up here. She had to get away from that constant pressure, even if it was just for a few minutes.

That big boob of a husband of hers, though, had insisted on turning on the television, so they still couldn't get away from what was going on in Texas.

She hated Texas. To her way of thinking, nothing good had come out of that state since Lyndon Baines Johnson and the Great Society.

Now it had given her the worst crisis of her Presidency, hard on the heels of those fiascos in Laredo and San Antonio.

She stared at the TV screen, where the same image was still being broadcast: the big, ugly store and the empty parking lot. Except for the graphic superimposed in the bottom corner of the screen that read LIVE, and the occasional passing shadow cast by a circling helicopter, the picture on the screen might have been a still photo. Nothing changed.

But things were going on inside the store, if the reports of gunshots were to be believed. More than likely, American citizens were being killed, and sooner or later, she would be blamed for their deaths by her political enemies. She was sure that was how the conspiratorial right-wing bastards would behave.

Her foot began to tap nervously on the floor. "I'm going to have to *do* something," she said.

"What?" her husband asked. "It's too late to withdraw our support from Israel. It wouldn't do any good. And even if it would, that would be political suicide. Trust

me on that. You don't want to piss off the Jews. You'd
lose too many votes."

"You think I won't lose votes if I stand by and do
nothing and those bastards blow up that store and kill a
thousand people?" she snapped.

He shrugged. "Not as many as you will if you turn
your back on Israel. Hell, you're never gonna carry
Texas anyway, no matter what you do, and in the long
run, people in California and New York aren't going to
care if a bunch of rednecks get blown up. The middle of
the country doesn't really exist as far as they're concerned anyway."

She knew he was probably right about that; she
trusted his political instincts. That was about the *only*
thing about him she trusted, but still . . .

"All right. We can't negotiate with the terrorists. We
can't appease them, can't give in to their demands. We
have to go in."

"They've got bombs on the entrances," he reminded
her.

"Those bombs can only go off once."

"Detonate them on purpose, you mean, and then go
in with SWAT teams right afterward?"

"Or Special Forces. I think this has gone beyond
SWAT teams."

"Yeah, you're right about that," he admitted, "but
you're talkin' about deliberately causing the deaths of
several dozen hostages."

"Several dozen casualties is better than a thousand.
Besides, the way they've been shooting in there, we already have multiple casualties."

"You're probably right about that, too." He considered
what she had said. "Going in would make you look
tougher, all right. You could probably use a dose of that

in the polls. If they've got a pocket nuke in there, though, an attack will just force them to set it off."

"If they've got a pocket nuke, they're planning to set it off anyway," she said. "It's just a matter of time. Maybe if we can get some men in there, they can stop the terrorists from setting off the bomb."

He shook his head slowly. "That's a mighty big gamble you'd be takin'."

"Somebody has to."

"Maybe you ought to run it by those folks down in the Oval Office—"

"Why? I'm smarter than all of them put together." Now that her mind was made up, she didn't see any point in wasting time. Ignoring his dubious, worried look, she picked up the phone on the bedside table and said, "Get me that FBI agent who's in charge at the scene."

She didn't have to say what scene she was talking about.

Today there was only one that mattered.

"There's something new going on in there, sir!" one of the technicians in the command center told Walt Graham in an excited voice.

Graham leaned over the man's shoulder and asked, "What is it, son?"

"A noise of some sort." The tech took his headset off and held it out to Graham. "Take a listen, sir."

Graham did, fitting the buds into his ears. He immediately heard a high-pitched wailing. The noise wasn't very loud because the walls of the store muffled it, but it was very familiar. After a second Graham was able to recognize it.

He turned to Bastrop in surprise and said, "The fire alarm's going off in there."

Bastrop snapped at the technicians operating the high-powered surveillance cameras, "Look for any sign of smoke."

Graham handed the headset back to the first tech. "Keep listening and let me know if there's any change."

Then he and Bastrop waited tensely to see if the store was really on fire.

After a couple of minutes, the techs at the monitors handling the feeds from the various cameras all reported no signs of smoke coming from the building.

"That doesn't mean the place isn't on fire," Bastrop said. "It could be that the smoke just hasn't found a way out yet."

Graham nodded and was about to say something when his cell phone rang again. He answered it, halfway expecting the voice that he heard on the other end.

"That's right, Madame President," he told her. "There were more gunshots about ten minutes ago. We haven't been able to figure out what happened yet . . . Ma'am?" As he listened, he looked at Bastrop and shook his head. "With all due respect, ma'am, I'm not sure that's a good idea. There are bombs planted at the entrances . . . I know you're aware of that, ma'am, but the hostages . . . I see."

He covered the bottom half of the cell phone with a big hand and told Bastrop in a whisper, "She's trying to yank us out and send in the army! My God, this is gonna be worse than Waco!"

Then he returned his attention to the person on the other end of the phone and said, "Ma'am, there are things going on that you don't know about yet, things that have just happened. The fire alarms inside the store have just started going off . . . No, ma'am, we don't know what that means. It doesn't appear that the store is actually on fire, but it could be . . . We don't know how the terrorists are going to react to this . . . Ma'am, I know you want to send in the Special Forces, but you don't have to." Graham was grasping at straws now, trying to find some way to keep this . . . this *politician* from acting too hastily and ruining everything. "The Special Forces are already in there . . . Well, one man anyway, but I'm told he's one of the best . . . Ma'am? . . . His call sign is Jackknife . . ."

CHAPTER 56

Water poured in high-powered streams from the sprinkler heads on the ceiling, instantly drenching the men as McCabe waved them forward. They dashed behind the counter and began grabbing guns from the broken cabinets.

McCabe went for the ammunition, yanking open the big drawer that held boxes of it. The lock on the drawer was broken. It had been pried open with a screwdriver during the first attempt by the hostages to get their hands on some weapons.

The men who had accomplished that now lay dead on the floor at the feet of McCabe and his companions. There was no time now to honor their sacrifice, but with any luck there would be later.

McCabe pressed boxes of ammo into the hands of his men and told them in a low, urgent voice, "Find a hole somewhere and load your weapons, then lie low. The terrorists are going to be looking for us, so let them come to us." He was changing the plan on the fly, but sometimes that was what you had to do.

The men nodded in understanding and hurried off,

splitting up and heading for different areas of the store. This standoff was about to turn into a guerrilla war, a deadly game of cat and mouse.

McCabe was the last one to leave the sporting-goods area. He still had one of the machine pistols tucked behind his belt, but he carried a fully loaded deer rifle with him now, preferring its precision to the automatic weapon. He didn't want to go spraying any more bullets around than he had to. Stray bullets had a habit of hitting the wrong people.

Staying close to the wall, he circled toward the front of the store. That was probably where the leader of these terrorists was, where he could keep an eye on the Americans who no doubt had the place surrounded by now. McCabe had a feeling that if there was a big bomb, it would be with the leader. It had to be neutralized before anybody could get out of here safely.

It was hard to hear much over the screeching of the fire alarm and the pounding of the water from the sprinklers, but the sound of gunshots from another part of the store suddenly penetrated the racket. The sharp whipcrack of rifle fire was interspersed with the chatter of a machine pistol.

The first confrontation between the terrorists and one of McCabe's men was taking place, and he wished he could be there to help.

He kept moving, though. He had his own job to do, and if he failed, there was a good chance that everyone in here would die.

Terry realized how close she had come to dying before the fire alarm going off and the sprinkler system kicking in distracted Hamed. She knew that as soon as he recovered from his shock he would still try to kill her.

She was damned if she was going to die without putting up a fight.

Before she could move, though, she was just as surprised as Hamed must have been, only in her case the cause of her shock was the sight of Ellis Burke leaping up from the floor and lunging at the terrorist.

Burke moved faster than Terry would have thought possible, probably fueled by desperation and sheer terror. One of the machine pistols started to stutter just as the lawyer crashed into Hamed. The terrorist went over backward. One of his pistols slipped out of his hand and flew into the air.

Since Terry was already on her feet, she was able to throw herself forward and make a grab for the gun. She got her hands on it, drew it in, stumbled forward trying to catch her balance as she fumbled with the weapon. After what seemed like forever, her hand went around the grip and her index finger found the trigger.

She turned and saw Burke and Hamed struggling on the floor. Burke had hold of the wrist of Hamed's gun hand with both of his hands and was pounding it against the tiles, trying to knock the second gun free from the terrorist's grip. At the same time, Hamed clenched his other hand into a fist and slammed it into the side of Burke's head. Burke managed to shrug off the punishment somehow and maintain his grip on Hamed's wrist.

Meanwhile, the other hostages were panicking. They screamed and scrambled to their feet and ran while they had the chance. Hamed squeezed the trigger of his remaining machine pistol and flame spurted from the muzzle. Several of the fleeing hostages cried out in pain and went down as bullets tore through their legs.

Terry lifted the pistol she had plucked from the air, but she couldn't get a clear shot at Hamed. She turned then to look for her daughter, and saw to her horror that Ronnie was running toward Hamed and Burke, instead of away from them. Allison Sawyer was with her.

"Ronnie, no!" Terry called. "Get away, get away!"

Ronnie ignored her. While Allison threw herself on Hamed's left arm and hand so that he couldn't keep using them to hit Burke, Ronnie kicked at the gun in the terrorist's other hand. She had the athleticism of youth and she had played soccer for quite a few years as a child.

She kicked the machine pistol right out of Hamed's hand. It flew through the air for a few feet, hit the floor, and then skidded even farther.

Disarmed, Hamed gave a cry of incoherent rage and bucked up from the floor, throwing Burke off and shaking himself loose from Allison. He twisted and kicked at Burke, driving the heel of his shoe into the lawyer's jaw. Burke rolled away.

"Ronnie! Allison! Move!" Terry screamed.

The two young women leaped out of the line of fire. As soon as they were clear, Terry pressed the trigger of the machine pistol. She had a firm grip on the weapon with both hands, so she was able to keep the recoil from making it ride up as she fired a short burst at Hamed.

The terrorist was already moving, though. The bullets chewed up the floor where he had been sprawled a second earlier, but now he was on hands and knees, scrambling away and powering himself up into a run. He disappeared into the shoe department as another burst from the gun in Terry's hands ripped a display of women's shoes to shreds.

Terry heard footsteps slapping the floor behind her

and whirled around to see one of the other terrorists running toward her. She didn't stop to think about what she was doing. She just pressed the trigger again and blew the son of a bitch away. The slugs punched bloody holes through his body and flung him backward like a giant hand.

"Mom!"

The sound of her daughter's voice made Terry turn again. She saw Ronnie and Allison trying to help Ellis Burke to his feet. The lawyer's shirt was bloody under his coat, and Terry knew he'd been hit by those shots Hamed had managed to get off.

"Mom, Mr. Burke's hurt!"

"I can see that," Terry said as she hurried over to them and added her strength to Ronnie's and Allison's. Together, they got Burke onto his feet. "Can you walk?" Terry asked him.

He nodded his head weakly. "I . . . I think so."

They were all soaked now, and the floor was slippery with water. Being under the sprinklers was like being caught in a heavy rainstorm. Terry had no idea how long the sprinklers would run before they shut off.

"Let's head for the front of the store and see if we can get out of here," she decided.

Gunshots were coming from all over the store now, along with shouts and screams and the continuing ear-numbing wail of the fire alarm. Terry knew they might have to fight their way out, but she didn't want to just stay put and wait for the terrorists to come and kill them. She remembered one of the things Jack had told her about dealing with trouble.

Once you have to move, keep moving until you're clear.

That was what Terry intended to do. She took the point, walking in front of Ronnie and Allison as they helped Burke limp along between them. Both of Terry's hands were wrapped tightly around the machine pistol, ready to fire it at a heartbeat's notice if they ran into more trouble.

If it hadn't been for Ronnie's presence, Terry realized, she would have almost wished that she *would* run into some more of the terrorists. She had endured what seemed like an eternity of paralyzing fear—even though it was probably only a couple of hours—and she didn't like it. Somebody was going to pay for putting her and her daughter and everybody else in here through that hell.

The old saying had it right.

Payback was a bitch.

And this bitch has a gun, she thought with a savage grimace that might have almost been a smile.

CHAPTER 57

Hiram Stackhouse pounded his thigh, chortled with glee, and said over the blaring fire alarm, "Pardon my French, missy, but it sounds like my boys're openin' a real can o' whoop-ass on your friends out there."

The female terrorist just glared at him, her eyes blazing with hatred over her flaring nostrils and the gag in her mouth.

"I wish I was out there with 'em," Stackhouse went on. "I was right in the middle o' that little dustup out in Arizona a while back, when that Mexican gang tried to take over an American town, and I never had so much fun in all my life. Makes a man feel mighty good knowin' that he's fightin' for what's right. Course you wouldn't know anything about that, seein' as you ain't a man, and any fightin' you've done has been on the side o' evil. You and yours made a big mistake when you came over here and tried to take us on, missy. You look at those damned politicians in Washington and you think that Americans've gone all soft an' mushy. And you're right about too blasted many of 'em. But there are still plenty o' folks in this country who've got steel at their core, little lady. They may not show it . . . hell, they may not even know it . . . but back 'em into a corner and you'll sure as shootin' find ou' mighty quick what they're made of."

Stackhouse rubbed a hand over his jaw and then went on. "You see, this is a good country, full o' good people. We don't like to fight. We'd rather live in peace, even with folks like you who hate us. That's why we bend over backwards tryin' to work things out, then bend over some more if that don't work. But you can only bend so far 'fore you have to snap back, and different folks got different snappin' points. You get what I'm sayin', ma'am? We'll put up with you pokin' us with a stick . . . for a while . . . but sooner or later we're gonna take that stick away from you and use it to paddle you good an' proper. Even the folks in Washington you think you've got buffaloed . . . well, I've got a hunch that if you push even them far enough, they'll fight back.

"Ah, well, I'm done with the speech-makin'. Wish I could get out there and help my boys."

He was looking toward the swinging doors that led into the store when the woman lowered her head and charged him, ramming him in the stomach with her head as hard as she could. Stackhouse doubled up and went over backward, his revolver flying from his hand.

The woman rolled over and lurched to her feet, then started hobbling toward the doors. She couldn't move very fast because her wrists were still tied to her ankles. But she had made a surprising amount of progress before Stackhouse got back the wind she had knocked out of him and struggled to his feet. He looked around for his gun but didn't see it.

Then he caught a glimpse of the revolver in the woman's hands as she shouldered through the swinging doors and disappeared. Stackhouse started after her, but then stopped and winced. He lifted a hand and pressed it against his side where pain throbbed.

It felt like she had busted a rib when she butted him like a crazy bull. He sank back against some crates and tried to catch his breath without inhaling too deeply and causing that pain to shoot through him again.

He wanted to go after her. McCabe had trusted him to keep an eye on her, after all.

But even though she had his gun, she was still tied up, and she was a woman to boot!

Just how much trouble could she cause anyway?

Hamed was filled with fury the likes of which he had never known. That fury warred with the shame he felt at being overpowered and disarmed by infidels. Where had the strength of the warrior that had filled him earlier gone? Had Allah deserted him?

He was instantly sorry for thinking that. He told himself he would make amends by finding Sheikh al-Mukhari and fighting at the holy man's side against the godless Americans. Perhaps the sheikh would even let him press the button that would detonate the nuclear device and bring this sacred quest to an end. He didn't deserve such a chance at glory, he knew, but he prayed that Allah would give it to him anyway.

It would have been even more satisfying to kill the lawyer and the blond woman with his bare hands, but evidently that was not to be. Surely by now they had fled—although they would find that there was really nowhere for them to run. They were still trapped in the UltraMegaMart.

Still doomed to die.

Hamed stumbled through the downpour from the sprinklers and emerged from the shoe department. As he did, a pair of swinging doors in the wall to his left burst open. He whirled in that direction, prepared to take on one or more of the infidels in hand-to-hand combat, but to his shock he saw Shalla Sahi stumbling toward him in an awkward, bent-over position because her wrists and ankles were lashed together with a belt. A gag was tied in place in her mouth.

But she was free other than that, and she had a gun clutched in her hands.

Hamed sprang to her side, realizing as he did so that the Americans must have captured her somehow and held her prisoner back in the vast stockroom at the rear of the store. But she had gotten away from them, and now Allah had brought the two of them together again. Hamed knew there had to be a purpose behind that.

She sagged against him as she recognized who he was. He took the gun from her, set it aside on a shelf for a moment, and untied her. As she flexed her fingers to get full feeling back into them, he worked the gag loose.

"Hamed!" she gasped. "The Americans—"

"I know," he said as he picked up the gun again. "They think they can overpower us and defeat us. But they have no chance. Our victory is the will of Allah!"

She grabbed his arm. "We must find Sheikh al-Mukhari. He must be protected until he can detonate the bomb. There are preparations that must be made—"

Hamed's eyes widened in surprise. "The bomb is not ready to trigger?"

"Would you have had it go off by accident before we

were ready?" she snapped. "It will not take long. Five, perhaps ten minutes."

It had been at least five minutes since the fire alarm and the sprinklers had gone on. If the sheikh had started preparing the bomb for detonation as soon as the trouble started, he might be almost ready to set it off.

But if he had been delayed for any reason, then the time he needed had to be bought somehow, and he had to be protected while he was readying the device. Hamed's original idea of heading for the front of the store had been a good one.

He took Shalla's hand and said, "Let's go!"

Before they started running, though, he took one last look at her. Her black hair was wet and plastered to her head, and the strain they were all under showed on her face.

But even though her head was uncovered and she wore immodest American clothes, Hamed realized at that moment she was beautiful, and he leaned closer to her and pressed his mouth to hers in a quick, hard kiss. She was startled at first before her lips responded.

But it lasted only a couple of seconds, and then they were hurrying toward the front of the store as fast as they could.

From one end of the long building to the other, the Battle of the UltraMegaMart was being fought. The wailing of the fire alarm and the drenching downpour from the sprinklers made it seem as if everyone in the store was caught in a thunderstorm in hell, with the roar of gunshots standing in for the rumble of thunder.

Two of the men Jack McCabe had freed from the stockroom died in their first encounters with the terrorists who were spreading out to look for them, chopped down by automatic-weapons fire.

But the terrorists began to fall, too, as men who had handled rifles for years—and other men who had never even fired a gun before—found reserves of strength and courage and icy nerve within themselves that they had never known were there before.

At the same time, since the terrorists were unable to watch their prisoners as closely as they had before, most of the hostages made a break for freedom, surging in a human tide toward the front of the store.

They came to an abrupt halt, though, as the prisoners who had been placed near the small bombs at the entrances screamed at them to get back. Those hostages knew what would happen if the others came stampeding through there. Scores of people would die.

So for a moment the mob hesitated, uncertain whether or not to continue its panic-stricken flight. Then common sense began to prevail. As the fighting continued elsewhere in the store, a few brave souls hurried forward to grab the hostages near the bombs and drag them away from the explosives. Everyone held their breath, fearing that the bombs would start to go off, but the motion sensors must have been turned outward, to prevent a rescue attempt from outside the store.

No one dared try to move the bombs themselves, though. Any jostling of them would surely set them off. That left hundreds of people crowded into the front third or so of the store, behind the long line of cash registers and checkout stands. They milled around, uncertain what to do next, cold and wet and still very, very scared.

But it was only a matter of time now until they all got out of here. That feeling was growing. Gunshots still rang out here and there, but the crisis was nearly over.

Soon, they would be going home.

CHAPTER 58

"My God, it's a war in there," Eileen Bastrop breathed as she clutched her boss's arm. She and Walt Graham stood just outside the mobile command center, listening to the roar of gunshots coming from inside the Ultra-MegaMart. They didn't need sophisticated listening devices to hear the sounds of battle anymore.

There was nothing sexual in the way Bastrop leaned against Graham. She was just shaken by the knowledge that innocent Americans were dying in there, and he knew that because he felt the same way himself. Feelings of rage and impotent frustration filled him.

"We've got to find a way to get in there," he muttered.

"We can't," Bastrop said. "Those bombs are still in place at the entrances. If anything comes too close to them, they'll go off."

"I know that." Graham was seething. "If there was just some other way in . . ."

His eyes swept the vast expanse of asphalt surrounding the store. The MegaMart trucks that had been parked behind the building to be unloaded when the hostage situation erupted had all been moved out to the very edge of the lot—after they had been swept for explosives, of course. Now they sat there like silent behemoths, forgotten because of everything else that was going on.

Graham stared at the trucks for a long moment and felt his heart began to slug harder in his chest. "I've got an idea, Eileen," he said. "They have all the doors rigged with bombs, right?"

"Right. As far as we know. Nobody wants to risk going in the back to see if they have bombs there, too."

"Well, then, it's simple." Graham smiled for what seemed like the first time in days. "If we can't go in the doors that are there . . . we make a new door."

McCabe moved fast because he was going the long way around, avoiding the fighting that had erupted throughout the central area of the store between the terrorists and the men he had freed. He heard the crack of rifles and the stuttering roar of automatic weapons, even over the racket of the fire alarm, and from time to time he saw muzzle flashes from the corner of his eye.

He hated to let someone else do the fighting like that, but his own mission was important, too. He had learned during his years in the Special Forces to never lose sight of the primary goal.

Which in this case was to make sure that the Ultra-MegaMart didn't turn into a smoking, possibly radio-active hole in the ground.

The worry that the terrorists had some sort of pocket nuke gnawed at McCabe's guts. The technology had become so advanced that something no larger than a brief-case could pack devastating power and also be "dirty" enough to contaminate a huge area. With the northwesterly winds at this time of year, a nuclear explosion here would send fallout all over Fort Worth and Dallas. In the long run, thousands more people would die from radiation poisoning . . . maybe hundreds of thousands. And the huge metropolitan region would be rendered unlivable for hundreds of years. It would be the worst attack ever on United States soil, eclipsing 9/11 by far.

So McCabe raced past sporting goods, past housewares, past auto supplies, sticking to the outer edge of the store's retail floor where he was less likely to run into any of the terrorists. By pet food, he turned and found himself in the main aisle, able to look all the way past the checkout stands to the other end where the produce area of the grocery section was located.

The aisle was thronged with people, as the hostages crowded forward looking for a way out of this store that had become their cage. McCabe bit back a curse. He would never be able to make his way through that mob in time. He darted out of the main aisle and began skirting the mob through the health-and-beauty section.

He came to a wall of shelves blocking his way. They didn't go all the way to the ceiling, though. Instead, they were only about eight feet high. He swept female products off the shelves and began climbing. The metal shelves bent under his weight, but supported him long enough for him to reach the top. He vaulted over and landed lithely in the open space directly in front of one of the store's main entrances.

He saw the motion-sensitive bomb to his right, part of the crowd of terrified hostages to his left. Straight ahead was the long, narrow clearing in front of the checkout stands, with the wall to McCabe's left being lined with a nail salon, photo studio, bank branch, eyeglass center, the customer-service desk, and the front restrooms.

McCabe's eyes searched for the leader of the terrorists, whom he had suspected would be up here somewhere, but he didn't see anyone other than the mob of shoppers, who were staying back behind the checkout stands because of their fear of the bombs at the doors.

Suddenly, near the far entrance to the store, there was a commotion among the hostages. They parted, and a woman strode through the opening carrying a machine pistol. McCabe's instincts started the gun in his hand swinging up, but then he froze as his stunned eyes recognized the lean, athletic shape, the blond hair, the proud stance.

Terry.

McCabe's heart leaped. His wife was alive! And not only alive, but also apparently unharmed—and armed. A second later, he got another pleasant surprise as he saw Ronnie come through the opening in the crowd, helping another young woman support a man who was evidently wounded or injured. Relief washed through McCabe at the sight of his daughter.

"Terry!" he bellowed. "Ronnie!"

They turned toward him, and even at this distance he saw their faces light up at the sight of him.

At that moment, two things happened. The sprinklers and the fire alarm finally cut off, leaving a silence that seemed empty somehow.

And McCabe's relief turned to horror as people in the crowd screamed and frantically got out of the way as two more figures stepped out behind Terry, Ronnie, and their companions. A man and a woman, the woman the female terrorist McCabe had captured earlier, the man tall, dark, and bearded, obviously one of her fellow murderers.

He had a gun in his hand—Hiram Stackhouse's revolver, a part of McCabe's brain realized—and it was swinging up to point at Terry.

CHAPTER 59

Terry couldn't believe it. Not only was Jack alive and inside the UltraMegaMart, but he was also armed and obviously had been taking on the terrorists already. She was about to break into a run toward her husband when the screams behind her made her glance back over her shoulder.

She saw Hamed emerge from the stampeding crowd. He had a woman with him, and in that split second Terry wondered if she was the female terrorist they had been looking for earlier. Shalla? Was that her name?

Terry didn't have time to think about it, because Hamed was lifting a gun he had gotten from somewhere, and from the crazed look in his hate-filled eyes, all he was thinking about right now was killing her.

He didn't get that chance because Ronnie let go of Ellis Burke and grabbed Hamed's arm, forcing it upward even as he was pulling the trigger. The gun roared, but the bullet went harmlessly into the ceiling.

"Ronnie, no!" Terry cried, but she was too late. Her daughter was already locked in a struggle with the terrorist, her lithe young strength a match for him, at least for a few seconds. Terry turned around, knowing there was no way she could risk a shot with Ronnie so close to Hamed.

She didn't get a chance to fire anyway, because in that heartbeat the woman who was with Hamed let out a yell and threw herself forward, launching a spinning kick that knocked the machine pistol out of Terry's hand. A second later, she slammed the base of her hand into Terry's sternum, knocking her backward.

Reacting instinctively, Terry blocked the next blow and threw one of her own, a good old-fashioned punch to the jaw. That rocked the female terrorist, but she didn't go down. She caught her balance and kicked again, aiming at Terry's knee.

Terry shifted at the last instant, bending so that she took the savage kick on her thigh. It staggered her. Knowing she was going to fall, she turned it to her advantage and lashed out with her other leg, sweeping her opponent's legs out from under her.

Both women crashed to the floor.

Terry didn't waste any time. She rolled over and flung herself on the other woman, slamming punches into the terrorist's face and midsection.

All the fear and anger and frustration that had built up inside Terry during the past couple of hours exploded then. She cried out incoherently as she continued the fierce attack, her pounding fists rising and falling almost too fast for the eye to follow.

She might have beaten the woman into insensibility, might have even killed her, if her maternal instincts hadn't kicked in and reminded her that her daughter was also engaged in a life-and-death struggle. Terry stopped punching long enough to look up and see if Ronnie was all right, and in that moment Shalla landed a stunning blow of her own, knocking Terry off and sending her into a place where the world spun crazily and she felt consciousness slipping away.

McCabe had never run track or anything like that. He had the quickness of a man who had survived for years in an extremely hazardous profession, but he was no sprinter.

He covered the ground along the front of the store faster than he had ever moved before in his life. His wife and daughter were in danger, and knowing that put wings on his feet that had never been there when he was just trying to save his own life.

He saw Terry struggling with Shalla, and felt a surge of pride when he realized that his wife was battling on even terms with the terrorist. Ronnie wouldn't last long against the man, though, and McCabe knew it. The element of surprise and her youthful vitality could only carry her so far against a mature killer.

In fact, just as McCabe was skidding to a stop a few yards away, the man clipped Ronnie on the jaw with the barrel of the revolver he held. The blow stunned the young woman and made her knees buckle. The terrorist raised the gun, clearly intending to strike again with it and crush Ronnie's skull.

McCabe leveled the machine pistol, ready to blow him away.

Before he could pull the trigger, the wounded man he had seen earlier, being helped along by Ronnie and a young blond woman McCabe didn't know, lurched between McCabe and the terrorist. With an angry shout, he tackled the would-be killer.

Both men went down. The revolver slipped out of the terrorist's hand and spun away on the tile.

The terrorist was clearly more experienced in hand-to-hand combat, and the other man was wounded to boot. The terrorist slammed the edges of his hands against his opponent's neck, where it joined the shoulders on either side. The wounded man stiffened, momentarily paralyzed by the blows. The terrorist flung him aside, came up onto his hands and knees, and went after the gun he had lost.

McCabe was already there. One of his work boots came down on the revolver, pinning it to the floor.

The terrorist looked up at him, eyes full of hatred. McCabe could have squeezed the trigger at that moment and exploded the guy's head with a burst of automatic-weapons fire. He thought about it. He came mighty close to doing it.

But he didn't.

Instead, his other foot lashed out. The heel of his boot caught the terrorist in the face, pulping the man's nose and sending him rolling over a couple of times. He came to a stop in the limp sprawl that meant he was out cold.

This was one of the bastards who was going to stand trial for the crimes he'd committed, McCabe thought.

"Daddy!" Ronnie screamed.

McCabe pivoted, letting his instincts do the work. He saw the woman Terry had been fighting with. She was on her feet again, and Terry was done, shaking her head groggily. Shalla had snatched up the gun Terry had been carrying earlier, and now she was bringing the machine pistol to bear on Terry.

McCabe didn't hesitate because the threat came from a woman. A heartless killer was a heartless killer, and that was McCabe's wife about to come under the gun.

He fired.

The burst of lead tore through Shalla, throwing her sideways as her eyes widened in shock and pain. Crimson welled from the wounds as she tried to stay on her feet, skidded, and fell. Ronnie grabbed the gun and wrestled it out of her hands, just in case Shalla had enough strength left to pull the trigger.

She didn't. Her fingers scrabbled against the floor tile for a second, and then her life came out of her in a long, harsh sigh.

McCabe lowered the machine pistol and hurried to Terry's side. He reached down with his free hand, caught hold of her arm, and lifted her to her feet seemingly effortlessly.

"Jack . . ." she whispered as she sagged against him and looked up into his face.

McCabe kissed her.

With his free arm around her, he held her tightly to him. Her arms came up and went around his neck. All the fear they had felt that they would never see each other again came through in that desperate embrace and that hungry, urgent kiss. A ton of emotions was packed into that moment.

"Very nice," a voice said. "Husband and wife reunited, I would guess?"

Something about the voice, some sinister quality that plunged daggers of ice into McCabe's spine, made him break the kiss, let go of Terry, and turn. He saw a middle-aged, professorish-looking man standing just outside the restrooms, where he had probably been hiding until now. The man was balding and had a short goatee, and in his left hand he carried a leather case that was several inches thicker than a regular briefcase.

McCabe knew what it was as soon as he saw it, and the chill along his spine suddenly filled his entire body.

"My young friends gave me the time I needed," the man continued. "All the preparations are made." He lifted his right hand.

McCabe saw a small black cylinder clutched in the man's hand. His thumb was over the end of it.

"Dead man's switch," McCabe croaked.

The man smiled. "That's right. If I release it, this entire store, and everything for half a mile around, will be consumed in a nuclear explosion."

"What do you want?" McCabe asked. His voice was a rasp now. "Safe passage out of here?"

The man laughed. "Do you know who I am?"

McCabe shook his head and said, "The leader of this bunch, I'd guess."

"I am Sheikh Mushaff al-Mukhari, infidel. I planned this holy mission. Do you think I would walk away from it before it was complete?"

McCabe didn't say anything.

After a moment, the sheikh spoke again. His words were clearly audible, because a tense hush had fallen over the entire store.

"You asked what I wanted. My desire is quite simple. I want you and all your godless, infidel horde to die. I want the new Caliphate to rise until it rules not only the Middle East but also the entire world. I want Allah to reign supreme. If the price for that is my death, I will pay it gladly."

He held the detonator out at arm's length, his thumb ready to come off the detonator.

Like the end of the world, a huge explosion filled the store.

CHAPTER 60

McCabe felt the vibration under his feet, and watched in amazement as the wall behind Sheikh al-Mukhari bulged and then flew apart in a thundergust of brick, mortar, twisted steel, and dust. The front end of a giant truck rampaged through the destroyed wall like a stampeding dinosaur. McCabe saw Mukhari's mouth open in a startled yell as he staggered forward, but McCabe couldn't hear anything over the grinding crash of the truck plowing through the wall.

He lunged forward at Mukhari, but someone else reached the sheikh first. The young blond woman who had been helping Ronnie with the wounded man flashed past McCabe and grabbed Mukhari's right hand with both of hers. She clamped down on his thumb, holding it secure on the dead man's switch.

McCabe knew how close they had all just come to dying. Another fraction of a second and Mukhari would have released the switch and detonated the nuke. That young woman had given them all a second chance at life.

McCabe wasn't going to waste that chance. He

dropped the machine pistol and grabbed the leather case, wrestling it out of the sheikh's hands.

Meanwhile, heavily armed men wearing helmets and body armor had begun to pour through the jagged opening made in the front wall of the store when the eighteen-wheeler crashed through it. Their progress was impeded by the hostages, who saw a chance for freedom and were grabbing it for all it was worth. They tried to pour through the gaps around the wrecked truck, but those bottlenecks were soon stuffed with madly struggling people.

McCabe knew the bomb was probably harmless as long as the sheikh's thumb didn't come off the dead man's switch. How long could the young woman hold it in place, though?

McCabe didn't want to find out. He set the case on the floor, gave it a shove with his foot that sent it sliding into the bathroom, and turned back to the struggling duo. Mukhari slammed his fist into the young woman's face, trying to knock her loose, but she held on as if her life depended on it—as, of course, it did.

McCabe's right arm went around the sheikh's neck from behind. "Hang on!" he shouted at the young blonde as Mukhari began to writhe frantically. McCabe's left hand gripped his right wrist as his right arm clamped across Mukhari's throat like a bar of iron. He bent backward from the waist as he began to apply pressure.

In a movie, this was the moment when the hero would either utter a wisecrack or try to rub the villain's nose in defeat. McCabe didn't think of himself as a hero. He was just a tired, scared man who didn't have time for any foolishness.

So with a heave of his arms and shoulders, he just broke the terrorist bastard's neck instead.

Mukhari went limp. Panting, McCabe told the young

woman, "Hang on, hang on! Don't let go of his thumb, whatever you do!"

She was white as a sheet and her eyes were so big around she looked like a character in a Japanese comic book. But she managed to nod and say, "I've got it. Don't worry, I've got it."

"I'm going to put him on the floor," McCabe said. "Come down with us. Easy, easy now . . ."

He wound up on his knees next to the sheikh's corpse, which stared sightlessly at the ceiling. The young woman sat on the other side of the body, maintaining her double-handed grip on Mukhari's hand and the dead man's switch.

"Now what do we do?" she asked raggedly.

Terry was up, having recovered from the brief moment when she had almost passed out. She sat down beside the young woman and put an arm around her shoulders.

"You're going to keep on saving the lives of everyone in this store, Allison," she said. "I don't think you've met my husband. This is Jack McCabe."

He smiled at the young woman. "Nice meeting you. Now hold on for just a little while longer."

He got to his feet and looked around. One of the armed men who had followed the truck into the store came over to him and said, "Jackknife?"

The man was tall and broad-shouldered, and a handsome black face peered out through the clear plastic shield attached to the helmet. "You SpecOps?" McCabe asked. "Or Company?"

The man shook his head. "Neither. FBI. Name's Walt Graham. You *are* Jack McCabe?"

"Yeah," McCabe said as sudden weariness threatened to overwhelm him. "There's a pocket nuke in the bathroom and a detonator with a dead man's switch in the hand of that guy over there on the floor."

"Just another day at the office, eh?" Graham said.

"Yeah. You think you can do something about it?"

"You bet I can." Graham turned his head and yelled, "Somebody go back to hardware and get me a hacksaw, damn it!"

Allison turned her face away so she didn't have to watch as the big FBI agent sawed Mukhari's right hand off at the wrist. Then several of the men who looked like a cross between regular soldiers and Imperial stormtroopers from the *Star Wars* movies lifted her to her feet.

"Get her into the command center," Graham barked. The huge RV filled with equipment had enough jamming, deadening, and shielding technology so that no electrical signals could get out of it once everything was working like it was supposed to. All Allison had to do was hang on to Mukhari's hand and keep the switch in place until then.

The Special Forces troopers had finally gotten control of the situation enough so that they were evacuating the former hostages in an almost orderly fashion. A couple of bulldozers had been brought in to widen the gaps around the wrecked MegaMart truck. McCabe looked over at the massive vehicle and grinned as he realized it was the one he had brought down here from Alliance Airport earlier that morning. Only a few hours had passed since then, but it felt like a month.

"Whose idea was it to ram that eighteen-wheeler through the wall?" he asked Graham as he stood near the truck with one arm around Terry and the other around Ronnie.

"Mine," Graham replied with a note of pride in his voice. "I was in the cab while I got it rolling, too. Jumped out just before it hit."

"Kind of a risky plan considering that you didn't know what was gonna be on the other side of that wall," McCabe commented.

"Not as risky as waiting to see what those bastards were going to do. If we'd let them write the ending to this little drama, it wouldn't have been a good one."

"You've got that right," McCabe admitted.

Graham looked around the store. Most of the merchandise had been ruined by the sprinklers, and when the truck was pulled back out there would be a gaping hole in the wall. "It's going to take a while to put this place right again," he said.

"Ain't gonna be put back right," a voice said from behind them.

McCabe turned and saw Hiram Stackhouse standing there. The billionaire went on. "I'm gonna raze this store. Take it right down to the ground and start over. Not gonna build another one, though. There's gonna be a damn nice park here instead, dedicated to the memory of every American who was killed here today, as well as to the ones who lived through it."

"That'll cost you some money," McCabe predicted.

Stackhouse snorted. "Shoot, I can build a park like that ever' day for the rest o' my life and still have a few billion dollars left over. I reckon I'll survive, and so will MegaMart." A sly grin spread over his face. "Besides, I already got another location in mind for the *next* UltraMegaMart. Question now is, what am I gonna call this place? How does Whoop-ass Park sound to you folks?"

McCabe didn't bother answering. Instead, he took his wife and daughter and went home.

They would finish their Christmas shopping some other day.

"The death toll from the hostage situation at the UltraMegaMart in Texas now stands at fifty-seven, including twenty terrorists who were killed in the fighting that broke out inside the store. The government is downplaying reports that civilians led by a former member of the U.S. Special Forces launched a counterattack against the terrorists and overcame them. Instead, a Justice Department spokesman attributed the relatively low loss of life to the actions of FBI Special Agent in Charge Walter Graham, as well as to other dedicated professionals who negotiated with the terrorists and tried to achieve a peaceful solution.

"Likewise, the White House Press Secretary and the Secretary of Homeland Security have both said that there is no credible evidence at this time that the terrorists ever had in their possession a low-yield nuclear device. The White House statement said in part, 'There is no need for scare tactics based on partisan politics to make this terrible tragedy any worse than it already is. The United States is as safe and secure tonight as it has always been.' A spokesman for the opposition party agreed, saying, 'That's true—and it's exactly the problem, too.'

"In related news, Hiram Stackhouse, founder and CEO of MegaMart, who was on hand for the incident today, has announced that the store will be torn down and replaced by a park dedicated to the Americans who lost their lives there today, as well as to those who survived the hostage ordeal. Stackhouse also vowed to build an even larger store in an undisclosed location.

"Meanwhile, the death toll from the bombings carried out by the same group of extremists earlier in the day continues to climb, and now stands at nearly four hundred, making this the deadliest day for terrorist violence in the United States since 9/11.

"Overseas, while representatives of foreign governments have expressed relief that the hostage situation was resolved and sorrow at the loss of life, speculation is growing, especially in Arab countries, that the whole incident has been overblown and in fact may not have even happened. Interviews with people on the street in Egypt and Saudi Arabia revealed the belief that this was, as one man put it, 'just another American trick to make Arabs look bad.'

"And while the incident in Texas may have put a damper on holiday shopping there, that didn't prove to be the case in the rest of the country. Retailers are still predicting a record year for sales . . ."

EPILOGUE

"We dodged a bullet," the President's husband said. He shook his head. "As bad as it is, if that damned nuke had gone off . . ."

"There wasn't any nuclear device," the President snapped. "You heard the statement we issued."

He just looked at her.

"Damn it, every news report for the next week will insist that there wasn't really any nuke," she said, her voice rising angrily. "Who do you think the American people will believe?"

"You'd better hope they believe you," he said softly. "If they decide you're lyin' to them about this, you can kiss any chances for reelection good-bye."

She sank down on the sofa in the White House's second-floor living quarters and covered her face with her hands. "I know," she said, her voice muffled. When she raised her head and spoke again, it was like the cry of a wounded animal.

What am I going to do if I can't be President anymore?

* * *

Ellis Burke leaned back against the pillows propped behind him in the hospital bed. His side hurt like blazes where the terrorist's bullet had gouged a deep furrow in it. He'd lost quite a bit of blood, the doctors said, and he would be hospitalized for at least a couple of nights, maybe longer.

Burke intended to keep an eagle eye on all the doctors, nurses, and the rest of the hospital staff. Medical malpractice ran rampant these days, and if he witnessed any, he knew a lawyer who would be very happy to file suit against the hospital and everyone involved.

Some things never changed, he thought with a painful grin.

But some did, and he knew he would never think about the world situation quite the same way again. It hurt to admit it—maybe not as much as that bullet in his side, but still—it hurt to admit that he had been wrong about some things. Evil *did* exist in the world, and some people just couldn't be reasoned with. Never again would he feel any sympathy for terrorists. He knew them now for what they really were—despicable monsters.

Burke shoved that thought out of his mind. There would be time enough later for pondering political philosophies.

Right now, he preferred to think about Allison Sawyer and how she had stopped by the hospital to see him on her way home. She had put a hand on his, resting it there for a moment as his hand lay on the crisp hospital sheets, and her touch had been warm and soft.

"What the hell," he told himself softly, speaking aloud since he was in a private room, "she's too young for you, old buddy-roo. You're just dreaming."

But that was part of life, wasn't it? You had to have a dream or two, even if you were a cynical, ambulance-chasing shyster in a state full of redneck yahoos.

Some of whom, Burke had to admit to himself as he started to feel sleepy, weren't really so bad . . .

Nate looked up when she came into the room, ran to her, and threw his arms around her. Allison lifted him and cuddled him against her, even though he was really too big for her to be doing that.

At this moment, she wasn't the woman who had saved the lives of thousands of people, maybe hundreds of thousands or even millions in the long run. She was just a young single mother who was glad to be home and reunited with her son. She hugged Nate so fiercely that after a minute he started to squirm and said, "Hey, I can't breathe!"

"Sorry, ace," she said as she set him on his feet again in the living room of her neighbors' apartment, wondering how in the world Mrs. Sanchez had kept him from finding out what was going on today. It was obvious from the way Nate was acting, though, that he didn't know how close his mother had come to dying. "What did you do today?"

"Oh, watched DVDs and played video games. The usual. Was the store crowded?"

"Yeah," Allison said. "Really crowded. You wouldn't have enjoyed it."

"I guess not." He frowned a little. "What happened to your face? It looks like it's bruised."

"Oh, I . . . ran into something."

Sheikh al-Mukhari's fist, to be precise, had run into her face, as he was pounding on her trying to get her to let go of that switch so he could blow up the whole place. But she didn't feel much like explaining that to Nate right now.

And he didn't seem all that interested anyway. All he said was "Oh." Then he looked up at her, eyes wide, and got down to the business at hand.

"What'd you bring me, Mom?"

"Nothing today, silly," she said with a laugh. "You'll have to wait until Christmas for your presents, like everybody else."

The new house Hiram Stackhouse was building for them ought to be ready to move into by then.

McCabe had just sat back in his recliner and put his feet up when the cell phone in his pocket vibrated.

He thought about not answering it. It had been a long day. Getting home had been a lot lengthier and more complicated process than he'd envisioned. He and his wife and daughter had spent hours answering questions from Walt Graham, his second in command Eileen Bastrop, and countless other government officials.

But now he was in his own house at last, in his own chair, with his eyes closed and the pleasant sounds of Terry and Ronnie moving around in one of the other rooms drifting to his ears. He was *home,* damn it! Couldn't they stop bothering him?

Evidently not, and he wasn't the sort of man who could easily ignore a ringing phone. So he slipped it out of his pocket, opened it, and held it to his ear.

"Yeah? This had better be good."

"Hey, Jackknife. I hear you saved the day." The voice belonged to Lawrence "Fargo" Ford.

"A lot of people saved the day," McCabe said, "including half-a-dozen MegaMart employees who were killed fighting those crazy sons of bitches."

"Word is that you got a few prisoners."

"I don't expect the government to admit it any time soon, but four of the terrorists were captured."

"Oh, they'll admit it," Ford said. "Everything's got to be open and aboveboard now, remember? No more of this illegally detaining prisoners like we used to. No more doing whatever it took to get information out of them we needed to save innocent lives either."

McCabe grunted. "Yeah, I forgot. Anyway, it's over. Nothing blew up real good . . . this time."

"Yeah, I've been thinkin' about that," Ford drawled. "You know what these guys are like, Jackknife. They're like cockroaches. You stomp one of 'em, there are always a dozen more running around, hiding from the light and fouling everything up for everybody."

"And your point is?"

"How'd you like to come back to work for the Company?"

"I can't do that," McCabe answered without hesitation. "I never worked for the Company to start with."

"You know what I mean," Ford protested. "You're too good at this sort of work to just sit around, McCabe. Don't you miss it?"

Again, McCabe didn't hesitate. "Not a damned bit. In fact, I already turned down one job today."

"FBI?"

"Hiram Stackhouse. He wanted to make me his new head of security. Seems he's not too happy with the old one. Can't say as I blame him."

"But you told him no."

"I told him no," McCabe said. "I'm a truck driver these days. That's plenty of excitement for me."

"I don't believe that," Ford said.

"Believe whatever you want, I don't care. Was there anything else you wanted?"

Ford didn't say anything for a moment; then a chuckle came from the phone. "No, I guess not. Oh, Brad Parker says to tell you hello."

"Right back at him. He gonna be all right?"

"Yeah, he'll be fine. He'll be back in the field before you know it."

"Fighting the shadow wars," McCabe said.

"Yeah. Somebody's got to do it."

For a second McCabe felt that old familiar pull.

Then his wife and daughter laughed in the kitchen, and it went away.

"Good night, Fargo."

"It's morning over here—" Ford began, but McCabe closed the phone and didn't hear any more after that. He turned the phone off, set it on the table beside his chair, picked up the remote, and turned on the TV. Nothing on the networks but special reports about what had happened today, he realized after a minute or two of flipping through the channels. He found a rerun of an old sitcom, heaved a sigh, and sat back to watch.

By the time Terry looked into the living room a few minutes later, McCabe's eyes were closed and his chest rose and fell regularly.

Terry smiled and let him sleep.

Hamed al-Bashar sat on the bunk in the tiny cell, unmoving, his hands clasped between his knees. He didn't know exactly where he was, but he knew it didn't matter. He would tell the infidels nothing, no matter what they did to him. He would never betray his fellow warriors in the cause of jihad.

And soon the infidels would give him a lawyer. Despite the fact that he was not an American citizen and had come to this country only to do it grievous harm, the fools would bend over backward to make sure none of his "rights" were violated.

The Americans didn't know it, but they had only one real right—the right to die, crushed by the inevitable tide of Islam that would sweep over the entire planet sooner or later. Today's mission might have failed, but there would be another, and another, and another, and as always, the Americans would slumber on until it was too late.

In the end, Hamed knew, he and his compatriots wouldn't even have to defeat the Americans. They were doing it to themselves with every day that went by when they refused to admit the true extent of the danger they faced. They brought themselves one step closer to extinction with each sneering, sanctimonious newscast, with each march by chanting, sign-waving "peace" protestors who had no idea what true peace cost, with each Supreme Court decision that took power out of the hands of the people and placed it in the greedy grasp of liberal politicians.

In the gloom of the cell, a smile spread slowly across Hamed's face. He was nothing, a speck of dust in a great wind blowing from the east, a wind that one day would scour the earth clean of the infidels and their corruption. If it was the will of Allah, he would live to see that day.

If not . . . well, he was secure in the knowledge that it was coming anyway.

A quiet sound that no one else heard came from the cell.

Laughter, and a whispered *"Allahu akbar!"*

GREAT BOOKS,
GREAT SAVINGS!

When You Visit Our Website:
www.kensingtonbooks.com
You Can Save Money Off The Retail Price
Of Any Book You Purchase!

- All Your Favorite Kensington Authors
- New Releases & Timeless Classics
- Overnight Shipping Available
- eBooks Available For Many Titles
- All Major Credit Cards Accepted

Visit Us Today To Start Saving!
www.kensingtonbooks.com